MW00975818

THE SCHOLAR AND THE SPHINX SERIES

The Scholar, the Sphinx and the Fang of Fenrir

Book Two
The Scholar and the Sphinx Series

A. R. Cook

MITHRAS BOOKS
London • New York

MITHRAS BOOKS

34 New House
67-68 Hatton Garden
London, EC1N 8JY
&
244 5th Avenue, Suite 1861
New York, New York 10001

First published in Great Britain and the United States in 2014 by Mithras Books

Copyright © A.R. Cook 2014

The right of A.R. Cook to be identified as author of this work has been asserted by her in accordance with the Copyright, Designs and Patents Act 1988. All rights reserved.

A CIP catalogue record for this book is available from the British Library.

ISBN PB 978-1-910282-07-6

Typeset in Janson MT Std

Printed in the United States of America and the United Kingdom.

This is a work of fiction. Names, characters, places and incidents either are the product of the author's imagination or used fictitiously.

www.mithrasbooks.com

Dedicated to my husband David, who reminds me every day that there is magic in the world; and to my family, who has shown me the power of stories my whole life long.

Prologue

...What Came Before...

I see in three.

I have seen it. I see it now. I will see it.

We see in three.

You will see as well. But what lies ahead will come soon enough. What you see now is what echoes behind us.

This moment is the Past. You need to know what came before, if you are to understand the design of your Present. Both Past and Present are woven into your Future.

It is the Past of a young man who is much like you, and of course, much unlike you. It is the Past of a myth who is true, whose bloodline influenced the fate of kings and heroes. It is a Past that, at first, you may think is far removed from your own. But all Pasts intertwine, so it is as much your Past as it is theirs.

Well, that was a good blather of pretentiousness, wasn't it? You'll have to forgive me. The first of my three minds tends to ramble on with "profound pontification." My third mind barely says a thing, which is equally as frustrating. I, on the other hand, like getting straight to the matter.

And I will get to the matter. But one cannot get anywhere unless you start at the beginning. So be quiet. I don't like to argue with myself. Now, let's see…ah, I remember.

It takes only one reckless decision to change a life—to better it, worsen it, or end it. It takes only one decision to make someone a hero, or a fool.

This is about David Sandoval. Sixteen years old in the year of 1852, and itching for something more wondrous than his home of Cervera, Spain. It is also the year of the beginning of the restoration of Paris, France, under the reign of Napoleon III. David receives an invitation from one of Paris' most prominent architects, with an offer to become his apprentice to help with the restoration. The young prodigy is more than happy to accept. But happiness can be an elusive white stag. When you believe you see it within your reach, there is always a lion in wait ready to snatch it away.

On his journey to Paris, David stays at an inn within the city of Orleans, and finds an evening's entertainment with a caravan of performing gypsies passing through town. After winning a contest proposed by the caravan's juggler, the Scotsman Gullin, David is given a dagger as a prize. The dagger does him little good, however, when an intruder breaks into his room at the inn later that night. When the intruder escapes, David has an irrepressible urge to hunt down his mysterious assailant, whom he is sure is hiding with the traveling gypsies. If only he had known what he was chasing after, he might not have slinked into the gypsies' camp late in the pitch blackness of night; he may not have stolen a peek into that strange looking nest within one of the wagons; and he would not have come face to face with a living, breathing sphinx who would decide, now that he had seen her, that he could not leave.

Stolen away by the sphinx and her gypsies, David is thrust into another world unlike his own. It is a world of legends and myths, of blood-craving dolls known as Jenglots, of singing sirens that welcome visitors to their hidden island—this is the world behind the Curtain, the magic that masks the "unseen" from the human world. It is also the place where the sphinx's cruel cousin, the half-fox, half-man Nico the Teumessian, wishes nothing more than to cause the sphinx humiliation and grief. Playing upon David's desire to return home, and knowing the sphinx has an unusual attraction towards the boy, Nico tricks David into getting lost in the Curtain. The Curtain sends David back to the human world, but into the foreign lands of Kyoto, Japan.

I forgot the part about David giving the sphinx a name, and by doing so he unwittingly proposes his life to her. Also the part about the night goddess Nyx's Shade being inside of the sphinx, draining her of her cunning and her life essence…

I was getting to that. I swear, I envy those who have only one voice in their head.

Yes, David gave the sphinx a name so he could address her as something more than "Sphinx," but he was unaware that in her people's culture, bestowing a name on a sphinx is the same as a marriage proposal. Perhaps that was why Acacia, as this was her new name, felt such a draw to him. Or it could be because of the oracle she had been given ages ago by a Grecian diviner, that a man fitting David's description would release her from the deadly grasp of Nyx's Shade within her, and save her life. Whatever the reason, she was determined to find David and see that he was safe.

David, rescued from Japanese bandits by the shape-shifting badger Tanuki, is welcomed into the home of Yofune Nushi. Yofune, a seemingly harmless old man, grants David the opportunity to open a dream path into the realm of Sleep, so that he might connect to Acacia's mind and help her find her way to him. The master of the Sleep realm, Hypnos, assists David in locating Acacia, where the boy and sphinx reunite, both having a better understanding of one another. But Nico abducts the gypsies and steals them away to a secret underground location, guarded over by an ancient monster, the Sleepless Dragon.

Yofune and Tanuki agree to help David rescue the gypsies from Nico, and Yofune reveals that he is in fact a sea dragon that can track down Nico's lair with his sense of smell. While Yofune fends off the Sleepless Dragon, David, Acacia and Tanuki make their way through Nico's lair and free Gullin and the gypsies from their prison. But Nico has a trap lying in wait, as hundreds of fire sprites pursue them and threaten to burn them alive. By summoning the Southern desert winds, Acacia was able to snuff out the fire sprites, but the magic is so taxing on her Shade-weakened body that the exertion brings her inches from Death's grip.

David goes to the Sleep realm to ask Hypnos for help, where the god of dreams imparts the oracle that Acacia had been told centuries ago. The oracle spoke of a Singing Turquoise, an enigmatic stone with special restorative properties that is in the possession of an earth spirit in North America. Traversing through the Curtain to get to the American Great Plains, David, Gullin and Tanuki encounter the Lakota tribe, whose shaman informs them that the earth spirit they sought was Ptesan-Wi, the White

Bison. To find her, he would have to take a spirit quest, which David must do alone.

It does not take David long to find Ptesan-Wi, but in order to attain the Singing Turquoise, she has to test him for his worthiness. David is swept into his buried memories, of his time as a child when he first met the woman who would become his favorite tutor, Señorita Catarina. He relives how he had come to care for her, and how he lost her when she married and left town with her new husband. He relives the pain of loss and heartbreak, but by understanding that he has to accept this loss, and not allow it to taint his heart, he is able to pass Ptesan-Wi's test and earn the Singing Turquoise.

With the healing power of the Turquoise, David captures the Shade plaguing Acacia within it, and restores her health and spirit. This does not bode well with Madam Nyx, however, who pulls both of them into her realm at the edge of the universe. She reveals that she has been planting Shades not only in Acacia, but within many magical creatures in order to attain their most prized abilities. These gifts she intends to pass along to her incarnation, a fragile gray-winged boy that will come to succeed Nyx when she will eventually fade from existence. While Nyx has become too weak to restart the process of draining Acacia for her intelligence, she is strong enough to drain it from a suitable replacement—in this case, Nico, who has been in Nyx's employment and failed to ensure Acacia's fatal fate. Madam Nyx, bestowing a mysterious modicum of benevolence, permits David and Acacia to leave her realm unharmed.

David returns to his world, to resume his life and future in Paris—although it is with a heavy heart that he says goodbye to Acacia and his new friends. For the next two years he apprentices as a landscape architect, and finds local acclaim as an author of children's stories. He finds new love in the kindly Florence, who becomes his wife. Yet, it would seem that his dealings with the world across the Curtain may not be done, as a present is left upon his doorstep shortly after his wedding—that of a matching sword to accompany the dagger that began his life-altering adventure…

Am I done? Good.

That was all before. This time is the Now.

CHAPTER ONE

She did not raise her eyes to look at him. *You've come to kill me.*

He leaned in close. ***Yes. You knew this was to be.***

Indeed, I foresaw this. You would dare do this, to your own mother?

You are not my mother. Mothers nurture. Mothers love. You merely created me.

You are *me. You are everything that I am, and more. For centuries, I slaved to give you the most valuable gifts from the most powerful creatures—*

Do you expect me to be grateful? To be compassionate because of your intentions for me?

No. But you could allow me to simply fade away, like the rest.

You have the one gift I truly want. If I do not take it, it will fade away with you.

The gift of prophecy can be a curse. You will foresee terrible things that will befall you. I have seen them. You will have no power to stop them.

No,* you *had no power to change what you prophesized. But I am more powerful than you ever were. I will make sure my future is secure.

Such foolishness. Such talk is almost…human.

Ah, there is the difference. You are from the time of gods when you relied on the faith and reverence of humans to give you strength. Without them, you cannot exist. I, on the other hand…it will be my word that decides whether they—whether all things in this world—continue to exist or not.

And even though she had foreseen this moment, even though she had already known of the agony to come, the scream of the ancient goddess Nyx sliced through the endless cosmos as she was torn asunder…

The scream sliced through the serenity of the house with the sharpness of broken glass.

David's head snapped up instantly at his wife's panicked cry. He shot up from his writing desk, his daily journaling forgotten, and he pursued the sound of the breathless sobbing as the manic rap-rap-rap of shoes skittering down the staircase.

"Florence?" David folded his arms around her as she flung herself at him. "Florence, calm down. What is it?"

"S…sn…sn…" Florence gulped in air as she clung to David's shirt collar. "Snake! Upstairs… horrid, black as sin…"

David crinkled his eyebrows. Paris was not exactly a city crawling with reptiles, especially in their neighborhood. How a snake would have gotten all the way to the bedroom, let alone into the house at all, was a mystery. Yet in the eleven months that David had been married to Florence, he had never seen her fly into frenzies over figments of her imagination. She must have truly seen something to be this panicked. "All right, all right. Calm down, I'm sure it's harmless. I'll take it outside."

"No, no! Do not go up there!" Florence pushed him towards the front door. "You haven't seen it. It's…it's not normal."

"Not normal? How?"

Florence took several deep breaths to steady herself. She tucked a stray strand of her strawberry-auburn hair behind her ear before replying in her crisp, elegant British dialect. "I was in the collection room to dust my tea sets, and it was there, on the bureau. It stared at me. And I swear, this…this thing was *smiling.* I don't know how to describe it, but it was smiling, and *leering* at me. It had…" She seemed torn between embarrassment and terror. "Eyes! I mean, eyes like you and me. I swear to you, David! *Human eyes*!"

Such a story would have at one time made David laugh at its ridiculousness. But he had witnessed events in his life, not so long ago, that made him aware that the impossible and fantastic could, in fact, exist. Most men of eighteen, going on nineteen years, may have dismissed such a story, or at the most felt a twinge of curiosity, but David froze as a ripple of icy anxiety scurried up his spine.

"You think I'm mad," Florence said when he didn't respond.

David shook his head. "No, Florence. I want you to wait outside while I take care of it. It's probably a garden snake. Maybe the light in the room made its eyes look different than they really are. But it may come down to me having to make a bit of a mess, so I'd prefer if you wait on the porch." He took her gently by the elbow and started leading her towards the front door.

"What if it's poisonous? We should go find someone who handles animals, or get a constable—"

"I'll join you in a minute. I won't go near it. Don't worry." With a firm hold, he guided her out the door and onto the stoop. The sounds of Paris rattled around them, business as usual. The day was bright and brisk, hardly the kind of weather that reflected the supposed doom slithering about inside the house.

"David, please, be careful," Florence warned.

David smiled at her with reassuring warmth. "I'm going to close the door in case it slips past me and tries to sneak out. I'll be back shortly." He gave her a comforting kiss before he stepped back inside and closed the front door. The fact was, he did not want to contain the snake because it might get out and attack someone else. If it had wanted to hurt Florence, it could have already done so. Florence was correct; something was not right about this animal, and David knew this because he could already sense an achingly bad presence in the house. Perhaps it was because of his past encounters with the demonic and deadly, but he had acquired a subconscious siren in his mind that was now screaming even louder than Florence had.

This snake—this monster—had come looking for him.

Armed with an iron poker from the fireplace, David ascended the stairs with soundless steps. His hand gripped the poker's handle tightly enough to cause his knuckles to turn white. He climbed to the top, looking down the hallway towards the collection room. Even from a distance, he could hear a faint rustling from that room.

His throat tightened. The collections room had originally been a guest bedroom which he had converted into his personal "Parlor of Collectibles." It housed his rarest books and a few special trinkets he had unearthed from oddity shops and traveling salesmen. It also was the room in which one special box was kept—a long, polished wooden case that concealed two irreplaceable gifts from…her…

No snake had need of anything in that room. No snake would try to steal anything from that room. Definitely, no snake had the means with which to pry open a locked case to steal the sacred gifts held within.

No snake could do such things, but this was not a normal snake.

David crept down the hall, willing his feet not to sprint lest he alert the animal. The poker in his hand seemed to vibrate with an anticipation to bash in some foul beast's skull. Just outside the door to the room David paused and waited for another sound from within. The silence only made the rapid thudding of his heart feel all the heavier, sound all the louder.

He noticed the sudden stench. He didn't realize snakes could have odors, and he couldn't decide at first if this was a good smell or a bad one. It was a meaty, earthy scent that seared his nostrils—it was potent enough that David covered his nose and mouth with the collar of his shirt. He slowly inched towards the edge of the door, tipping his head forwards to take a look into the room.

At first, he couldn't spot anything out of the ordinary: his book shelves lining the walls, the glass display case of foreign coins and knick knacks, the polished bureau upon which were Florence's china tea sets and one of David's displayed violas, the gothic-style mirror above the bureau, the two plump crimson armchairs placed across from one another, the marble pedestal with the Grecian vase. It was all there, not a thing out of place.

There it was again. That rustling noise, a rough surface rubbing against another. It was faint enough that it wasn't easy to determine where it was coming from—at least, not for anyone who didn't already know what an intruder such as this would be after.

David crept towards the bureau, his eyes locked on the bottom drawer. His forehead wrinkled in intensity as he noticed the drawer had been pulled open, no more than half an inch. Using the curved tip of the poker, he hooked it onto the drawer's handle, standing away at arm's length as he slid open the drawer to look in.

There was the long wooden case, and a moment of relief washed over David to see it still in its hiding place. But that little black-green tail wiggling out from between the barely-parted lips of the case was new. As the drawer opened wider, a flat head wriggled out from the case and looked up at David. Two glistening, pin-head-sized eyes stared at him, and a bright red tongue flicked out, almost in a mocking manner rather than to taste the scents in the air.

David stared at it for a little longer, and then let the hand wielding the poker drop to his side. He smirked. This is what Florence had been so frightened of? This miniscule, bug-eyed, barely six inches long…

He paused. He narrowed his eyes at the snake. The reptile stared back at him steadily, as if it had been expecting him. David noticed that its tongue was a bit too bright red, its scales a bit too glossy, its eyes a bit too aware. And, indeed, those eyes were not the solid black of other snakes' eyes, or even the yellow or green variety with slitted pupils. Silvery-white orbs with tiny red irises were locked onto him.

"Who are you?" David asked.

The petite python flicked his tongue at David again. It blinked.

The snake—a species that possesses no eyelids—blinked.

David's teeth clenched, and he brought the poker up slowly. "I don't tolerate thieves in my house."

The snake looked at the wooden case, and then back at David. "Oh, is this yours? I was sure this belonged to someone else."

David was taken aback by the deep voice that came out of the tiny animal. It was a voice that was as dark and sticky as pitch, a tone that could make a tiger cower. "You're not really a snake, are you?" he asked.

The snake curled around so its head was upside down. "And you're not really who I think you are. You don't look it, anyway…not right side up, not upside down. Perhaps inside out? Would you shed your skin so I can see? Or I could help you peel it off."

"I've faced dragons and demons before," David informed the snake. "I'm not afraid of you."

The lips of the snake pulled back into an awful, hate-filled smile. "Then you're a fool."

The snake raised its head higher...and higher...and higher...as its body inflated, its scales elongated, and its head widened and bloated. In a few seconds, it was as tall as David, and its oily coils were spilling out of the drawer. But it was its face that made David reel back, for it was not a serpentine façade glaring at him. The red and silver eyes shrunk back into craggy eye sockets, while the protruding nose flattened into a snout and a pointed chin jutted out. The scales on the face lightened into a grayish-green hue as a wide forehead ballooned from the top. It was a human face, albeit not a handsome or remotely pleasant one.

It opened its mouth to reveal several rows of serrated teeth, and a wildly delighted look shined in its eyes. "Oh, and what fun fools are...both to play with and to—"

The poker came crashing across the right side of the snake-beast's head. It flew backwards, its head smashing into the mirror above the bureau as its coils twisted about in a frenzy. It swiped Florence's tea sets and David's viola clear off the bureau and they clattered into irreparable pieces on the floor. It burst apart the drawer it had been sitting in, sending the wooden case with David's secret gift tumbling out.

"You owe me for all those things you broke," David remarked, readying his poker for another strike.

The snake laughed as it came back around to face him. It was hysterical, manic laughter, as if having been bashed in the face by a poker was the most humorous thing the snake had ever been subjected to. "You are amusing, Señor Sandoval! For a human to fight back against an Ilomba, is like a gazelle in the grip of a crocodile's jaws. I hate it when humans cower and whimper when threatened, like that dainty little morsel that went screaming out of here before."

Rage brewed in David's gut, the heat seeping up into his chest and limbs. "Don't you ever go near my wife again."

The Ilomba swiveled its head from side to side. "Or else, what? Will you hit me with your iron stick again? Or maybe your sphinx will come and save you?"

David froze, his rage blotted by surprise. "How do you…you've been sent by Nyx, haven't you?"

The Ilomba slithered slowly towards David, who stood his ground. "It will drive you mad, won't it? If you don't know the truth. You feel in control if you know everything. But why? Why live in the stifling confines of order and knowledge, when madness is so much fun? To try to be in control is to be controlled. Everyone wants you to act as they do, to be 'sane,' so they feel safe. There is no such thing as safe."

Everyone is out to get you! shouted one of the chipped tea cups on the floor.

David watched out of the corner of his eye as the broken porcelain cup began hobbling slowly towards his foot. It did not seem strange to him, nor did his cracked viola craning its neck towards him with the shuddering of a snapped-necked swan. But he was not paying them mind, for the Ilomba's eyes held him, enticing and paralyzing him, blending David's dread and fascination into a concoction beyond his logic.

The Ilomba's scales brushed David's leg, as the beast slinked up around his waist. "All this time, you've been trying to find answers to the most pointless questions, but you don't even realize that your mind is being consumed by confusion, blinded by fear…but Madness is freedom from fear, freedom from pesky, paranoid thought…"

Don't think! Thinking hurts! begged the painted roses in the wallpaper, twittering in childlike unison.

Above David, his mother—wasn't she supposed to be back in Cervera with *Padre* and his *hermosos*?—sat in a fine chair on the ceiling, hanging upside down but looking perfectly composed. *"What is Florence going to say about that broken tea set? Didn't I raise you better?"*

David's reflections in the broken mirror shards began conversing among themselves. *What did he say about a sphinx? Where is she? We need her right now… She could twist this snake into knots…*

The books in the room began flying like bats around his head, hooting words like confused owls. *Sphinx…minx…drinks…thinks…stinks…*

Scary scary scary! chirped the tea cups.

A multitude of clamoring, laughing voices clustered around David, and they nipped and scratched and dug into every inch of his consciousness. Among the throng, he heard his own voice from somewhere outside of himself. *Why do I attract these monsters to myself... What if I am a monster? What if I grow fangs and claws and wings and start eating everyone in Paris?*

One of David's shoes giggled, murmuring, *I bet Parisians taste like cheese...*

The voices were all silenced, the talking objects rendered inanimate again, by David's agonized scream as the snake's teeth clamped down on his arm.

Scorching pain flooded David's arm and chest, forcing him to drop the poker. The Ilomba swatted the poker away across the floor with a flick of its tail, as it dug its fangs deeper into David's flesh. David grasped the Ilomba's face with his free hand, desperately trying to pry the beast off, but he could feel himself growing weaker by the second. Terror stung his heart as he watched the Ilomba bloat even bigger, and he realized that the snake wasn't pumping venom into him—he was feeding off of him.

When the Ilomba suddenly produced a second neck, upon which sprouted a second smiling human-reptilian head, David nearly vomited.

"Shame. I was expecting more from you," the second head said. "Don't worry. You won't be dead for too long..."

David stopped listening to the Ilomba long enough to realize that the wooden case that had tumbled out of the bureau was within his reach, and the lock had unclasped when the case had hit the floor.

He launched himself at the case, extending his free arm while the Ilomba clung on to his other. His sudden leap caught the Ilomba off guard, and the second head smacked against the floor as David fell heavily on his side. He got close enough to the case to flip it open. He grasped one of the items within—a dagger that curved like a basilisk's tongue—and drove it into the neck of the Ilomba's primary head.

The second head wailed as David stabbed again, and this time the dagger sliced clean through. The decapitated head released David's arm, plunking to the floor and rolling a few inches before dissolving into a pile of dark mush.

David reached for the case's other item, a long sword that was the dagger's brother in style and material. He staggered to his feet, both blades pointed at what remained of the Ilomba. Already, the snake was slowly deflating in size, having lost its food source.

The creature bared its teeth, its eyes bleeding fury at David, but his gaze no longer held its hypnotic power over David. Then its face melted. All of its facial features dripped away in viscous sludge, leaving nothing but a smooth surface of black-and-white-stripes, a convex shell of painted glass. Yet without a mouth, its raspy voice screeched. "The Night may fear you… even Death may fear you…but Madness fears nothing!"

David raised the sword over his head and brought it down with all his strength to slice the snake in half, but the Ilomba darted away and the sword's blade clattered on the floor. The Ilomba, returned to its puny worm size, slipped into a crack in the wall, and was gone. It left no trace of itself behind except for the oily trail of ooze that it had bled—but after a few moments the trail fizzled and evaporated like the fading wisps of a bad dream.

David collapsed, straining to gulp air into his body. He dropped his sword and dagger to inspect his wound. The flesh around the snake bite pulsated purple, but then faded rapidly to blue, to greenish, and then returned to David's normal skin color, that of milk-kissed breakfast tea. Even the puncture marks sealed up and smoothed over, as if concealing some horrible secret never to be uncovered.

The sound of shoes rapping up the stairs caught David's attention. He breathed deeply, figuring that if the Ilomba had poisoned him, the effects would happen quickly and no rushing to a medic would save him. But his heart continued to beat, his body was not racked with the acidic heat of venom…although, why did his arm look so vein-riddled…and why did he feel so weak…

"David? David!" Florence rushed into the room, kneeling down next to his hunched figure. "I heard a horrible crash from outside, and I thought…"

She stopped, dead silent. David turned his face up to look at her. Florence's eyes were wide, and her breath caught in her throat. She shot up to her feet, staggering a few paces back. Her hands, the givers of gentle gestures and comforting touches, pressed against her lips to keep a scream from escaping.

"Florence…" David immediately noticed his voice did not sound the same. It was raspy, tattered. He picked up one of the broken mirror pieces on the floor and looked at himself.

An old man, with hair the shade of cobwebs and wrinkles of a lifetime of decay, stared back at him.

CHAPTER TWO

There were curious minds and hushed whispers in the neighboring flats as the doctor's carriage sat quietly outside the Sandovals' townhouse. He had arrived shortly before the supper hour, and was allowed into the house by an unusually shaken, pale Florence Sandoval, who normally invited all guests into her home with confident eyes and a bright smile. Now, her gaze was downcast, and she ushered the doctor in quickly before shutting the door tight behind them.

Being somewhat of a local celebrity, it was difficult for secrets to be kept when it came to David Sandoval. An apprentice to the highly praised and highly sought-after landscape architect Antoine Roland, and the author of a small collection of well-received stories that sold in most of Paris's bookshops, David had made a very good name for himself at his young age. While it was no secret that he spoke more often of what stirred in his vast imagination than what happened in his real life, Paris society respected him and admired his skills. It was an immense change to David's life only a few years ago in his hometown of Cervera, Spain, where his stories and imagination had been given little attention and patronizing smirks of amusement.

David missed his mother, father and brothers, but his Paris apprenticeship with Monsieur Roland had opened so many doors, including his eventual meeting and courtship of Florence, who had traveled all the way from England solely to meet her favorite new author. His journey to Paris had also initiated what may have been the grandest, most incredible adventure of his life...

It was a tale he would never tell. He had been sure it was over, and it was one he wished to keep pristine and untouched, locked away in his mind and soul. But it seemed that some stories were determined not to end easily, and a snake had been sent into his garden of happy endings to foul it.

When the doctor walked into the bedroom and saw David in his decrepit condition, he had extended a hand to introduce himself, positive that this was some ailing family relative that the Sandoval couple had taken in. When a tearful Florence explained to the doctor that it was, in fact, David sitting there, the doctor blinked a few times, adjusted his spectacles on his nose, and after a long minute of silence, cleared his throat.

"Well, this is new," he muttered. "Let's get to the bottom of this, *oui*?"

As David predicted, the doctor could not make heads or tails of his condition. He had never encountered such a condition before, although he had heard rumors about patients with rapid-aging diseases in a certain hospital in London. There had been no official studies or documents about such a disease, however, and all the doctor could say was, "Perhaps you are like that man from the American story, Van Winkle. Maybe it works the other way. Rest, get plenty of sleep, and perhaps you'll wake up young again?"

David wasn't sure if that was meant to be a joke, or if the doctor was a tactless idiot.

Once the doctor departed, Florence sat down next to David on the bed. "Perhaps there is something to what the doctor said. Maybe we need to get away from the busyness of the city for a while, and go to the country. The fresh air, the sunshine, and the quiet might make you better again."

David sighed. "Not to mention, someone will stick his nose in here soon enough, and then all of Paris will know about this."

"We'll say you have an ill relative back in Cervera that you need to attend to, and that you went on ahead of me. If we run into anyone, I will say you are a great-uncle that came to bring us the news, and that you are escorting me to Spain. We'll leave first thing in the morning."

"You're not ashamed of what's happened to me, are you Florence?"

Florence touched David's face gently with her fingertips, giving him a sad smile. "Of course not. I could never be ashamed of you. But you have a reputation, and I wouldn't want anything to damage it. I know you will recover from this, darling. And if you do not, I will still love you and take care of you."

David took Florence's hand and kissed it. He knew Florence was telling the truth, but a dark corner of his heart chastised him, saying that she deserved better than to be saddled with a brittle old man for the rest of her life.

The carriage rumbled briskly on the road leading out of the hustle and bustle of Paris. As much as David would have loved to return home to Cervera, he didn't want his family to know what had befallen him, particularly since his younger brothers had no capacity to keep their lips sealed about anything. He and Florence were headed towards the countryside in the south of France, to stay at a small country inn where no one would recognize them. They had traveled through the area before, and Florence had fallen in love with the endless fields of golden-burst sunflowers. David could hardly feel excited about the trip. In his elderly state, merely getting from the house to the carriage had been exhausting, and his uncooperative muscles were making him testy. He said little, fearing that he would inadvertently gripe at Florence in his foul mood. It didn't help that he honestly believed that the coachman, being of practically bear-sized stature, would cause the entire carriage to tip forward and flip over due to his weight. He hadn't been able to tell much about the coachman other than his unusual size, for he was huddled inside a massive leather coat and wore a ludicrous hat that looked much like an upside-down Dutch oven.

Florence hadn't taken notice of the coach driver. She patted David's hand, and gently caressed his gray hair. David knew how fortunate he was to have such an understanding wife. Yet, every now and then, his thoughts would drift to a different face, one remarkably different from Florence's. A sun-tanned face of feral beauty, long tresses of dark hair and stunning, golden eyes…

His thoughts returned to the present, and he saw that Florence had drifted into a deep sleep. It struck David as unusual, as Florence had never napped while in a carriage before; the jostling from the bumps in the road would keep her wide awake. Yet she was sound asleep, and even a sudden dip in the road that caused the carriage to bounce aggressively didn't wake her. But her serenity had an effect on him, and he settled back with a few creaks in his joints, and closed his eyes.

Instantly, he knew he was not alone in his slumber.

It is good to see you again, David Sandoval.

He knew that voice. It was one he had not heard in years, yet he was aware that the owner of that voice had been watching over him from this Realm of Sleep for all of his life. The shifting rosy hues of the realm were leaking into David's vision, and a peace took hold of him that let him know there was nothing to fear.

"*Hypnos,*" David replied—or thought, as it was unnecessary to speak aloud in the Dream world. "*It is good to hear from you, although I wish it was during a better time.*"

The indistinct form of Hypnos took shape before him, a man who shifted through many visages of the human ideal, although the two blue wings that extended from his head above his ears remained consistent. ***Given what could have happened to you, I would contend that it could be a far worse time.***

"*You see what happened to me, don't you? To my body?*"

I see how everyone views themselves in their mind's eye. You have always appeared much older than you truly are. An old soul, I believe the saying goes. But you could be lacking yours right now, had the Ilomba finished what it started.

"*Is that what it was trying to do? Steal my soul? Why? Who sent it? Was it Nyx?*"

Hypnos made an abrupt gesture towards David, silencing his thoughts. It disoriented David, not just from being silenced without warning, but the urgency of the gesture was unlike Hypnos. The embodiment of Sleep had always been a calm, tranquil being, at least from David's experience. He sensed there was a tense apprehension in the god now, the feeling of being trapped in a dream where the dreamer has no control.

Refrain from using that name, Hypnos said with hushed caution. ***It would***

be best not to draw unwanted attention, although I fear there is nowhere in my realm that we cannot be watched. We must make this brief.

"Then tell me, quickly. Who sent the Ilomba?"

His name would mean nothing, as you nor I would be able to find him through name. But you have seen his face.

David was going to ask when, but then the thought came to him. The Ilomba's face had changed once it had started to grow stronger, into that horrible man-like visage, before melting into the striped mask.

An Ilomba adopts the face of the one who sent it, Hypnos confirmed, sensing David's realization. ***Such creatures are created by practitioners of black magic, but I fear your assailant is an entity that cannot be contained, cannot be reasoned with. Its presence signifies that there will be great chaos in the near future, and it will grow stronger from that chaos. Yet it is in opposition with forces that could threaten its existence, and thus it wanted to claim you before its adversaries did.***

"Me? Why?"

You are aware you have a rarer fate than most humans. A fate that could change the destinies of many others. Whoever owns your soul, owns your fate.

David paused, hoping Hypnos would add more, but the lingering silence indicated that he wasn't going to. "*Hypnos, if you aren't going to give me straight answers, then why are you here? Are you helping me as...a favor to someone?*" A surge of hope rippled in David's essence, as the face of a dear friend flashed in his mind.

You think of the sphinx. No, she is not aware of what has happened. But soon she, as many others whom you have known from her world across the Curtain, will be aware of the worst to come. The rise of Madness is only the beginning. While I do not bear the gift of prophecy, it is clear to me that you may be tied into what will occur. And you will do no good in the state you are currently in. There is someone you must see in order to undo that curse upon your body, and I can send you to him.

David wanted more than anything to take Hypnos's offer, to be sent wherever he needed to go to become his old—young—self again. He paused, however, a heavy weight on his mind. "*I'm traveling with my wife to the country. I doubt she'll understand about all of this "worst to come" that you speak of, or that the god of Sleep is sending me away to see someone, somewhere, I've never met before."*

She will be fine. She is in my realm at the moment. I will give her a dream to make her believe that you are going to the country because you were exhausted from work and needed fresh air. She will think she dreamt your aged condition, as will the doctor who visited you. She will awaken once you have been restored, and returned.

"So this person you want me to speak with, will return me to normal?"

You need only pass a simple test to see him, and then he will help you. Maybe.

"Oh, that's reassuring."

Let him know that I sent you. He will be more willing to help you then.

"He's an old friend of yours, I take it?"

He's my brother.

"Please tell me that being irritatingly cryptic doesn't run in your family."

It would do you well to not be so curt. I have guarded over humans for millennia, thus I have come to tolerate your kind's...less admirable qualities. He, on the other hand, is not so patient. Offend him even slightly, and you will lose your chance to return to your original self forever.

"Very well, I understand. So, this test you mentioned..."

The fisherman will explain.

"The...who?"

David's eyes opened, although for a minute he wasn't sure that he was awake. He should have been in the carriage, beside his sleeping wife, watching the French countryside roll by. But there was no carriage, no Florence, no countryside. There was a rickety, leaky boat that he sat in, bobbing on a churning sea that stretched out to infinity in every direction. The sky, which had been joyously sunny before, was painted in mirthless overcast, not threatening a storm but not offering any comfort. The only thing that remained from before was the coachman, the same abnormally large man in the leather coat and pot-shaped hat. His reigns had been replaced by oars the size of ship masts. David felt severely small, sitting face to face with this man.

The man removed the Dutch-oven hat from his head, revealing a tangled mass of earthen-dark hair. A thick beard devoured the lower half of his face, and as he sat up straighter, he showed that he was even taller than David had first thought.

This was not a man. This was, in both body and presence, a giant.

"Name's Hymir," the giant bellowed. "You ready to go fishin', old man?"

Having returned from the Dream realm, David grunted at the stiffness and chill in his flesh and bones. He had never been fond of boats—not that he was fearful of water, as he could swim fine—but the constant swaying and the spray of sea foam in his face was rapidly unnerving him. Being seventy years older than he should have been didn't improve matters, either. Everything ached and creaked and wouldn't work properly. Something as simple as craning his neck to look around was an effort. "*Dios mío, ser viejo es insoportable*," he muttered.

"What's that?" boomed the giant, as he brought the tree-sized oars around in another powerful stroke.

"I said, 'being old is a pain'," David explained.

The giant nodded. "Can't argue with you. I turned 1,132 last month. It's no walk in Valhalla, I'll tell you."

David cocked an eyebrow. "Granted, that's *viejo*. Are you immortal?"

"Can't be sure. Most of us giants don't live to ripe old age. Usually there's a war, or a plague, or you trip and fall down—for a giant, tripping and falling is not a trivial thing. Many never get back up, and there's an earthquake's worth of destruction to clean up afterwards. But me, I stay away from all that. My place is out here, on the water. Lots of fish, lots of clean air. Used to run a tour guide business for centuries, taking folks out here to fish for legendary catches. But my last one..." Hymir shook his head, with a hearty laugh. "Crazy Thor, trying to catch Jormungandr like some eel on a hook! I laugh now, but I tell you, that rattled me so badly, I swore off the fishing guide business for life!"

David should have been curious to learn more about the story, as tales of great adventure held a soft spot in his heart, but his concentration was elsewhere. He was scanning the horizon. "How far do we have to go to find Hypnos's brother? I don't see a spot of land anywhere."

Hymir cast his gaze to the sky. "Don't get impatient. The stars are pointing us the right way. It won't be long now."

"Hypnos said you'd tell me about a test I need to pass to see this…who am I trying to find, anyway?"

Hymir pulled another mighty stroke through the water. "Ah, test, yes… there is one of those, isn't there?" He was quiet as he paddled along a few more times. "Can't imagine you need to be too athletic for it, if Hypnos thinks you can pass it."

David glared at Hymir. "You don't actually know what this test is, do you?"

"Now now, give me a minute to think. I'm working with a 1,132 year old brain here."

"Yet you remember a fishing trip with your friend Thor that must have happened, what, a millennium ago?"

"That's different! You don't forget something like that. We're talking about hooking a monster whose whole body could curl around the entire world! With a mouth full of teeth that could grind mountains into pebbles!" Hymir shivered at the memory. "Mountains…that rings a bell…I think climbing is part of that test. But it's not really climbing if it's underwater, is it? Why wouldn't you just swim upwards…"

"Did you say, 'underwater'?" David nearly bolted up out of his seat, but the precariousness of the rocking boat kept him down. "Wait, I don't have to…" He looked over the side of the boat, into the frothy dark depths. "That's ridiculous. My body's too old to do an easy swim on the surface, let alone dive underwater!"

Hymir shrugged. "Sorry, old man. Geras likes his solitude, and there's no place that has more solitude than down there."

"Why do you keep calling me 'old man' when you're over a thousand years older than I am!"

Hymir tapped a meaty finger to the side of his head. "It's all in the mind.

I don't think like an old man. I don't focus on things like achy backs, or what I can't do because I'm 'too old' to do it. Therefore, I'm not anywhere as 'old' as you are."

David was going to argue that Hymir didn't think about those things because he clearly had selective memory, but the giant did have a point. David was still himself, whether eighteen or eighty, and he had faced much more daunting obstacles than this in his life. "All right, I understand. So, what was that name you said? *Gyro?*"

"Geras," Hymir corrected. "Not familiar with 'im myself. But if he's anything like that devious hag Elli that tricked Thor into a wrestling match, you best be on your toes. She didn't look like she could lift a feather, but she pounded the God of Thunder flat as *pannekaken*! They may look like harmless, shriveled skin bags, but the older you are, the more you know, and the more you know, the more dangerous you can be."

David knew how dangerous certain 'clever' people could be. His memories of Nico, the Teumessian, who valued cunning over all else and had tried to have Acacia killed in order to become the most cunning creature alive, had not faded with time.

Acacia…it was hard enough to hear the word "sphinx" without a pang in his heart, but to think of her name, to mentally hear it sing in his mind…and then to hear her gentle voice, see her golden eyes and smile in the weavings of his imagination…

"We're here," announced the giant. He let the oars rest in the water, as the boat's pace gradually slowed.

David was thrust back into the present, and audibly groaned at having been torn from his reverie. But it was just as well that Acacia was a memory, and not here in the flesh. For her to see him as he was, to see what would have undoubtedly been revulsion on her face, would have destroyed him.

Funny, that he was more concerned with what Acacia would think of him, rather than with Florence's reaction upon his transformation. It was probably because of how comfortable he was with Florence, knowing she would still care for him despite his condition. Besides, she was eventually going to see him as an old man anyway, as they aged together over the years. He could never grow old with Acacia; her kind didn't seem to age physically, given that she was centuries old and still had the face of a youth. Not that it was even a thought to concern himself with; wherever she was, the sphinx had another life to live that didn't involve him. She had let him go so he could lead a happy, prosperous, stable life in Paris.

She had let him go…

"Are you wandering off, old man? I said we're here."

David looked over the side of the boat again, and gulped. "You mean, this is where I…disembark."

"How's about something to give you a bit of courage?" Hymir leaned over the pot he had been wearing on his head, which he had placed on the floor of the boat between his feet. David had thought it was empty, but as he sat forward to look into it, he saw a frothy brew had burbled up inside of it.

"Not like the cauldron I once had. Now that was a beautiful piece, a mile deep, with enough brew to satisfy all the gods and giants together. Lost it in a wager. To my own son, no less." Hymir sighed. "My *modir* gave me an earful about losing that cauldron, all night long. The old lady's got one tempest of a temper."

David smirked, figuring Hymir's *modir* was his mother. "Mothers are good at that. Mine has given me enough tongue lashings in my time."

"Bet your *modir* doesn't have 900 heads to scream at you with." Hymir held out the cauldron to David, who almost dropped it from its weight. "Drink up. You'll need the energy."

David hoisted the cauldron to his lips and managed a tentative sip—and instantly spat the liquid out. "*Qué repugnante!*" he coughed. "What's in this?"

"The ale of the gods. And some lime juice. And ox blood. Puts some hair on your chest." Hymir laughed deeply, as he took the cauldron back and enjoyed a long swig of the nasty brew. "Now, I wish you good luck. Keep your wits about you."

"Wait, you still haven't told me what the test—"

David was never able to finish his sentence, for Hymir picked him clean off of his seat with one hand and pitched him over the side of the boat. David thrashed in the water, sputtering and gasping for air as his frail limbs did no good keeping him afloat. As he sank beneath the tumultuous waves, he heard Hymir call out, "No, down, old man! You want to swim down! And hold your breath, that'll help..."

CHAPTER THREE

Perhaps it was because Hymir was more familiar with giants and gods then humans, that it hadn't occurred to him that tossing an old man overboard into freezing, unforgiving waters was a bad idea. The sea closed in over David's head as his arms and legs wore out after a few seconds of frantic paddling, and the soundless, opaque blueness enveloped him. He remembered the time that he had tried to go through the Curtain from the hidden world of legends back into his own world: he had left the island that the Sirens called home, into the rolling thunderclouds of the Curtain, and then plummeted into bleak darkness as an unknown ocean rose up around him before waking up in Japan. He prayed that this was like that time. This had to be the entryway into one of the Curtain's many openings, and that any second the water would dissipate and he would find himself in some strange, bewildering place.

He sank deeper. His body grew colder. No reprieve from the suffocating water was coming.

The dread that he had been struggling to keep at bay was now the one and only thought beating in his brain: *I'm drowning. I'm going to die.*

What he found more surprising than that realization, was the fact he wasn't that bothered by it. Something in his creaky, weary body was murmuring that it was just as well, it had put up a good fight but now it was time to rest. He had a good, long run—

No I haven't! I'm eighteen! I'm not really an old man! I have to get back to Florence! I have to keep fighting!

David summoned his limbs to begin moving again, to forget the aching and the freezing and to keep swimming.

And then he was swallowed whole.

Swallowed, perhaps, was not the most accurate term. Sucked into a swirling vortex was closer to what happened, but at the moment, the sudden sensation of being forcefully suctioned into a tunnel of darkness felt like being swallowed to David. Then he smacked into something hard, and he swore every bone in his body must have been shattered. He lay still for what felt like an eternity, but eventually it dawned on him that he could breathe again, and he gasped and gulped for air. He could also hear again, for somewhere around him, a voice crackled:

"Blast that κουτός Charybdis! Shaking up my house with all that whirling nonsense! Just when I was about to win, too!"

Somewhere in the cobwebs of David's memory, he recalled hearing the word "Charybdis" before…yes, Homer's *The Odyssey*, which was one of David's favorite stories. Was that the same Charybdis from the legend, the monstrous whirlpool that swallowed ships whole? If so, then David had a notion that he was in the right place.

He slowly opened his eyes. There was not much to see, at first—the space above him was an inky blue-black, and he could make out fleeting shadows darting through it. When he felt something spiny walk over his outstretched hand, he rolled his head to the side and found himself gawking at a vibrant red, spidery creature that was prodding at him with long antennae.

David scrambled to sit up and bat the creature away, but in his haste he pulled a muscle in his hip and let out a squawk of pain. The creature—a lobster—skittered away across the beach of polished rock that David had landed upon. The old man forgot his pain when he saw that it was not one lobster, but what appeared to be hundreds, possibly thousands, cluttering the ivory-hued beach. They were all different sizes, different shades of reds, blues, and pinks. David gasped as he noticed a brown lobster so large, its claws could have cut a horse in half.

He paled as that monster lobster started to crawl its way over to him. Without any weapon, and not finding any loose rock near him to throw, David defended himself by picking up one of the smaller lobsters, about the size of a trout, and threatened to swing it at the giant lobster.

The giant lobster paused, its antennae twitching. "I know you humans are peculiar, but you would use a lobster to fend off a lobster?"

David placed his small lobster down, which scurried away to bury itself amid the piles of other shellfish. "I apologize. I thought you intended to eat me."

"Now that would be ironic, wouldn't it? A lobster, eating a man?" The lobster chuckled. "You're not immortal, not from the smell of you. But I'm not particular. We do need a fourth for Bastra. It's more interesting with four players than three. Follow me."

"Bastra? Players?" David carefully got up onto his feet with a grunt. He was vaguely familiar with the card game Bastra, although he had never played it. "Since when do lobsters play cards? And it looks like you'd have plenty of players here."

"What, these fellows?" The giant lobster waved an idle claw towards the others. "No, no, I like having them around because unlike people, they'll never wither away and die. Did you know that? Lobsters can live forever, if kept safe. They just get bigger and bigger, until some κουτός fisherman catches them or some larger fish eats them."

"No, I didn't know that." David hobbled behind the lobster, taking care not to step on any of the smaller ones. "My name is David Sandoval. I was hoping to find someone named Geras. You wouldn't happen to know of him, would you?"

"GERAS!" A feminine but bombastic voice crowed from somewhere beneath them, causing all the other lobster to scatter in a clicking stampede. "Geras, get your keister back in here! We're in the middle of a game!"

"Hold your hippocamps, Elli! I'm coming." The giant lobster sighed. He turned a beady black eye towards David. "Imagine having to deal with that for centuries. These Nordic women could make thunder shut up."

Elli…hadn't Hymir said something about an Elli?

The glassy beach suddenly sloped downwards, and somehow the lobster, Geras, was able to keep skittering down without sliding. David, on the other hand, hesitated as his feet slid precariously. "Geras, sir, I confess, I'm not used to moving in such a…I mean, I'm not really this…my reflexes are not—"

"Stop babbling." The lobster came back to him, taking David in one massive claw and picking him up. David made an "oof" noise, as Geras was not being all that gentle. "And I know you're not naturally old. You smell spring green. I hate that smell. But I figure, soon enough you'll start smelling a nice winter gray. Time fixes all problems."

"You consider being young a problem?"

"The world's biggest problem. Every horrible thing in this world comes from being κουτός, which comes from the young not knowing their head from their tail end."

David squirmed in the lobster's claw, and held his breath for a moment as they descended. He was beginning to think this was not a beach at all, but more of a mountainside. "No offense, but I've known plenty of older folk who have done silly things as well—"

The lobster laughed. "Anyone you think is 'old' is a child to me. All you humans are children. You value youth so dearly, and fear *me* so greatly! And someone like you, you are blessed with not having to deal with the faults of youth anymore, yet I bet my bones that you've come to complain to me about it. κουτός, I tell you. κουτός!"

"You use that word a lot, 'κουτός.'"

"It means 'stupid.' In fact, that's what I'm going to call you. κουτός. At least it'll be easy to beat you at Bastra."

David prided himself on being smart—he cherished books, he taught himself new things outside of his traditional schooling, he was apprentice to a prominent architect, and it was by his intellect that he had survived his ordeal against Nico and Nyx. To be blatantly called "stupid" sent a furious fire through his skin that made him want to boil that cantankerous crustacean.

The slope continued to curve down, and down, until Geras was walking perfectly vertical towards a round opening below. David stiffly craned his neck back to look up the way they had come, and now he could see the shape of the structure that they had been walking on. The glossy surface, the iridescent ivory coloring, the spiraling ridges going up and around—

they were on a towering, mother-of-pearl shell.

Geras continued crawling along, entering the shell's opening upside down as he skittered along the ceiling. Eventually he walked across to the side, gliding along the wall and down to the floor, much to David's nauseous relief. There was a glow emanating from inside the shell, and soon the two were in a humble little kitchen. In the middle was a round table made of coral, and at the table sat two elder women. One was taller and ganglier than the other, with wisps of frosty-white hair and long, lithe limbs. She grinned two rows of worn, chipped teeth as Geras and David entered the room.

"There you are, you old crab!" The woman cackled gleefully, shuffling a deck of cards in her willowy hands. "And you brought a fourth player! And he's cute!"

The other woman, round and squat, smoked a foot-long pipe, the bowl of which was carved to look like a crow's head. Long tresses of silver flowed from her head, and a long pointed nose protruded from the deep ravines of cracks in her face. She eyed David, not saying a word, and only puffed tendrils of white smoke into the air. The smoke curled into the shapes of birds and cats that danced around her wide-brimmed hat.

Geras set David down on the floor. A rattling sound, like sand shifting through fingers, leaked from between the plates of Geras' shell as he began to shake all over. David scooted back when he noticed that Geras was, literally, falling apart, and bits of him were raining onto the floor. Those bits started to scuttle about, for they were hundreds of tiny hermit crabs, toppling over one another and flooding the kitchen before they fled out the exit. When the last hermit crab fell from Geras' body, a frail, shriveled man stood where the lobster had been. He held a gnarled walking stick, gray-white with droxy and scarred with deep creases in its bark. David couldn't help but think how similar Geras looked to his cane.

"Men, always making a mess," the taller woman sighed. "Some things never change, no matter how old you get. Speaking of change…" She held up the deck of cards. "…are we starting a new game, or would you prefer to talk philosophy all night again? You Greeks, with all your philosophy."

"You Scandinavians, with all your battle lust. You'd rather be playing with swords than cards, Elli." Geras hobbled over to the table and sat down. He glanced over at David. "Ever play Bastra before?"

"Can't say that I have."

"Good." Geras gestured with his cane to the taller woman. "This is Elli. Let her win. Everyone will be happier. And this..." He gestured to the other woman, who continued to eye David steadily. "This is Jadwiga, but most call her Baba. Baba, Elli, this is κουτός."

David grimaced at the insulting pet name, but he did his best to bow to the two women, cracking his back as he did so. He groaned as he straightened up again. "Actually, it's David. David Sandoval. And I was hoping—"

"You are the one who defied the Night," Baba murmured, her teeth clenched around the stem of her pipe.

Her accent was thick, one that David had difficulty deciphering at first. She sounded much like a man he had met at the Paris Opera, a visiting composer whose opera had become so popular in his home country that word of it had spread all the way to Paris. *Ruslan and Lyudmila,* he believed the opera was called. Yes, Mikhail Glinka, that was the man's name. Where had he been from...Russia. This woman, Baba, sounded Russian.

Geras and Elli froze at the sound of Baba's voice. They glanced at each other, and turned their amused expressions towards David. "Ah, you're *that* David," Geras said. "Yes, I have heard of you. It's a special occasion for a human to meddle in the affairs of my mother and escape, unscathed."

"Your brother, Hypnos, sent me here to speak to you," David explained. "A snake, a Ilomba, took away my youth. At first I thought it was one of Nyx's—"

Geras made a rasping sound like a hiss, and he pounded his walking stick on the floor. Elli and Baba both cringed, and their gazes turned sour.

"Do not use that name in this place," Geras ordered.

David paused, hoping he could continue without angering the Old One further, lest he should lose his chance to regain his youth. "Has your mother become so hated, even by her own children, that no one can hear her name without loathing?"

Geras' hateful stare softened, but barely. "It is not my mother that fills me with loathing, although I had but little love for her. No, it is the other one."

"The 'other one'?" The memory somersaulted to the front of David's thoughts, as he recalled a small, frail, gray-winged boy that had sat at Madam Nyx's feet the last time he had been to the Night Goddess's realm. "You mean, her incarnation? The little boy she is stealing others' most prized abilities for?"

"Not anymore," Elli muttered.

"Why not anymore?"

The three elders did not respond at first. Geras appeared agitated, even nervous. Elli shuffled the deck of cards absentmindedly. Baba puffed on her pipe, as tiny clouds of toads hopped into the air around her head.

"Has she stopped?" David wanted to feel hopeful, but something told him that was not the case. "Has she realized how wrong it is to kill others just to—"

"She is dead," Baba said flatly.

The concept of Madam Nyx being dead didn't register with David. He honestly thought the old woman was joking, but no one was laughing or grinning. "Th…that's not possible. She's a goddess. Gods can't die."

Geras snickered, but it wasn't pleasant. "Oh, gods can die, boy. And it is often more agonizing and horrible than any death a human could comprehend. Yes, my mother is gone. And what she allowed to fester in her stead is a blight, a thousand times worse than her deadly Shades."

This revelation could have spawned a thousand and one questions from David, but one tumbled from his lips without thought. "Is he going to go after Acacia?"

Three stunned stares bore into David, until a rupture of laughter filled the room. Elli practically fell from her chair, as she threw her head back in wild cackling. Geras had to grasp his walking stick with both hands to keep from shaking out of his skin, he was laughing so hard. Even the stoic Baba couldn't hold back her chortles, and her smoke wisps took on the forms of laughing ghost faces the joined in.

"By the gods, even in an old man's body, he still thinks like a child!" Geras gasped between laughs. "All this lovesick nonsense. The whole world could go straight to Hades, and he's worried about one female who happened to fancy him, once!"

It was a good thing David was too feeble in his current state to do what he had the impulse to do, which was to clock Geras on the head. He also had enough wits about him to know that striking the Old One would not bode well for him.

"That's one of the millions of problems with youth," Geras said, his laughter subsiding. "All those pheromones smelling up the world, the dreamy eyes, the ignorance that love conquers all, when it rottens as easily as beached fish in the sun. Disgusting.' He spat on the floor. " You're one of the lucky ones. You'll wise up faster than the rest of your kind who have to wait decades to get to where you are now. A few days in that body, and your brain will catch up."

"But I don't want my brain to catch up! I need you to help make me young again!"

Geras' frown was as heavy and cold as iron. "And what makes you think I can do such a thing? Youth is that twit goddess Hebe's territory. I'm just Old Age."

"But…but Hypnos said…"

"Hypnos is a twit as well. Now, if you're going to be our fourth, sit down. If not, get out. I don't have time for whining intruders." He turned back to Elli and Baba.

"Please," David bowed his head, his voice softening. "If there is something, anything you could do, I will be forever in your debt. I will do any task you ask of me. I will take…any *test* you put before me."

Elli cocked an eyebrow, and gave Geras a look that said, *See, he already knows.*

Geras grumbled. "Hypnos, you κουτός…" He turned to look back at David. "What makes youth so much better than old age? Why do you want it back so badly?"

David blinked, as a rapid fire string of answers was ready to burst forth from him. But he held back, sensing that this was not an informal question.

"No answer? And you thought you were so smart. That's it, isn't it? Your brain worked faster when you were younger. You hate being called κουτός. You were smarter as a young lad, yes?" Geras asked.

David started to nod, but he stopped. Hymir's words echoed in his ears: *the older you are, the more you know, and the more you know, the more dangerous you can be.*

"No, that's not it," David said. "After all, wisdom comes with age."

"It's because he was stronger when he was a foal!" Elli said, leaning forwards on the table. "Must be horrid, being weak and slow. You miss having all that strength, eh?"

She had a point. Aching muscles and brittle bones were something David would love to unburden from himself. But once again, he heard Hymir's voice, telling him about how Elli had wrestled the Thunder God and won. David suddenly realized: Hymir *had* been telling him about Geras's test all along! He had been giving him all the answers. What else had Hymir said about being old?

"No, there are elders who can be much stronger than younger men. To survive life for as long as you do, you would have to be strong," David replied. His eye peeked over at Baba, who he expected the next question to come from.

Baba shook her head, whether in disbelief or to snub him, David was not sure.

"Bravery, perhaps?" Geras piped up. "Certainly a young man, who can be a solider, a warrior, a hunter, has far more bravery than some old hermit."

David scratched his head. "I thought I was brave before I had to face the Teumessian, and the night goddess, and all the monsters I had to fight on the other side of the Curtain. But I didn't know what courage I really had until after I survived those trials. There is a difference between courage and foolishness, and an old man who has had to face so many trials has more courage than a young man who only dreams of overcoming such dangers."

"Then what?" Geras demanded. "If you are wiser in Old Age, and stronger from life's challenges in Old Age, and braver in Old Age, then what does Youth have that you covet so much?"

David found that he was struck dumb. This should be an easy question. But any answer he could think of—having more time, more pride, more opportunities—did not feel right. After all, time was relative; someone with very little time could use it more wisely and happily than a fool who wastes years away. Pride was not always a good thing, either—the young could be more arrogant than proud, and true pride came from years of work and accomplishment. And as for opportunities, normally a person had found most of what he needed in life by the time he was old. What was the need for more opportunity if one had already attained them?

In fact, the more he thought about it, the more being aged didn't seem so bad. Being young came with too many worries, too many fears, too much to lose. Being old, what did one have fear of losing? David slowly walked over to the table, and took a seat next to Geras. There was a calm but smug smile on Old Age's face, and he patted David on the shoulder.

"See, I knew your brain would catch up with you," he said.

David stared down at his wrinkled hands resting on the tabletop. My brain…my mind…

It's all in the mind. I don't think like an old man. I don't focus on things like achy backs, or what I can't do because I'm 'too old' to do it. Therefore, I'm not anywhere as 'old' as you are.

Being old wasn't merely in the body. It was a state of mind as well. David was thinking like an old man because he looked like one. What would eighteen-year-old David say? What would he say as the boy, who was so optimistic, so infatuated with heroic stories, who, even when he and his friends had been in the grip of Death, he had never let go of…

"Hope," he murmured.

Again, the three elders paused, staring at him.

"Hope?" Baba echoed. "What, you are saying old people do not have hope?"

"I'm not saying that. Not exactly. As long as you have hope, you believe that life will go on. That life will get better. If you believe in life…if you don't dwell on how growing old will change things, but you simply live, then you're not really 'old.' But when you get to that point that you don't concern yourself with the future anymore, then you pass your hope along to the next generation. You give them your hopes, so they can believe in a better life. Some may call hope foolishness, or uncertain, but it's what keeps us going. It's meant to be passed down. And it's what I do not want to lose, even if some day I don't need it anymore. Someone else—a child, a friend, an heir—will need my hope to become their own. That's what youth has, what it needs, that is so important."

There were no replies for a long, quiet minute. The one sound was the soft rustling of the cards slipping out of Elli's fingers and falling like autumn leaves on the table.

Baba's pipe dangled loosely from her lips. But her eyes, for the first time since David had entered the room, glimmered with a subtle awe.

Geras's lips, meanwhile, twisted into a frown. He leaned back into his chair, as his fingers rapped on the top of his walking stick. "That might be the most naïve answer I have ever heard." He sighed. "Spoken from the heart of a child. Honestly, if I kept you around here with all your talk of hope, I'd start hoping again, and then what would I be? I'd have no one to pass it on to, and gods know I don't want to be some κουτός in heart or in mind."

He looked over at David, and gestured with his cane towards the door. "Get out."

David was flabbergasted, and shot up from his seat. "But I answered your—"

He caught his breath. His voice…

He looked down at his hands. No wrinkles, no creases. He touched his face, feeling the familiar smoothness, the defined cheekbones, and firm jaw.

"I said, beat it," Geras said. "We old timers have a game to play. No time for babysitting children."

"Shame," Elli said as she gathered up the cards. "He was cuter with the gray hair. Ah well, I can wait. What's another seventy years? Be sure you outlive your wife." She cackled again.

Baba removed the pipe from her mouth, preparing to say something. A trail of smoke from her pipe suddenly changed from white to coal black. She stared at the smoke, as it took the shape of a savage head, with a long muzzle full of gruesome teeth. All the color drained from her face.

"Boy," she rasped. "You bring Death upon us all—"

There was a shrill wail from above, and a vicious rumbling that shook the walls and the floor. There was an ear-shattering crunch, and David gasped as a series of sharp, yellow-ivory stalagmites punctured through the walls of Geras's home, and the walls rapidly closed in on them. A smothering, lung-burning air filled the space, seizing David's lungs and stopping his breath.

He dropped to his knees, covering his mouth and nose with his hands, gagging. The walls burst into pieces, and the stalagmites—no, he could see now that they were teeth—rushed in to grind him to bits.

The last thing he heard before the darkness overwhelmed him, was a Russian accented voice saying, "I would rather not be a wolf's dinner today, would you?"

CHAPTER FOUR

There was a peculiar smell wafting in from...somewhere.

David opened his eyes, squinting at the sunlight flowing in through the window. It bathed the room in morning's saffron glow, lighting the gossamer white curtains with a buttery hue. He tentatively moved his hands, patting at the plushy, soft blankets beneath him. He recognized the familiar texture. He rolled his head left, then right, observing the bedspread, the striped wallpaper, the nightstand, the matching vanity and chair set painted sterile white.

This was his bedroom. He was home.

Anyone else, awaking to this, would have sighed, rolled over and closed their eyes, presuming any ordeals involving giants, lobsters, Old Age, and a Mouth of Death would have been a fantastic dream. But not David. The remnants of the bristling terror that had gripped him still ran electrified in his veins, and he knew he had not dreamed such events. He sat up, and breathed deeply. Again, he smelled something fresh and fragrant, the smell of something cooking.

Florence...was she cooking downstairs in the kitchen? But she was supposed to be at the country inn, where they had been heading before David was spirited away. Perhaps Hypnos had given her a dream, telling her to come home when she woke up and found David gone. He prayed that he could explain his absence to her, if Hypnos had not already constructed a dream that made her believe some fabrication of his disappearance. He honestly wished the God of Sleep had come to him to let him know what on earth had happened back there, at Geras's home.

Now that he thought about it, why hadn't David seen Hypnos in his sleep? In fact, awaking from that slumber had felt different than before. It had felt stagnant…empty…

He got up from the bed, passing the vanity. He checked himself in the vanity mirror. The dark brown hair, the tanned wrinkle-free skin—he was completely himself again. At least that would be one thing he and Florence would not have to worry about. He walked out of the bedroom and started down the stairs. Four steps down, he stepped on something and it let out a loud screech.

David pulled back, nearly losing his balance as a soot-gray cat scrambled down the stairs. It made a beeline for the kitchen. David regained his footing, but stayed put. Since when did they have a cat?

"No crying to me, lazy bones," came a voice that was definitely not Florence's, from the kitchen. "You sleep on stairs, you get stepped on. Now off with you. You'll get cat hair in pot."

David crept quietly down the remaining stairs. He knew that voice, that thick accent speaking in broken English. He rounded the corner and peeked into the kitchen, to see the Russian woman stirring something in a pot which simmered on his cast iron stove. She removed the ladle to taste her concoction, and scrunched her nose. "Eh, such inferior ingredients. All cheese and sugar. Nothing to put meat on bones." She withdrew a turnip from her sleeve—David had a feeling that her sleeve had been empty a moment ago—and plopped it whole into her stew. There was a short scream as the turnip hit the boiling broth. Some of the stew sloshed onto the floor, which the cat padded over to the spill to sniff at it.

Baba shooed the cat away with her ladle. "Shoo, greedy thing!"

David took one step into the kitchen. "Baba?"

"Ah, so the Death Caller awakes," Baba said with a mock sweetness. "Convenient you awake now, after I save you and the danger is long gone."

David tightened his lips. "And how convenient that you can speak my language. I expected Geras and Elli to speak in any tongue, since they are more than human. But you…what exactly are *you*?"

Baba laughed. "Let's say, I am what I need to be, when I need to be it. As for speaking as you do, I have what I call 'magic ear.' You, too, have such an ear, yes? Can speak another tongue without having to learn?"

How did she know? David had once drunk enchanted water from the river-dwelling kappa in Japan, that allowed him to understand and speak in Japanese. Perhaps she too had such magical water in her possession. Or did his "ear" allow him to understand Russian too? No, then Baba's dialect wouldn't sound broken. "I don't think my 'ear' is as diverse as yours," he replied.

"Be glad you still have ears, or a head at all. You may have tricked the Old One to make you young again, but you are still cursed, little man. The wolf will hunt you again, and it won't matter if you on this side of Curtain, or the other side. When he desires his prey, he does not stop."

"Wolf? Is that what that thing was, that ate Geras's house? What happened to Geras and Elli?"

"They take care of themselves. Have for centuries. I doubt the beast would keep them down—they probably taste like rotten shellfish. I, on other hand, prefer not to be eaten. Much better to eat others, than be eaten." She smiled widely at David. He gulped when he saw that her teeth were gray and metallic—iron. She chuckled at his uneasiness. "If you afraid of old lady, you don't stand chance against wolf. You would have been snack if not for Baba Yaga."

Baba Yaga…that rang a bell. David had read that name somewhere, he was sure of it. He could not place where he had read it, but the word "witch" surfaced in association with that name. "Why *did* you save me?" he asked.

"Eh." Baba shrugged, and removed a handful of salt from her sleeve and chucked it in the pot. "There is something strange about you. Strange things intrigue me."

David stepped closer to her, trying to sneak a look at what she was cooking. Baba turned around, advancing on him and poking him with her ladle. "No interfering. Soup will be ready when I say it's ready. Meantime, you don't make any more smelly thoughts. Wolf will find you if you think too strongly. It smells it."

"What are you talking about? That wolf can smell thought? That's imposs—" David caught himself, realizing he was about to say something was impossible when, given how his day has been, nothing seemed to be so anymore.

Baba Yaga frowned. "Why you think it come to Geras's home, eh? To play cards? Peh! Most people have simple thoughts, fleeting thoughts. They come and go and don't cause a stir. But you—you have very strong thoughts. They hang in air, like scent of sage tied up to dry. You thought about something the wolf wants. He smelled what you were thinking, and came to devour it. So no thinking!" She rapped David on the head with her ladle, and then went back to tend to her soup.

David rubbed his head, wincing from how hard she had whacked him. "What kind of wolf is bigger than a house and can smell thoughts?" He narrowed his eyes on Baba. "And how do you know all of this? I don't suppose you might know about Ilombas as well—I was told practitioners of black magic create them." He glanced back towards the boiling pot again. "You're not summoning any other evil creatures with your cooking, I trust."

Baba Yaga sighed. "I know nothing about such things as Ilombas or whats-its. But wolves—I know of wolves. There are always wolves. Wolves in the shadows, wolves in the storm, wolves ready to gobble you up. But this, this is very bad wolf. Wolf that will do worse than eat a house, or swallow an ocean."

"This must be that 'worst to come' that Hypnos warned me about. But what was I thinking about, that it came to hunt me down? What was it really looking for?"

Baba shrugged again. "You tell me. They're your thoughts."

"I was thinking about what that snake did to me—about being young again. And Ny—" David paused, casting a weary glance at Baba. "The Night goddess. But she's gone, so that can't be what the wolf wants. Does it want to find the incarnation? The little boy with the gray wings?"

The old woman smirked. "Not so little now. But I do not think wolf is ready to hunt gods. Not yet. It is still not strong enough for that. But something smaller, something less powerful, perhaps." Baba took what looked like a brown lizard from her sleeve and threw it in the pot.

David groaned, throwing his hands up in the air. "You're the one who said I shouldn't think, and now you're making me think about all this…this madness! Why won't you tell me what that beast wants, instead of feeding me all these riddles…"

Riddles…I remember. She was the best at solving riddles. It was in her nature. It dawned on him what else he had been thinking about.

Baba looked over her shoulder, and grinned at him.

"Acacia…I was thinking about Acacia too." David ran his fingers through his hair, feeling his face flush hot. "Is the wolf after Acacia?"

Baba stirred the soup again. "Best you don't think of her. Your thoughts about her, particularly strong. Stink up whole town."

A cold, heavy weight sloshed in David's stomach, and clawed upwards towards his chest. "But why? Why would it want Acacia?"

"You ask me? I know much, but not all. It is wolf, she is part lion...perhaps dog likes to chase cat?"

The gray cat, lazing on the windowsill, lifted its head and gave Baba a sharp look.

Baba hoisted the pot off of the stove and set it to rest on the kitchen counter. "Give moment to cool. Then, you eat."

David sniffed at the simmering slop. He did his best to keep from coughing at the stench. "What is it?"

"Wolf knows your scent now, knows you know the sphinx. This soup will cover your smell, so wolf won't find you. Also show you why Russian cooking better than French." She dipped the ladle in the pot, and held it out to David. "Eat."

David took the ladle from her, staring at the bubbling spoonful. He glanced at the cat. It shook its head at him.

"Keep opinion to self, mangy furball," Baba warned. "Or next time I throw you in pot."

David held his breath, and then raised the ladle to his lips and sipped. He managed to swallow the liquid, but gagged. Tears filled his eyes and he snorted as if to sneeze out the horrible taste.

Baba clapped her hands, seeming delighted at his reaction. "See? Will make you hearty. Grow much hair on chest. Now finish it."

David forced himself to down what was left in the ladle. "There," he gasped, pounding his fist on his chest a few times to get the soup down.

"There, nothing. I said, *finish it.*" Baba pointed to the pot.

Dios mío, I should have let the wolf eat me, David thought.

Despite the stew gurgling in his stomach like an irritable boar, David went to the coat tree by the front door and gathered one of his coats.

"And where do you think you're going?" Baba asked. She had planted herself on one of the settees in the parlor while David had finished her scent-masking soup.

"My wife Florence is at an inn a day's journey south from here," David explained as he threw on his coat. "Now that your stew will hide my scent from the wolf, I can go to her without putting her in harm's way. She must be worried sick, all alone and not knowing where I went."

Baba leaned back on the settee, as comfortable as if she were in her own home. "I would not worry about pretty little yellow-hair. You will see her very soon."

David halted, his hand on the door knob. "What do you mean? Is she all right?"

Baba shrugged. "What do I know? I'm just old lady."

David walked over to her, nearly tripping over her cat again. "You know much more than you want me to believe. Clearly you know magic. Do you have a spell that can let me see where Florence is?"

"Should not bother. Will see her in short time." She took her crow-headed pipe from one of her sleeves and a small pouch of tobacco. She began preparing her pipe to smoke. "But perhaps you would like to see how another is fairing, someone far away who you care much for?"

"You mean Acacia."

"For that, I would give you a moment to see. But it would come with price."

David turned from Baba, pacing the floor over to the window. His desire to see Acacia, even if it was a momentary image, burned in his heart like star fire. But should he tempt himself to it, when Acacia could no longer be a part of his life? He had a settled life now, with a wife, an apprenticeship that had opened so many doors to him, and a good social standing. Acacia had wished him to have such a life, and had severed her ties from him so he could have it. Would seeing her bring him more anguish than he could bear? Would he even like what he saw? What if she was hiding in fear from the wolf, or what if the new Nyx was sending more creatures after her to drain her of her cunning, as the old Nyx's Shade had almost done? What if the wolf or Nyx had already found her…what if she was…

"There is always a price for every choice we make," David said. "You can't take without giving something, no matter how small. What would you ask of me, to show me Acacia?"

Baba snapped her fingers over the bowl of her pipe, and a spark ignited the tobacco inside of it. She puffed twice, and the white smoke was born to the air. "Let us agree, you would owe me favor. Sometime, someplace. I promise it will be in equal value to what I give you, no more, no less. And you will not argue or try to make me change my mind when the time comes that I ask for your favor. Deal?"

"It is a dangerous thing to make ambiguous deals with witches."

Baba Yaga smiled, her iron teeth glistening. "You are in more danger than you could imagine, boy. Face it or flee. It matters not to me."

David returned to Baba, looking her straight in the eye. "No false illusions. You guarantee you'll show me the truth?"

"I guarantee nothing."

David glanced at the cat, who was rubbing itself against his legs. He looked back at the witch. She watched him steadily, breathing out smoky trails that formed the shapes of cats that prowled around her hat. One smoke trail blossomed into a larger feline shape: the sleek but muscular body of a lioness, with a long mane around its fierce but human face, and two feathered wings extended from its shoulder blades. A Grecian Sphinx.

David knew Baba was producing this image to entice him, to lure him into accepting her offer—and the ache to see the real thing, the true sphinx, was so great, he thought his entire chest would burst.

"Tell me what you need," he said.

After gathering a silver tea tray from the kitchen and pouring a film of water onto it, David set it on the floor in the parlor at Baba's feet. Out from her space-defying sleeves, the witch withdrew a small red pouch. She sprinkled the black powdery contents within it onto the water in the tray, and mumbled a string of words that rumbled in her chest with the foreboding of a distant storm. Shortly, the water began to swirl, the powder darkening the liquid before it started to glow with a greenish radiance.

The cat hissed, but didn't run away. David kneeled down to the tray, staring into the glow. He could see nothing at first, save the swirling colors of the water, reminding him of a serpentine dragon's coils twisting through a dusk-laden sky.

Then, he could see it forming…her face…it was so close…

She was in a dark place. There were candles encircling her, dimly illuminating her features, but did nothing to help reveal what sort of place she was in. There were walls, but they rustled and wavered as if made of fabric.

She was not alone. A form stood before her, an abominably tall stretch of materialized shadow. Even in the lack of light, its eyes glistened like orbs of mirror. Its back looked massive in comparison to its slender legs and thin face, but for a moment, its back expanded outwards into two distinct wings before folding up again.

"What do you want?" the sphinx asked. Her voice was laced with warning.

The shadow presence took three steps towards her. Acacia lowered her head, snarling one corner of her lip to show her canine tooth that could rip flesh.

"I have come to offer you refuge," the presence replied. "The worlds that you know will cease to be. There is a Devourer coming to make a feast of all living things. For the cruel actions of my predecessor against you and others, I wish to make amends by giving you safety in my realm, where the Devourer cannot follow."

The sphinx bared her teeth fully, and the muscles in his shoulder blades tensed. Her obsidian claws flexed from her paws. "Why should you care about me, or any of the victims that your mother's—no, you and she are one in the same. Why do you care what your Shades did to us? You benefitted from our suffering. You took our talents, our strength, and many of us, our lives. What need do you have for me now, unless you intend to try and drain me of my cleverness again?"

The winged shadow rippled like a reflection in water. "I am not the same as the goddess before me. I am more than she was. I have foreseen the future with her gift of prophesy. The mortal world, and yes, your world across the Curtain, will be consumed. We gods exist to herd, as much as your kind exist to be herded."

"If you are so powerful as you claim, why not stop whatever will consume the worlds?" Acacia's tail whipped back in forth like a pendulum from an impatient clock.

"Why should I want to stop it? I have no love for your kind's world, or the human-mastered world. I have my own realm. My benevolence is limited. But there is a shard of it for you, perhaps because the Nyx before me was so drawn to you and your cleverness. There will be no place else for you to go, to survive. Accept my offer, if you are not foolish."

Acacia sat back on her haunches, holding her head high. "Tell me, first, how it feels to live countless lifetimes and have no one or nothing to love, or to love you. Then, perhaps, I can judge if it is better to live as you do, or to perish with those whom I have loved. Somehow, I am led to believe the former is more horrible."

"Those whom you love…You refer to the humans that you tended to all those years. Your pretend 'pride' of gypsies."

"They were as real a pride to me, as your heart is pitch black."

"They will all die, Sphinx. Whether it is due to the Devouring of the Worlds, or to their short lives, they will die. Let them go from your heart. Come to the Night and embrace the eternal."

Acacia closed her eyes, and inhaled deeply. When she opened her eyes again, they held a cold but collected serenity. "Thank you, but I refuse your offer. You would be wise to never summon me again."

The shadow reached within the folds of his robes—if he indeed wore robes, and it was not his bare skin--and brought forth an object. It was a blackish bubble, as if blown from tar or oil. "Let me leave you with a parting visage, Sphinx. A glimpse of the near future, a taste of the horror that will come from the one who would end your world, and all worlds touched by light."

Acacia narrowed her eyes on the bubble. The shadow-being dropped the bubble, where it splashed into a pool of night, spilling out around her feet. Acacia hissed, stepping back from the liquid with the urgency of evading acid. The pool did not burn her, however, but clung to her fur with sticky molasses tendrils. A shape inflated up from the pool, something that could have at first passed for a malformed log or a crocodile's backside, but soon solidified into what was clearly a human, prone and still.

The intense look on Acacia's face faded, dissolved into horrified heartbreak. The shape before her was a young man with dark hair and dark unblinking eyes, lying dead in a soaking mess of his own blood. Most of his middle shredded and mauled to threads.

"No!" she howled. "You lie! You deceive me!"

"My gift of prophesy must reveal what is to be. I cannot alter the design of the future, just as the previous Nyx foresaw that she would not attain your intelligence, no matter how badly she willed and worked to change her vision. I cannot deceive you, Sphinx. He will be destroyed. His murderer will relish in his slow, excruciating death."

The sphinx was silent, a frozen living corpse. All of the strength seemed to melt from her being. She slowly, shaking, placed one paw upon the cheek of the corpse before her. The body popped into nothingness, and the murky pool soaked into the ground.

Acacia's eyes flared white-hot venom, and she growled, "Who would do this?"

"It will be the one called Fenrir. Your beloved human's fate is tied into confronting him. They will fight, and Fenrir will win."

Acacia curled her claws, digging into the earth. "Where is Fenrir now?"

"He moves swiftly and silently. Despite his great size and his path of destruction, he is difficult to track."

"But not impossible. He will wish he never left his prison. Your vision will never come to be, Nyx. Like the Nyx before you, you believe you can foresee all, but you cannot predict everything." She turned away sharply, and vanished into the surrounding darkness.

The image in the tea tray blinked out. All that was left was the remaining bits of powder floating in the water.

David looked up at Baba. "I don't understand. That man, he kept saying 'the Nyx before him.' He can't be Nyx's incarnation, is he? He was a little boy when I saw him two years ago. He couldn't have turned into...*that*... And who is this Fenrir that will kill...someone Acacia cares about..." David wiped a hand over his face. "Who was that, Baba? Who did Acacia see in the pool?"

Baba cocked an eyebrow at David. "You know well who that was. Who do you think Sphinx would mourn so greatly for? Who would be in danger of death that she would do anything to prevent it? Only one man she knows has crossed paths with wolf lately, yes?"

"The wolf? What does the wolf have to do..."

David felt a tapping on his ankle. He looked down to see the cat, holding a leather-bound book in her mouth and batting his leg with her tail. It was a large book, so the cat must have dragged it along the floor to bring it to him. David recognized the fake gold-plated lettering on the cover; it was a book from his Collections Room library.

"Why did you bring me this?" He knelt down and picked up the book, reading the title: *The Poetic Edda.* He remembered it now; he hadn't read this book since he was about ten years old. His parents had brought it from Cervera, as well as a chest-full of his other childhood books, when they had attended his and Florence's wedding, thinking he would want them for his personal collection.

He recalled it was a compilation of poetry from the 13th century, about gods and heroes, magic and monsters from the far North. Yet for some reason, he remembered that he had read it once, and then never desired to read it again. Why? It should have been everything he loved about myths and heroic tales. He rejoiced in such stories. David started to flip through the pages, taking in the familiar scroll-work drawings, the worn print, and soon it came back to him why he had detested this book.

Ragnarok—the End of the World. There were poems in the *Poetic Edda* about all the heroes that would one day be destroyed by the monsters, the gods killed and the world devoured. Ten-year-old David hadn't been able to stand it. Heroes didn't lose! Monsters couldn't win! Even in the Greek myths where heroes occasionally met their doom, at least most of them won the day before their untimely deaths, thus it was an honorable sacrifice. But for all the Norse heroes to be eaten or slain and the world to come to an end? That was unacceptable. Thus he had tossed the book aside and stayed devoted to his tales where the heroes triumphed and the villains got their comeuppance.

David froze when he got to one page. He had almost missed it, but the word had somehow leapt off the paper, snaring his eyes. It was in the story about how the father of the gods, Odin, would someday battle the son of a traitor god, Loki. Loki's son would kill Odin, thus slaying the mightiest god in the world.

Loki's son was named Fenrir. On the opposite page was a sketch of a white-bearded god wearing a crown-shaped helmet—it must be Odin—riding on an eight-legged horse, and he was battling a monstrous black wolf.

David snapped the book shut, closing his eyes. "The wolf, he is Fenrir, isn't he?"

"Ah, so boy is not so stupid." Baba Yaga picked up the tea tray from the floor.

David opened his eyes. "And Acacia thinks Fenrir is going to kill me. *Dios mío*! She is going to go after that wolf!" David dropped the *Poetic Edda* on the settee, and marched over to Baba, coming so close to her that she had to step back. "Why did Nyx show her that vision, if there is nothing she can do to change it? He must know Acacia would go after Fenrir by showing her that. Nyx must want her to go after him. What does he want?"

Baba shrugged. "I'm just an old lady—"

"You are not just an old lady! You know something you're not telling me, and I need to know it, right now!"

Baba's eyes darkened, and the grimace on her face could have turned ravens' feathers white with fear. "You should be grateful Baba Yaga tell you anything at all. But now you owe her, remember? It would be best you thank her for her kindness towards you. You wouldn't want to make her angry. Make her decide that you should do something quite nasty to pay for her services, no?"

David pulled back. He looked away from her poisonous gaze. "I deeply apologize, Baba. I am thankful for your help. I did not mean to offend. My emotions got the better of me."

"You should calm yourself. Would not want to be temperamental to your arrival."

David did not need to ask what "arrival" she was referring to, for the sound of the front door opening caught his ear.

David dashed from the kitchen to the front hallway. There, standing in the doorway, was a bedraggled young woman, her blonde hair hanging in tangles around her panic-stricken face. The bottom hem of her dress and her shoes were coated in mud.

"David!" Florence exhaled the word, as if all the relief and fury were pouring out of her in that one breath. "Why did you leave me alone?"

CHAPTER FIVE

There were no words spoken for several minutes, as David sat side by side with Florence on the settee, holding her close. He gently stroked her hair, kissed the top of her head, but nothing elicited a reaction from her. He could feel her trembling, not from a chill or fear, but she was restraining her emotions that were welling up inside of her, ready to erupt.

"Please, Florence…I am so sorry, I…I was…"

"You were gone," Florence said softly, tensely. "I awoke, and I was alone, lying on the side of the road, out in the middle of nowhere. It was dark, I was in the grass and mud, but I couldn't remember how I got there. I know I wouldn't go that far from the city without you. But you weren't there. No one was. Not even a horse, a carriage, nothing to tell me how I had gotten so far out there. So I started walking, hoping I was heading the right way. Eventually a farmer and his wife rode by in a cart, and gave me a ride back to town." She turned to look at David. "I don't know how to feel. Why couldn't I remember anything? And why were you here, at home, not worrying about what had become of me?"

"I was worried! I was worried sick! But I…I couldn't…"

"We thought you were lost to us, dear." Baba Yaga came hobbling from the kitchen, with a clean tea tray and a piping fresh pot of tea in hand. At least, it appeared to be Baba, although her hair was pulled back into a clean, smooth bun, and her face was rosier and brighter. "Poor man, out looking for you all evening, but could not find you. Lost track of the bandits that kidnapped you. He searched everywhere until it got too dark to keep looking. I told him, best to come home and start again in the morning."

Florence stared at Baba, as the old woman set the tea set on a side table next to the settee. "Oh, I didn't know. I thought…who are you?"

"David, you don't introduce your own grandmother to your wife?" Baba said, with a smile. David noticed that Baba's teeth were now pearly white and flat, not the row of sharp daggers they had been. She even looked cleaner, more radiant, as if layers of grime and dust had been washed away. She exuded a presence of calm comforting.

"Oh, of course. Florence, this is my *abuela.* Remember that ill relative I mentioned, who was coming to stay with us a while?" David held his breath, hoping that Florence's lack of memory would allow him to fabricate things. He also hoped she would misconstrue Baba's Russian accent for a Spanish one.

Florence glanced between him and Baba, and she gave Baba a tired smile. "Of course, how good to meet you. But, you were saying something about bandits?"

"Yes, dear. Broke into house while David was out taking me to see the doctor. Must have hit you hard on head. We came back, and we were so terrified. David went out right away to catch up with the bandits to get you back. Thank heavens you are all right."

"Yes, thank heavens." David hugged Florence tightly and kissed her.

Florence took a deep breath, and then she took David's hand. "I don't remember any of that. I should have known you wouldn't leave me. Oh darling, it's so good to be home!" She embraced him, burying her face in his neck.

David held her for a long time, rubbing her back. "It's okay, Florence. You're safe now."

Baba huffed, rolling her eyes.

David ignored her. He helped Florence to her feet. "It would be best to get you into clean clothes and into bed. I'll bring you up some supper."

He helped Florence up the stairs to their bedroom, and then left her to change out of her clothes. He came back down the stairs, passing Baba who watched him with concern. She followed him into the kitchen, where the gray cat sat patiently on the counter, her violet eyes glistening like two polished amethysts.

David began to move towards the pantry to gather some items to make

Florence's dinner, but Baba patted him on the shoulder, and motioned him towards a chair. "You let Baba worry about making supper. You sit."

As Baba went about preparing Florence's meal, chopping up some vegetables on a chopping block, David was trying to figure out why she had become so motherly. She certainly hadn't been this way before Florence came in the door. He felt a soft nudging on his leg. He looked down to see the cat.

Was it grinning at him?

Baba abruptly stopped what she was doing. She looked at the vegetables on the block, at the knife in her hand, and blinked in confusion. She ran her fingers over her head, feeling how neat and smooth her hair was. Her face turned bright red, and she slammed the knife down on the counter. "You flea-bitten feline! How dare you trick me like that!"

The cat dashed to hide under David's chair, peeking out from behind his legs.

"Baba, what are you—" David started.

Baba yanked the pins from her hair, allowing the tresses to run wild again. "It is that horrid cat. I don't know why I keep her around. You think I like being all lovey-dovey, sugar and spice? No! I wanted to see how you would wriggle out of that problem with your wife, but no, cat felt sorry for you. Wanted me to intervene."

David looked down at the cat again. "You mean, the cat asked you to help?"

"No ask! Just does what it wants! Cat can…influence others. Make them act…" Baba shivered at the notion of the next word: "Nice."

The cat mewed. David admitted, something about being near the cat made him feel calmer, even a bit happier. He leaned down and gently scratched the cat on the head. "Well, whether or not your help was willing, I thank you for putting Florence at ease."

"Bah. You fix supper. I've done too much work for one day."

David stood up and went over to the chopping block, while Baba took over his chair and went about smoking her pipe again. He went about preparing supper half-heartedly, as his mind was elsewhere. He sighed. "I can't leave Florence in this state. But how can I stay here, knowing what danger Acacia is in? What danger everyone is in, with Fenrir running around?" He looked over at Baba. "Am I meant to become entangled in that world again, in the Curtain, or am I meant to be in my own world?"

"What matter is it to me? This world, other worlds get eaten by wolf, eh. I'm sick of world anyway. So, you stay with wife, Wolf eats Sphinx, eats everyone, eats moon and sun and stars and planet. You go help Sphinx, you have very angry wife. I can see your problem."

David glanced at the cat again. "I don't suppose your cat could help… soften Florence to the idea of me going away for a short while? Or maybe, you have a spell that would make her not realize I am gone? Maybe she could sleep again…"

Baba laughed, coughing up clouds of smoke. "Oh, yes, why not put wife in coma so you can run off and do whatever you so please! Heck, why not turn her into stone, then she can wait forever." Baba's gaze turned dark again. "Or maybe, crazy thought, you can be man, and take responsibility for choices you make. Either you stay or go, there will be consequences. No cheating at life, little man."

David knew Baba was right. It wasn't fair to Florence to put spells on her so he could get her to comply with his decisions. She was his wife; he had promised to be there for her and take care of her. But, had he not also pledged himself to Acacia, when he first named her? It had been unknowingly, as he had been unaware at the time that giving a sphinx a true name was the same as proposing to one. She had agreed not to hold him to such a promise. She had let him go.

Perhaps Acacia would be fine. She was a sphinx—powerful, fierce, clever. She could outsmart a wolf, no matter what kind of monster he was. And surely there were those on the other side of the Curtain who could subdue Fenrir. According to the *Poetic Edda*, Fenrir had been captured before. It wasn't David's burden to bear. He had no obligation to go risking his life, to go up against some beast that could destroy the world, and everyone he loved. He didn't have to fight against "the worst to come." Right?

"Tell me one thing," David asked. "If Acacia fights Fenrir, can she win?"

Baba shrugged. "I don't see into future. But I know of the past. Sphinx was almost destroyed by Night, yes? Had life sucked out of her?"

"Yes."

"Then think: your sphinx, almost killed by a god. If wolf gets strong enough, it can kill gods. Do you think Sphinx can beat a thing that is stronger than what nearly killed her?"

David inhaled deeply, hoping to bring his fear under control. Acacia had fought monsters before: her cousin Nico, the Sleepless Dragon, plus who knew what else. But Fenrir was not Nico. Fenrir probably ate fox-demons and dragons for breakfast. Acacia was in mortal danger. As much as he loved Florence, she would be safe here. In fact, she was probably safer without David. What if Fenrir tracked him down, despite Baba's spell to hide his scent?

Why do I want to go find Acacia so badly?

"You know answer to that," Baba said.

David hadn't realized that he said his last thought out loud.

David stood at the door of the bedroom, Florence's supper in his hands. He took a deep breath—and another, and another—and quietly opened the door.

Florence lay in bed, propped up against a pile of pillows. She was clean, wearing a fresh cotton nightdress. She smiled as David walked to her, placing the dish of cooked vegetables and cheese in front of her. "Thank you, Darling. It smells divine. Did you not want any supper for yourself?"

"No, I'm not hungry." He honestly wasn't, as his stomach was twisted into knots at the moment. He sat on the edge of the bed as Florence ate. All he could do was stare at the floor, his hands clutching his knees.

"Is something troubling you?" Florence asked, noting his quiet moroseness. "Are you worried that the bandits may come back?"

David looked at her. "No, I'm sure they won't bother us again. But there is something I must tell you."

Florence stopped eating, and placed her dish on the bedside table. "What is it? You look so shaken."

David scooted closer to her. He took her hand in his, rubbing the back of her hand with his thumb. “Florence, a dear friend of mine is in trouble. I must help. I…have to go. Tonight.”

Florence was quiet at first, as if she expected him to say more. “Oh,” was all she said. After a long pause, she asked, “Where are you going?”

“I need to go far away. I won’t be back for quite some time. I honestly do not know for how long.”

Florence’s eyebrows pinched together. “How far is far? Who is this friend of yours?”

David knew these questions were going to come up, and unfortunately he couldn’t come up with good answers for any of them. “It’s a delicate matter, and I wish I could tell you more. All I can ask is that you trust me, and know I will come home as soon as I can. I don’t want to leave you, after all that has happened. But my friend is in mortal danger. She could die if I don’t go.”

Florence’s eyes shot wide open. “ ‘She’? Your friend is a woman?”

Technically, no, David wanted to say. But instead, he replied, “I was friends with her before I began my apprenticeship with Monsieur Roland. I haven’t seen her since then.”

“How do you know she’s in trouble? Did you receive a letter from her? If she is so far away, does she not have family or friends near her that could help? Why must it be you?” The tone in Florence’s voice had changed; it was one David was not familiar with. It sounded like a cutting knife being sharpened against a whetstone.

David could have invented plenty of good excuses: yes, he did get a letter, or his *abuela* had heard word about it and told him, or even his lady friend was a member of the Roland family, and Monsieur Roland trusted no one better than David to handle the matter. But lying so blatantly to Florence was something David could not do; being cryptic about the matter was difficult enough. “If I don’t go help her, no one will. It could be mere rumor, or it could be true, but if it is within my power to save her life, I must do something. You would do the same, if it were your friend’s life at stake.”

Florence’s piercing glare softened. “I know you wish to go because you have such a kind heart. I do trust you. But what am I to tell our friends and neighbors? That my husband ran off to save a woman's life, not saying how she is in danger, or who she is? David..." She placed her hand to her quivering lips. "I don't know what to think. Why is everything falling apart so suddenly? I was kidnapped by bandits, and as soon as I come home, you want to go far away to someone I don't even know. It's as if something is trying to tear us apart. I...I don't want to be alone right now. I need to know that you want to be with me. Please, can you not send someone else to help your friend? If she needs a doctor, or a guardian, we could recommend plenty of those. Surely, there is someone—anyone—else who could help her."

David wiped a hand over his face. What was he supposed to say to that? How could he leave now, with Florence feeling this way? He did not have time to answer, as Florence's features fell before he even could. The fact he hadn't instantly agreed with her seemed to have struck her to the core.

"Your friend is that important to you," she whispered. She looked away, lost in thought. David wanted to say something to appease her, but his voice failed.

Florence took a deep breath, and exhaled slowly. "David, we have not been wed a long time, but everything you have done in the time I have known you, has been honorable and true. So I will trust you. Go to your friend, see that she is well, and return home straight away. Send letters to let me know you are all right. At least I will have your grandmother to keep me company for now."

David bit his lip. He wasn't sure if Baba would agree to such an arrangement, nor was he too keen on the thought of leaving Florence alone with a witch. Maybe he could convince her by owing her an extra "favor," if that was how Baba bargained. "I promise, I will not leave you waiting long. I will come home as quickly as I can. I love you, Florence. I would never abandon you."

Florence leaned over to him and kissed him. "I love you too. Be safe, and remember, write to me."

He nodded in agreement. Florence leaned back against the pillows and closed her eyes. The exhaustion of the day took hold of her quickly, and soon she was fast asleep. David held her hand a while longer, before he leaned over and gave her a parting kiss on the cheek. He gathered her supper dish and crept out of the room. He took one last look at his wife, sighed, and then closed the door behind him.

"You must be crazy," Baba snapped. She crossed her arms, slouching in her seat on the settee.

"Please, she doesn't want to be alone right now," David pleaded. "Just stay with Florence for a few days, until I find Acacia and see that she is all right."

Baba smirked. "And how do you plan to find your sphinx? How do you plan to get anywhere? Do you have magical sphinx-finding compass in your head?"

David paused. "I…was hoping maybe you could use another spell to show me where she is…"

"You already owe me favor! You like having mountain of debt? Besides, Sphinx moves fast. I show you where she is *now*, she will move on by time you arrive. You need a tracker, and I do not track." Baba glanced over at her cat, who was glaring at her from the floor. "Don't look at me like that. If you feel so bad for little man, you do something."

The cat cocked her head, thumping the tip of her tail on the floor. She had that funny grin on her face again. She mewed softly, batting her paw at Baba's skirt.

"No, not even you can track Sphinx," Baba replied to the cat. "Is not a mouse. He needs someone who knows how to find the unfindable. Someone who knows how to hunt what cannot be hunted." She laughed. "Little man is out of luck, no?"

Hunt what cannot be hunted…a master at hunting. A smile grew on David's face. "I don't need just anyone who can track. I need someone who knows how to hunt creatures from the other side of the Curtain, someone who knows how Acacia would think and where she would go. I need someone who knew her better than anyone else. Baba, that's it! I know who can find

Acacia. He's from the guild of Master Huntsmen. He's known her for years." His smile faltered. "But I'd have to go to Scotland to find him. That's several weeks journey, and I would need to secure a ship to take me there. There must be a faster way."

The cat mewed, clawing at Baba's skirt again.

"Now *that* is crazy," Baba said. "Boy already owes me favor. Not doing any more until payment."

The cat hissed at Baba.

"No, stupid cat! I know what you're up to. Baba is not a fool."

The cat rubbed her head against Baba's leg, purring sweetly.

Baba sighed, rolling her eyes. "All right, all right. I suppose it would be nice to get you out of my hair for a while."

"What did she say?" David asked.

"She said, she stay with your wife, while I take you to find Huntsman. My mode of travel, much faster than carriage or boat."

David looked at the cat. "I don't think Florence will settle for a cat as company. She will want a person."

Baba plucked a long, gray hair from her head, and removed her shawl from her shoulders. She leaned forwards, tying her hair around the cat's neck like a noose, and then draped the shawl over the cat's back. She murmured a few indecipherable words, tapping the cat on the head with her bony fingers.

In a matter of seconds, the cat ballooned in size. Her fur receded, except for the patch on her head, which lengthened and changed to pale gray. She stood up on her hind legs, while the shawl formed to her changing body, morphing into a simple brown dress. David gawked as there were now two Baba Yagas in the room, although the cat-Baba retained the vibrant violet eyes as opposed to the real Baba's gray-brown ones.

"Can she…speak?" David asked. "Florence may find it strange if my grandmother can only meow."

"Don't be silly," the cat-Baba said, in a voice much like the real Baba's, but more soothing, more delicate. "This is why I don't mind it when Baba puts this spell on me. It's the only time I can talk. And cook, which I do much better than she does. By the way, my name is Vasilisa. You probably wouldn't know otherwise, since Bony-Legs wouldn't have told you."

Baba's face flushed red. "What I tell you about calling me that? I do not have bony legs. I have good strong legs, unlike mangy cat. And if mangy cat does not watch mouth, Baba will gut her and turn her into violin strings."

Vasilisa chuckled. "She says such things, but she adores me. I will look after things while you are gone. It will be nice to spend time with a nice lady, instead of an old grouch."

"Why do I put up with you?" Baba huffed. She turned to David. "But now you owe me double, boy. Stupid cat may make me act nice, but Baba does not forget what she is due."

David nodded. "I will return the favor tenfold, I swear. But you said you have a mode of transport faster than boat or coach? You must know how to travel through the Curtain, then."

"Bah! Curtain is a mess. No, Baba has better way. As long as you have no fear of heights."

David swallowed, sensing that he was soon to be airsick. "You mean, we would fly. I hope you have a spell for that, unless you have a broomstick big enough for two—"

He yelped as Baba grabbed hold of his ear, yanking down on it with such surprising force that David had to drop to one knee.

"Now you've done it," Vasilisa said, shaking her head.

Baba flashed her iron teeth at him, like a mother bear whose cubs had been threatened. "You think you are funny? You poke fun at Baba with your 'broomstick' joke, because I am witch? It is not hard enough being Baba Yaga, with what people think of me, but now to be ridiculed with silly lies? I do not ride broomstick! I do not eat children, I do not wither crops, and I do not take nonsense from nasty boys who think they know everything!"

David wriggled in Baba's grasp, clenching his teeth in pain. "I'm sorry, I truly am! I won't joke like that again. You're trying to help me, and I'm being rude. I humbly ask for your forgiveness, Madam Baba."

Baba held him a moment longer, her scowl seething fire at him, before she let him go. "Do not call me 'Madam.' I know what I am, and it is not a 'Madam.' Now, you figure out what *you* are, and maybe I don't think you're so dense."

David scrunched up his brow, not having the slightest clue what she meant about him figuring out who he was. Given her irritated state, however, he wasn't about to ask for clarification. "May I ask, Señora Baba, how we will be flying to Scotland?"

"Same way I flew you here from Geras's house." She reached into a large patchwork pouch hanging from a belt around her waist. She took out a small stone mortar and pestle, the sort David had seen local chemists use to grind up herbs and minerals for medicine. "Outside. Come."

David took one more look at Vasilisa, who waved him on to follow Baba out the front door. "Your wife will be perrrrfectly fine." She caught herself, touching her fingers to her lips and chuckling. "I will try to keep my feline habits under control."

Baba and David trudged outside onto the front stoop. It was nighttime, and while Paris never slept, their street was empty of pedestrians. Most people at this time of day would either be at the opera, or out to a late supper, or tucked away at home. Baba set the mortar on the stoop, while keeping the pestle in hand. "You are ready for this? You realize, if you go find Huntsman, find sphinx, and then find wolf, you don't stand chance, yes? You saw what Night God showed Sphinx about your fate. You are no wizard, no warrior. You are scrawny boy who reads books. You plan to smack wolf with a book until he cries?"

David shook his head. "Of course not. The Huntsman must have some idea of how to fight a monster like that. Everything has a weakness. And I know how to fight. I've studied swordplay…wait, I'll be right back."

He dashed back inside the house and knelt down at the bottom of the staircase. He gripped the plank of the bottom step and pried it off with relative ease. He had moved the item he was looking for to this new hiding place after his encounter with the Ilomba, right before he and Florence had left for the country—it was Acacia's gift to him, the case with the matching sword and dagger. He lifted the case out, running his hand over the polished wood. He unlocked it and opened it, confirming that the two weapons were still there. Inside was also a burgundy velvet lining upon which the weapons lay, so he bundled up the sword and dagger in the lining and tucked them under his arm. He also retrieved the *Poetic Edda* from the settee where he left it, hoping it might contain information about Fenrir that he could use. He returned back outside to Baba.

The old woman shook her head. "Of course, you bring book. I was kidding about smacking wolf with book, but then he brings one." She regarded the wrapped bundle. "What is that? You have secret weapon?"

"I suppose you can call them that."

"Do you know how to use 'them'?"

"I studied swordplay when I was younger. And I've handled these before. Well…one of them."

Baba set her hands on her hips. "What makes you think because you have secret weapon, that will protect you from wolf? What makes you think you can protect anyone? Why put your neck on the line and not leave this to a real hero?"

David scratched the back of his neck, looking up at the night sky. He turned his gaze to Baba, his face set in determination. "If I don't go, people I care about could die. I couldn't live with that. I've been brought into this, and I have to see it through."

Baba scoffed a disdainful laugh, although something in her grin hinted at intrigue as well. "Then get in."

"Get in what? You mean get in that tiny mortar—"

Except it wasn't tiny anymore. In the time it took to snap one's fingers, it had surged up in height and width to the size of a hot air balloon basket. It looked far too heavy to take flight, however, as it was still made of solid marble. Baba slowly climbed into the mortar, but David had to give her a gentle boost (lifting her by the waist, hoping this was the least offensive place he could hold her) before he climbed in himself.

"I haven't traveled by mortar before," David noted, setting his bundle and book down at his feet. "This should be interesting."

"I would hold tight to edge, if I were you," Baba advised, placing her pestle over the side like a canoe paddle.

David gripped his side of the mortar, although he was thinking, *This thing can't possibly go that fast. It's like riding on a boulder—*

His brain froze, as well as his lungs, as the mortar shot straight up into the air as if it had been blasted out of a Roman candle. Paris became a landscape of tiny lights below, and the Eiffel Tower, Notre Dame, and Le Sacré Coeur were no more than toys on display. David's voice eventually found itself, as a scream the echoed through the night.

Baba laughed wildly over David's screaming. "How is this for 'broomstick,' little man?"

CHAPTER SIX

At what point the night peeled away to reveal the dawn, David couldn't remember. He had been too busy clinging to his side of the mortar so as not to tumble out from the pull of the wind, and too focused on not passing out or retching over the side. As the light crept up, bleeding the sky from blackness to purple to teal, David could see that they had left land behind and were flying over a vast stretch of water—they must be over the English Channel, or possibly as far as the North Sea. It reminded him of the time he had ridden upon the back of Yofune Nushi, the ancient sea dragon, when he had fallen through the Curtain and wound up in Japan. But that ride had been short and tolerable enough; this ride felt like it was going on for an eternity.

"Would you relax?" Baba Yaga said, who looked as at ease flying in her mortar as if she were drinking tea. "Baba won't let you fall out. Besides, we are making good time. My mortar always knows where to go—used to live on my bookshelf next to globe, taught it about all lands and oceans. Although it says it would like to know exactly where the house of your friend is. Scotland may not be as big as Russia, but it is hard to find one person in a whole country."

David swallowed down a lump in his throat. "The last time I saw Gullin, we met in a pub in London while I was traveling on business. He told me he lived right outside...I should remember this...it was the village that is widely known for its bath house with supposedly healing spring water. Muffet, I think..."

Baba huffed. "My mortar says you must mean Moffat. All this love and marriage mush, makes my stomach ache..."

"The sun's coming up, Baba. We don't have the night to hide us anymore.

Shouldn't you hide us with a cloaking spell so people below won't see us?"

"Well well well, look who knows so much about magic and such," Baba scoffed. "Why waste magic on cloaking spell, when people are so good at convincing themselves they do not see what they do not understand? If someone sees two people in a mortar fly by, they will wonder if they actually saw such a thing, and then decide not, because to believe such a thing would upturn everything they know. It is easier to pass off something as imagination than accept change in reality."

David remembered all the times when he was younger, and he would tell his parents, his brothers, his schoolmates, and the neighbors the fantastic stories he read in his folklore and fairy tale books. They would smile and nod, or chuckle at his naïve enthusiasm, or roll their eyes. They all believed it was imagination; he had believed it to be reality. How he wished he could show everyone how real his "imagination" was, that there were such things as sphinxes, and dragons, and true magic. Then again, he probably didn't want everyone to know about a world-eating wolf on the loose or a night god who could drain other's talents with body-inhabiting Shades.

"We should still try to avoid being seen," David insisted. "If we can find some remote place to set this mortar down not too far from Moffat, we can walk into town and ask if anyone knows Gullin." He swallowed back another lump in his throat as the mortar made a sudden unexpected dip downwards. "The sooner, the better," he wheezed.

David's nausea ebbed a little as he watched the tranquil beauty of the Scottish countryside whisk by beneath him. He had never seen any place so vibrantly green, not even in the gaudy shades of Paris's latest ladies' fashions. Here and there, weathered but cozy stone cottages with thatched roofs nestled in the earth like grand toadstools. The fields were dotted with hundreds of cloud puffs, an earth-bound stratosphere of sheep. Apparently, a large mortar flying directly over their heads did little to concern the sheep, as they meandered and munched contentedly on the grass.

Slowly, the mortar began to descend towards one of the fields, and a circle of sheep scattered as they approached to land.

"My mortar says Moffat is over the hill," Baba said, and huffed as the mortar thudded heavily into the ground, teetering for a moment before settling still. "Hope you're happy. You make an old lady have to walk through field full of mud and who knows what else with all these four-legged yarn balls."

David picked up his bundled weapons and climbed out of the mortar, as his shoes sank an inch into the muddy ground. He barely had time to turn around to see the mortar shrink back down to its pocket size, as did the pestle in Baba's hand. She picked up the mortar and plopped it and its pestle back into the pouch at her waist. She trudged ahead, glancing at David over her shoulder. "You go find your friend. I'm going to find a good drink."

After having spent his life in cities like Cervera and Paris, the main square of Moffat seemed to David like a one page illustration from a children's storybook.. It was refreshing in its rustic quaintness, but felt unnervingly intimate in the close cluster of white-painted homes, shops, and inns. David was hopeful that someone in this place must know Gullin, or at least had seen him recently. It would seem that in a town this small, everyone must know everybody who lived in the area.

Baba made a beeline for the first tavern she spotted. David followed after her. A tavern was as good as any place to start looking for Gullin, given that it was a pub where David had run into him last time.

He entered the tavern, and received curious glances from the patrons. David clearly stood out, not only because he was a stranger in a small town, but his fashionable Parisian attire was a remarkable clash with the simple rural apparel of the Scottish townsfolk. Yet no one appeared threatened or alarmed by him. From what Gullin had mentioned, hundreds flocked to Moffat to experience the rejuvenating waters of the bath house near the town hall—some even considered the waters miraculous. People of all types must have passed through this town, so an unfamiliar face was nothing new to them. For all they knew, he was another visitor wanting to try the sulphurous waters. Given that he had entered right after Baba, the patrons might think he was her caretaker, here to see that she was given the Moffat healing treatment.

Baba plopped herself down at a vacant table, and snapped her fingers at David. "Fetch me drink, and make it strong."

Now several patrons were glancing at David with amused expressions. David shrugged, and walked over to the bar. He could see movement beneath the counter, the backside of a white shirt. "Excuse me, could I have two drinks, please? A tea for me, and something that would incapacitate a bull for my friend."

A hand reach up to place two glass mugs on the countertop. David leaned in closer and lowered his voice. "I was also hoping you might know a man who lives outside of town. His name is Gullin. Has he been here?"

The figure beneath the counter stood up. David blinked in bewilderment at the brawny woman with a mass of sepia-brown curls that stood before him. "You wouldn't be talking about that no-good sauced scoundrel Alasdair Gullin, would you?"

David bit his lip. He was surprised, and slightly embarrassed, that he hadn't ever learned Gullin's first name—in fact, he had thought all this time that Gullin *was* his first name. "Well...he has copper-red hair, a beard, he's about a foot taller than I. He has a tattoo of a silver spear crossed by two golden arrows, with a white lily entwining them."

The woman brought up a bottle from under the counter and started pouring the liquid into the mugs. "Whatcha want with that lazy no account bum? Goes wandering off whenever he feels like it, prances around like he's the cock of the walk, never lifts a finger to help his gorgeous, darling wife who deserves a thousand times better than that lump of matted hair and skunk musk."

David smiled, giving her a small bow. "You must be Beatrice. Your husband told me all about you the last time we met, except he didn't mention you own a tavern."

Beatrice shot him a half-grin. "I only own it when my Da is laid up in bed with the shakes, or a booze-battered brain. Normally I'm just the help. As for what my husband might've said about me, don't believe a word that liar says."

"He said you were fierce enough to tackle a bear."

"He did?" She put the bottle down, and beamed. "How sweet. Or maybe you're just putting in a good word for him. How do you know him?"

"We met a few years ago, back when he was…traveling." David wasn't sure what Gullin had told Beatrice about his life before they were married. Did she know he had once been a Master Huntsman, a member of the secret guild that hunted mythical monsters and legendary beasts? Had he mentioned that he had been part of the traveling gypsy caravan that had been guarded over by Acacia? David highly doubted Gullin would have ever mentioned Acacia—not because Acacia was a sphinx, but because of old feelings that Gullin had harbored for her, and David was sure Gullin didn't want to dwell on them.

"Ah. You seem a bit more refined than the usual lot he makes for company. Shame none of your good manners rubbed off on 'im." Beatrice finished pouring the drinks and shoved them towards David. "On the house. A little Moffat hospitality."

"Thank you." David peered into the mugs at the dark swill. He thought better than to ask Beatrice about the tea he had ordered, and picked up the mugs. "So, is Gullin in town with you today?"

Beatrice nodded her head in the direction behind David. "He's hard to miss," she said.

David hadn't realized that the other patrons of the tavern had gathered around one table, and there was laughter and verbal goading emitting from the crowd. He could hear one voice among the others, a familiar male Scottish brogue: "Don't be expectin' me to go soft on you. I take my battles seriously, even if you be older than Hadrian's Wall!"

David set the drinks down, and dashed over, trying to squirm his way past the other patrons towards the table. His mouth dropped open as he watched Gullin, face set in eager determination, thick muscular arm propped on its elbow upon the tabletop, prepare to arm wrestle an equally eager-looking Baba.

"As do I, even if you be as thick as a wall," Baba replied.

David tried to step in, reaching forwards to grab at Gullin's and Baba's arms. The crowd was pressed in too tightly, and David had to shout to be heard above them. "Stop it, you two! Gullin!"

Gullin turned his head towards David. The intensity dropped from his face, and his eyebrows shot up. "David?"

Baba took advantage of the distraction, and slammed Gullin's arm backwards down onto the table. The crowd cheered and hollered, and a few coins were exchanged among hands from those who had placed bets.

Gullin glowered at Baba. "You cheated, woman!"

Baba leaned back in her chair, grinning. "I do not cheat. You do not take battles seriously."

"Enough!" David broke through the barricade of patrons and stepped up to the table. The patrons, seeing that the arm wrestling match was over, dispersed back to their respective tables. David crossed his arms. "I don't want to know how this started. You two should not be fighting."

"Then what's the point of making new friends?" Gullin asked.

"Yes, do not spoil fun," Baba agreed.

David wiped a hand over his face. "I forget how all of you people are crazy."

Gullin laughed, and stood up to clap David on the back. "How have you been, boyo? You came all this way to visit your good friend Gullin, eh? And you brought your grannie with you." He grasped David's shoulder with a hard grip, and leaned in close to whisper in his ear. "Your grannie who any Master Huntsman worth his salt can tell from a mile away is a *bana-bhuidseach*, so if she's put some curse on you to do her bidding, you tell me and I'll put that witch in her place."

David shook his head. "No, no, she helped me find you. She's good…I think. But Gullin, there's something I must talk to you about. It's important, and we may not have much time—"

"I'm guessing there's trouble on the other side of the Curtain, aye? Best we talk about it elsewhere." Gullin drew back, releasing David's shoulder and ruffling his hair. "Paris life has been softening you up. A hearty helping of my wife's cooking will fill you out. Are you staying in town? 'Cause I insist you save your coins and come spend a day or two at my place. Always plenty of room for a guest or two…" He smirked at Baba. "…and a half."

"Does not matter whether we stay in town, or stay at your house," Baba said. "Will smell you no matter where we are."

"I like her." Beatrice approached the table, smiling at Baba. "You're more than welcome to stay at our place. I could use some intelligent conversation for a change."

"You see this, boyo? See how the ladies all band together against me?" Gullin shook his head. "Thank the Lord we've got a son. I don't need a daughter siding with my wife."

"Speaking of sons," Beatrice said, digging her fists into her hips. "Where *is* Ian?"

Gullin blanched, and he dropped to his hands and knees to search beneath the table, his chair, and around on the floor. "Aye, the wee blighter couldn't have wandered far on such tiny legs…"

David was about to search as well, when he noticed a small hand clinging to the side of Beatrice's skirt. A face topped by copper-colored hair peeked out from behind her. Beatrice looked at David, and winked.

Gullin was crawling around on the floor to look under various tables. Sweat was rolling down his face. "Ian! Has anyone seen a wee one scuttling about?"

Beatrice rolled her eyes, and looked down at the little boy clinging to her. "Go to your father, before his heart explodes."

The little boy waddled out from behind his mother and tackled Gullin by wrapping his arms around the big man's neck. Gullin laughed, picking up the boy in his arms and swinging him about while Ian giggled wildly. "You and your mother are going to be the death of me!"

David laughed. "Your son can't be more than a year old, and he's already a troublemaker?"

Beatrice tipped her head at Gullin. "We know whose bloodline he's got to thank for that."

"Please, woman. If he were all your bloodline, he'd been born a dragon." He went over and kissed Beatrice to make amends for the comment, and she readily forgave him with a return kiss.

It struck David as funny that Gullin had such a sensitive, fatherly side, after knowing him as a veracious fighter and hunter. He knew the Scotsman was a fiercely loyal person as well; his wife and son couldn't be in more protective hands. David glanced over at Baba, and noticed there was a strange expression on her face—she didn't look sad, exactly, but more wistful. For some reason, it seemed to David the look of someone who was silently mourning the absence, or loss, of something beautiful in her life.

Before it grew too dark outside, Beatrice closed up the tavern early as her father had yet to recover from his ailment, which she was sure was his reoccurring case of bad indigestion. Beatrice with Ian in her arms, David, and Baba Yaga all clambered into a big wooden cart that Gullin had parked outside the tavern, along with an ivory-coated Clydesdale horse tied to a post next to a watering trough. David recognized the horse instantly—it was one of the six horses that had once pulled the wagons of the traveling gypsy caravan that belonged to Acacia. When the horse looked over at David, and gave him a long snort, David believed it was also the horse he had stolen in his one attempt to escape the caravan. The horse probably never forgave him for being stolen, or riding him straight into danger involving a group of blood-craving living dolls.

Gullin hooked up the horse to the cart, and climbed up into the driver's seat. He took up the reins, clicked his tongue, and the horse pulled the cart along at a casual pace. "Best we be getting back to the homestead now," Gullin commented. "Need to make sure the farmhand hasn't burned down the house."

The ride was four or five miles down the road east of Moffat. The cart rattled up to a modest plot of land, not the wide expanse of a typical farm but enough for a handful of sheep and goats to graze nearby the house. The house was built from large blocks of quarry stone with a thatched roof, with a three-foot-tall stone wall marking the perimeter of the Gullins' land. There was a crude stable in the back where the horse and cart were kept, and a wooden shed that could house a decent store of rations for the winter months.

As the cart approached, a young man dressed in a mud-coated work shirt and breeches came out of the house to greet them. David could tell from the first sight, even at a distance, that the man was not of Scottish heritage. His skin was a little more tanned, his hair as dark as raven feathers, and his eyes were smaller, shaped like slivers of almonds.

"Is that your farmhand?" David asked.

Gullin nodded. "Aye, he's a bit odd in the head. Was a vagrant, I suspect. He says he came from a country far away. One day he shows up, asking for work and a place to stay. Normally I don't need ruffians around, but he's proven to be a good man, hard worker. Has a gift for keeping the foxes away, and he looks after Ian when we need to be away."

"When *I* need to be away," Beatrice said, "and when *you* want to go cavorting whenever and wherever you darn well please."

The farmhand came up to the side of the cart as Gullin tugged at the reins to halt the horse. "Good day, Mister Gullin," he said with hesitant English. "I will take the cart…"

His tongue froze when he saw David in the cart. The farmhand stared, his eyebrows rising up almost to his hairline. David couldn't imagine what surprised the young man so; maybe it was so rare for Gullin to bring guests home, the farmhand didn't know how to react. But then a wide smile, bordering on laughter, blossomed across the farmhand's face. He took one step towards David with a childlike eagerness, but then he halted. He stepped back, his smile dropping into a sheepish grin.

"Ru, we have guests tonight," Gullin said. "This is an old friend of mine, David San…Sandy-something." He looked back at David with an apologetic shrug.

"Sandoval. And it's okay. I didn't know you had a first name until today."

"That's still more than most of his so-called friends know," Beatrice noted.

Gullin gestured towards Baba. "And this is his old lady. Treat them as you would treat my family."

"Yes, sir," Ru said quietly. He glanced back up at David, that funny cheerful smile on his face again.

Baba was giving Ru a long, good scrutinizing. She snorted, the corner of her lip twisting into something between a frown and a sneer. “Where are you from, *boy*?”

Ru turned his eyes to her, and David could swear the man was chattering his teeth. Ru turned his gaze down to the ground. “Far away,” he replied.

“I would figure. Don’t see much of your type,” Baba said.

David stood up to help Baba down from the cart. She pulled her arm away from him, giving him a nasty look. “Don’t need help from scrawny boy like you,” she said.

David lowered his voice. “What do you mean, ‘his type’? Why does he look scared of you?”

Baba chuckled. “Who is not scared of Baba? But he is nervous because I see him for what he truly is. But no matter. He is not dangerous.”

“What is he, really?”

Baba shrugged. “Who is anyone, *really*? But no worries. That one could do no worse than put lots of holes in garden.”

David helped Beatrice down from the cart, who gave him an appreciative smile before casting Gullin a glance that said, “See, *this* is what manners look like.” As the family and Baba walked into the house, David took one more look at Ru, who was guiding the horse and cart towards the stable. It struck David then, where he had seen those facial traits before. It had been when the Curtain had taken him to a faraway land, halfway around the world from France. It had been a place where he had made helpful allies, who had become good friends to him, and had helped him save Acacia’s life from Nyx’s shade.

But for a man to have come from that land, it would have taken him many months to travel that far, and that would have required money that this poor farmhand couldn’t possibly have. Unless…he could travel through the Curtain…

CHAPTER SEVEN

"So, boyo, what's that you got there?" Gullin gestured to the wrapped bundle that David carried under his arm.

David shifted the bundle so he held it firmly in both hands. "These were gifts. I might need to use them, but that's why I came here looking for you. I need your help, Gullin—or I was told, Alisdair?"

Gullin smirked. "Only the missus calls me by my first name, and only when her ire's riled. But hey, what's in a *name*, eh?" His grin faded into a tight grimace.

David had a feeling that Gullin was thinking about how a name could in fact mean everything—and how Acacia had chosen the name David had proposed for her over the one Gullin had offered. In sphinx culture, accepting a name was the same as accepting the vow of a life partner. David hadn't known that at the time—he had merely wanted to call her by something other than Sphinx. Gullin had known this, apparently, and David wondered if he would ever fully recover from the blow of rejection. Even a married man carried the scars of past loves, and they could still bleed from time to time.

David thought it best to get back to the point. "Gullin, have you ever heard of a wolf called Fenrir?"

The Scotsman's entire body seized up, his hair practically standing on end. He glanced over at Baba and Beatrice, who held little Ian in her arms. The women were sitting at the kitchen table, chatting away as if they were age old friends.

Gullin wrapped an arm around David's shoulders and led him towards the front door. "Why don't you and I take a short walk? Away from prying ears?" He turned his head around to look at Beatrice. "The lad's going to help me with the tanning for a while."

Beatrice gave him a dismissal wave. "Take your time. The longer you're out, the cleaner the house stays."

Gullin led David out of the house and around towards the stable at the back. Ru was brushing down the horse in its stall, and he stole a sideways glance at David as the two went into the shed adjacent to the stable.

Inside the shed hung a collection of furs and dried animal skins on one wall, and a variety of tools—sheering scissors, skinning knives, hammers, and wood-cutting saws—on the opposite wall. There were two racks on which large skins, bear and boar, were stretched. A workbench sat in one corner next to a low table.

"I see you've kept busy," David noted, as he set down his sword-and-dagger bundle on the table.

"Puts bread on the table and coin in my pocket. Can't have the missus do all the work around here." Gullin sat down on the bench. "Why don't you start from the beginning. Why did you come find me, and what's this about the big bad wolf?"

"You know who Fenrir is, then."

Gullin scratched his chin. "When you're a Master Huntsman, there are a few names of the worst sort that you can't help but be warned about. That name in particular has been hanging over my head for...well, a good decade or two now."

"Have you encountered him before?"

"No, no. From what I understood, Fenrir was supposed to be locked away, imprisoned until Ragnarok."

David digested the word. "Ragnarok...it's in the *Poetic Edda.* Ragnarok, as in, the End of the World?"

"It actually means Fate of the Gods. But same idea." Gullin sighed, rubbing his forehead. "You're about to tell me something about Fenrir that's going to make me sore as 'ell, aren't you?"

David explained what had happened to him, from the time that the Ilomba attacked him, to the meeting with Geras and Elli, to almost being devoured by Fenrir if not for Baba Yaga, to the vision he had seen of Acacia and Nyx's incarnation. "I think Fenrir is after Acacia, and I don't know why. But Acacia is also after Fenrir because Nyx tricked her into thinking he will kill me—at least, I hope it was a trick. Acacia could be in real danger right now, and I didn't know who else to turn to, who else would know Acacia well enough to know how to find her before Fenrir does," David said.

Gullin didn't respond at first. He stared at David, as if trying to judge if the young man had told him an elaborate fib or not. Finally, he exhaled in an exasperated voice, "Dear Saint Bridget…" He closed his eyes, his head tipping backwards, a pained expression scrunching up his face. "You've had a rough few days."

"That would be putting it mildly. So, what should we do?"

There was a slight creak against the wall behind them. Gullin's eyes snapped open, and he looked at the door of the shed. He stood up and marched over to the door, throwing it open so hard that it smacked Ru clean in the face, who had been standing right outside the door. The man reeled backwards, falling flat on his back.

"The first thing I'll do is give this snooping sod a good walloping for listening in on things that aren't his business!" Gullin bellowed.

Ru held up his hands. "I'm sorry! I wanted to know… Could not help it."

"Gullin, wait a minute," David said, getting in between the Scotsman and the farmhand. He helped the boy to his feet, and in a low voice, said a short greeting in Japanese.

Ru froze. In quiet Japanese, he replied, "Do you know?"

"I could tell you are from Japan. I've been there once before, and I picked up the language."

Gullin crossed his arms. "All right, what's going on here? What gibberish are you two tellin' each other?"

David put a hand on Ru's shoulder, switching back to English. "It's all right, Gullin. I'm familiar with Ru's culture."

"Are you now? Is it customary in his 'culture' to be eavesdropping on private talk?" Gullin rolled up his sleeves. "Look, there's some thinking I need to do, 'bout what you told me. Why don't you keep this one's nose out of trouble in the meantime?" Gullin walked towards the house, leaving

David and Ru to themselves.

"Maybe I can help you in the stable until Gullin gets back," David offered in Japanese. "Keeping busy would help pass the time."

Ru nodded, flashing his excited smile again. "You really *do* know, right?"

"Know what?"

The farmhand bit his lip, stifling a chuckle. "Nothing," he said. He turned and headed towards the stable. "Gringolet says he remembers you."

"Gringolet?"

"Master Gullin's horse."

"Oh, yes, I thought that was the same one from the…wait, the *horse* told you that?"

Ru's head dipped a little, and David could tell he was smothering laughter.

David followed Ru into the stable. "Tell me the truth. You're from the other side of the Curtain, aren't you?"

Ru lifted his hands palms up, shrugging. "I don't know what you mean."

"You know what I'm talking about. You talk to animals, you come all the way from the other side of the world, which is an impossible distance for anyone to do without money…and Baba said something about seeing you for what you truly are."

Ru grinned as if proud of something. "I thought you were pretending not to know because of Master Gullin being around. I must be getting much better at this, if even you can't tell."

David was becoming rapidly annoyed. "Can't tell what?"

Ru smirked, and went over to David. He leaned in close, and David was startled to see his eyes shift—from the dark brown irises of human eyes to solid black.

"Come on, David-san," Ru snickered. "You don't recognize your own spirit guide?"

David's jaw hung open, and the corners of his mouth upturned into a surprised smile. "Tanuki?"

Ru—Tanuki—laughed and grabbed David in a tight bear, or badger, hug. "See, I must be your spirit guide after all, if I come all the way here from Japan and found you without even trying. Or, maybe you found me. Wait, would that make you *my* spirit guide?" Tanuki scratched his chin in thought. "But usually I have sake to help me make my decisions…"

"It's good to see you again, Tanuki," David said. "I should've known it was you, when Baba said something about you digging holes in the garden."

Tanuki picked up a curry comb on a nearby stool and went into Gringolet's stall, where the horse was munching on hay. "You mean the old lady you brought with you. Yes, I figured she could 'see' me. But she seems good. I've met people like her, and they were not good. They put curses on people or hypnotize animals to do their bidding. You look fine, though."

David went over and leaned against the fence surrounding the stall. "So you can tell what she is, too."

"I can smell it. People who have magic smell a certain way. The clan that took me in taught me how to recognize the scent. They knew lots of good tricks like that." Tanuki combed Gringolet's back in rhythmic circles. "Speaking of which, you don't have your smell. Did the old lady take your smell away?"

"No, she covered it up. It's a long story." David sat down on the stool. "I'm curious, what is this clan you're referring to? Do you mean Master Yofune and Kappa?"

Tanuki was unusually quiet before he cleared his throat. "No, I mean the Tanuki."

"But, *you're* Tanuki."

"Well, *now* I am. I wasn't always."

David shook his head. "What do you mean?"

"I am a badger, yes? My family was the Badger clan. But I was born different from my brothers and sisters, since my grandfather Raiju, Lord of Lightning, blessed me with his ability to change shape. My mother didn't know what to do about me, so she kicked me out. But I went out into the woods and found the Tanuki. They were like me. They taught me how to use my gift to shift from one form to another at will. They accepted me, so I discarded my old family name and took up their clan name instead."

"I see. I'm sorry that your family turned you away."

Tanuki gave a quick wave of his hand. "Eh, they were boring anyway. I was three weeks old when I left, so it is not as if I knew them *that* well."

"What happened to the Tanuki?"

"Oh, they're still in the forest. I went my own way after a while. And then when Master Yofune took me in…" Tanuki went quiet again, but this time he began to shiver.

"Tanuki, what is it?" David put a hand on his shoulder. "Is something wrong with Yofune?"

"Oh, David-san! It's horrible!" Tanuki wailed, throwing down his comb and weeping into his hands. "Poor, poor master! I should have protected him! But what could I do? What could I do?"

"Tanuki, try to calm down. Did someone hurt Yofune?"

Tanuki wept harder, and he shifted into the form of a raincloud. His tears showered down in torrents, rapidly flooding the floor of the stable. "Dead! Dead! Master Yofune is gone, David-san! Murdered!"

"What?" There was a tearing sensation in David's chest, the agonizing trauma of a hundred carrion birds thrusting their beaks into his ribs and ripping out his lungs. "Murdered? Are you sure? I mean, who could kill a dragon—"

A crackle of lightning emitted from the Tanuki cloud. "Of course I am sure! I don't know who did it, but it was murder! May Lord of the Underworld Emma-hoo hunt them down and cast them into his torturous realm!"

"Tanuki, I understand your anger, but I need you to calm down and tell me everything. Can you do that, so I can help you?"

The cloud continued to thunder and rain a few seconds more, but slowly the storm dwindled. The cloud solidified into Tanuki's natural badger form, but the badger was more gaunt and ragged than David remembered him. Tanuki sniffled, wiping his nose with his paw. "Someone did it while we were sleeping. I do not know how I could not have heard or smelled anything. I was right there in the same room! But I woke up, and he was dead, with this…terrible look on his face. His blood, David…they took his blood! Not a drop left, not one drop spilt. Only once I had awoken, I smelled it—the demon had left behind the scent of Death. Not the smell of death that I've known…not natural death. This was nasty, bitter, hateful death…"

"Tanuki, was there any clue that might point to what sort of person or creature could have done this? A footprint, or something that the killer might have left behind?"

Tanuki scrunched his nose as he thought. "No, I couldn't find anything. I don't know how they could have gotten in, for none of the doors or windows had been tampered with. But…"

"Yes? Do you remember something?"

"I think…I was having a very bad dream before it happened. I was dreaming about being trapped. I can't remember all of it, but I…I think I dreamt I was cornered in some dark place, and couldn't get out. There was an animal keeping me there. It was bigger than me, with this twisted long smile…and lots of sharp teeth. But that's all."

David pondered on this. It would be helpful if he could ask Hypnos about any strange creatures that invaded others' dreams, but he feared something had become of Hypnos, and he had no way of knowing for sure. Acacia might know, when—if—they could find her.

"I tried to follow the evil scent, but it did not go farther than the house, so I could not track anything," Tanuki said. "So I knew I needed someone's help to find the murderer, someone who was good at hunting down hard-to-find evil things. Then I remembered the smelly man! He hunts monsters, so I went through the Curtain and ended up here. Normally I get lost in the Curtain when I go by myself, but the smelly man was easy to find. I picked up his scent right away." The badger rubbed his paws together anxiously. "But then I got all nervous about asking him for help—because he's scary sometimes—so I thought, maybe if I took the shape of a human, he would like me better. I spent a while in the town listening to people talk so I could learn the language. When I finally learned enough of it to come here and talk to him, I got nervous again, so I thought if I did some work for him, he'd trust me more. But I'm still too nervous to ask him what to do."

David sat down on the floor next to Tanuki, and gave him a scratch behind the ear. "I'll help you talk to Gullin about this, and I'll do whatever I can to find whoever did this. If we can find Acacia, she can help too. She may know what kind of creature could have attacked Yofune."

"I remember Acacia. She's the sphinx lady. I liked her. It would be good to have her help us." Tanuki stood up and waddled into David's lap. "Is there really a wolf after her? And was there really a snake that turned you into an old man? I couldn't help but hear you talking in there with Master Gullin."

David nodded. "I don't know what is going on, but we need to find her before something bad happens to her, or anyone else. I don't know what to do if we run into this Fenrir...I doubt even Gullin could stop him."

Tanuki rested his chin on David's knee. "David-san, why are there so many bad things happening to us and our friends? It's not fair."

David sighed. "No, it's not. But we'll make it through. After all, I have my spirit guide back. He can show me the way, right?"

Tanuki looked up at him, and smiled. His nose twitched, and his ears perked up. "Smelly man's back." He rolled out of David's lap and shifted back into his human form right before Gullin walked into the stable. David stood up, dusting off his trousers.

Gullin glanced back and forth between Tanuki and David. "Hope you two are gettin' well acquainted. 'Fraid I have to cut in. Here, boyo." He tossed a leather belt at David. The belt had two matching frogs for holding weapons, one frog being wider than the other.

'For your sword and your dagger," Gullin said. "Lucky I had a few spare frogs that should do the trick. I've an idea to find Acacia, but no matter what course we take, one thing's clear to me. We need to be ready for a fight, boyo. So before anything else, we need to make sure you know how to use those blades properly."

David swallowed hard. "You don't mean, fight Fenrir head on, do you?"

"Nah, I was thinking we could jab him in the tail end until he can't sit no more. What do you think I mean?"

"You can't seriously expect me to fight Fenrir by myself, with just a sword and a dagger!"

Gullin walked over to David, his face coming within an inch of the young man's nose. "First of all, you won't be by yourself. Even I'm not that daft. But if you think you've got 'just a sword and a dagger,' then you don't know what kind of strength you wield. Once, a boy with your name took down a bloodthirsty giant with no more than a slingshot."

David strapped the belt around his waist. "You're talking about David and Goliath. I know that story. But—"

"But nothing!" Gullin grabbed David by the collar of his shirt and pulled him along. "You've got a lot to learn, and not much time to learn it. Get outside, David. Your first lesson begins *right now.*"

CHAPTER EIGHT

It was going to be difficult for David to take sword-fighting lessons from Gullin, who would probably delight in walloping him for a few rounds before actually teaching him anything. It wasn't made any easier by the fact that Baba and Tanuki had decided to watch. The witch and the disguised badger eyed each other warily, but both were far more interested in the pending practice duel.

David prayed that what knowledge he already had of swordplay would prove to Gullin that he was more than capable of defending himself. The smirk on Gullin's face, however, hinted that the Scotsman was intending to have a bit of fun with him.

"So, you know some techniques, you say," Gullin said. "Mind tellin' me what you know?"

"I've been taught basic fencing, and I've had a few lessons in—"

Before David could continue, Gullin thrust his sword forwards and knocked the blade out of David's hand. David jumped away, readying his fists, even though Gullin's sword was pointing at his face.

"Apparently no one taught you to always be on your guard," Gullin remarked.

"You didn't say you were starting," David countered.

"Do you think Fenrir is going to give you a warning? Do you think he abides by fair fighting rules? He'll snap your head off before you have time to cry Mum. So keep your sword up, and focus."

David retrieved his sword from the ground and prepared himself.

Gullin withdrew a dagger from his belt, so he had a blade in each hand. "Since you have both sword and dagger, it would do you well to learn how to use them together. The dagger can be your defense while striking with your sword, and it is also light so you can make quick damage with it if you need to use your sword to block."

David took out his dagger, feeling the weight of each of his weapons in his hands. "I haven't practiced with two weapons before. Will it take long to learn?"

"Oh, many years, boyo. But we'll have to make do, won't we?" Gullin grinned. "Now, a wolf has its eyes in the front of its face, so it doesn't have much peripheral vision. And it has a big muzzle, so it'll have a hard time seeing an attack coming from below if you're in close."

Not that I want to be in close, David thought.

"So your best bet is to distract it with an attack coming straight forward with one hand, and then sweeping in beneath with the other, into the chin or the throat," Gullin said. "Take a swing at me."

"How? From the side, or overhead and straight down—"

"For God's sake, just attack me!"

David thrust straight on at Gullin, who easily blocked his sword with his dagger and then swept his sword blade towards David's legs. He stopped less than an inch from David's knee. "Now you try it," Gullin said.

As David and Gullin sparred, Baba and Tanuki watched on. Tanuki coughed as Baba smoked her pipe, its gray wisps spiraling around her head.

"Men, and their fancy knives," Baba muttered. "They think such tactics will stop Wolf? Peh. Might as well dig through a mountain with sewing needle."

Tanuki scratched his nose. "Mr. Gullin and David have a chance. They've fought big monsters before..." He stopped himself, glancing away from Baba.

"Ah, so you *have* met the boy before, eh? Perhaps you looked different then, much smaller, much hairier?" Baba puffed again on her pipe.

"I know you know what I am," Tanuki said. "And I know what you are, too. And if your magic was truly great, you could enchant David's sword and dagger to be powerful enough to defeat this wolf you are all talking about."

Baba chortled. "Fact is, Badger, there already lies a power in those weapons that David does not know about. A power than even my magic could not affect. He has to figure out how to make that power work…and not work *against* him."

Tanuki's eyes widened. "What power? David would feel better to know that his sword and dagger have special—"

"No good to tell him. Then he will either be too confident, thinking his weapons can do all the work, or he will obsess about trying to bring the power out. He will learn of this power in his own time. For now, he must focus on the task at hand."

Tanuki frowned. "I don't like keeping secrets from David-san. I am his spirit guide. I'm supposed to help guide him, not keep him in the dark."

Baba nearly choked on her smoke, as she coughed forth a dry laugh. "Spirit guide? You, little Badger? Then the boy is in real trouble."

"You don't know everything, even if you are old," Tanuki groused. "And my name is not Badger. It's Tanuki."

Baba shrugged. "Call yourself whatever you want. Doesn't change what you really are."

"Fine. So I'm a badger. And you're a grumpy old lady who smells like burnt hair, and cats, and onions, and…" Tanuki's glower softened. "And loneliness."

Baba raised an eyebrow at him. "Better to be alone than have annoying company like you."

But Tanuki noticed that the smoke wisps around her head took the shape of birds, and they all flew away in various directions, except for one. The one smoke-wisp bird shivered, as if cold, and then dissipated into nothing.

David was black and blue after his training with Gullin. He was also starving, and he was thankful when Beatrice called them all in for dinner. He felt better, though, feeling he could learn the new techniques well enough to defend himself against whatever creature might be out searching for him, or Acacia.

Before they sat down to eat, Gullin led David to their guest room to clean up in a wash basin. Beatrice brought David some ointment for his bruises, although Gullin said that David would have to start "toughening up" to the pain. But Gullin was not about to argue with his wife, who shot him a death stare and replied, "David is a guest. We do our best to make out guests comfortable, even if the two of you are roughin' up each other like dogs over the same piece of meat."

After Beatrice left the room, David turned to Gullin. "You said you had an idea of how we can find or communicate with Acacia. I thought about calling out to her in my dreams, but I think something could have happened to Hypnos, and without him…"

"Don't get flustered, boyo," Gullin said. "We'll find her, or she'll find us. Sphinxes have a way of knowing, you know?"

"Knowing what?"

Gullin walked out of the room, and didn't say another word about it all through dinner.

That night, David dreamt, yet was not dreaming. He had a sense that he was in a dream, for he certainly could not be awake—he was not in Gullin's house, or anywhere, for that matter. It was blank, empty space, although he could feel a pulsation around him. There were heartbeats, muffled whispers, and a twisting, gnarling sensation as if his spirit were being wrung out like a wet towel. It was not painful, but it gave the impression of being on the teetering edge of a nightmare, and something was waiting nearby to push him over into terror.

Then the word came to him, the word that described how he felt—trapped.

He tried to call out for Hypnos, but as was usual in the dream realm, he lacked a physical voice. He tried to think of Hypnos' name, but even his mind was too hazy to do so. His brain felt like buttery mush.

Then there was something near him, and he felt what he could only interpret as a chill, or a burn…something not right.

Do you want to know a perk of being dead, David?

It was a voice, but not a voice. Yet its familiarity sent screams of panic throughout David's being.

It means I can do things I couldn't do when I was alive. Well, alive as I once was.

For instance, I can detach my soul from my body, and each entity can be perfectly fine. And my soul can skip about in this realm as much as I please.

David wanted to run, but there was nowhere to run to. He desperately commanded his body to wake up.

No no no, you'll wake up when I say so. And you will, this time. You're more useful to me in the waking world. But your usefulness will run out. I suggest by then, you remain awake as long as you can.

David couldn't see it, but the image of a long, twisted smile full of sharp teeth flickered in his thoughts.

As for my body, well... it's seen better days. Still functional, even if not as illustrious. But I don't blame you or my cousin for the current state of my body. What I do blame you for is destroying my life. It's only fair that I return the favor.

A surge of anger permeated David's consciousness. That anger spoke for David, asking the awful essence to stop taunting him and be done with whatever horrible thing it planned to do.

No, not yet. Like I said, you still hold some use to me. Besides, I want you alive long enough to witness me at my finest hour, when I finally get the justice I seek. And I want you to see your beloved sphinx bleeding to death at my feet.

"LEAVE ACACIA ALONE!"

David was sitting bolt upright in his bed. Sweat drenched his body, and his muscles ached all over. He tried to regain his breath, but he was so shaken that tears began to form in the corners of his eyes.

He tried to steady himself, realizing his scream might have awoken someone in the house. When he turned his gaze towards the door, he jumped to see Baba already sitting in a chair next to the door, staring at him.

"Nightmare, boy?" Baba asked. "Believe me, you haven't seen anything yet."

As much as David was in no mood to continue his fighting lessons the next day, Gullin made him get up before the dawn peeked over the horizon. Since David had not gone back to sleep after his nightmare—not that he wanted to, even if he could—he figured it was just as well to get up and keep his mind and body busy. He guzzled down his breakfast of porridge with the expectation to start back into the lessons right away, but Gullin passed him a wooden bucket instead.

"Even with wolves around, there are still chores to do," Gullin said. "You help me get them done, the sooner we get back to lessons. Go help Ru in the stables. You can fill the horse's food and water and clean out his stall."

David went to find Tanuki, who slept in his own secluded room next to the kitchen. He was sleeping on a thin straw mat with a few blankets, and even as a human, Tanuki had dug himself into the blankets and was curled up like a kitten, snoring. David hoped that the evil entity that plagued him last night wasn't bothering Tanuki, but Tanuki didn't appear to be distressed.

I'll give him a while longer to sleep, David thought. *I can feed and water the horse without help.*

David went outside with the bucket and filled it at the water pump. He could see across the field that Gullin was tending to the sheep, getting them ready to take out to pasture. David hoisted the full bucket and walked towards the stables, taking in the tranquil stillness of the morning. He hadn't been on a farm in years, not since he used to visit family in the Spanish countryside when he was young, but the peacefulness of the country eased his troubled mind.

He went over to Gringolet's stable, but the horse was missing.

David froze, scanning the stall as if Gringolet could be possibly hiding somewhere. Also, there was no door on the stall anymore. It had been torn clean off of its hinges. When he looked over towards the back of the stables, there was the door, with a massive bite mark in it, lying splintered and broken on the ground.

Right by the feet of the most terrifying animal David had ever seen.

David dropped the bucket, the water spilling all over and soaking his boots. His eyes were locked with the animal's, paralyzing him. The animal was so large, it had to lower its head to fit within the stable, and even then its shoulder blades were touching the ceiling. There was no doubt in his mind, from the night-black fur, to the cold ravenous eyes, to the saw-toothed maw, everything that had been depicted in the drawing within the *Poetic Edda*, who this creature was.

"The horse was filling enough," the wolf growled. "but there is always room for more. Come here, little meat-ling."

David had to use every ounce of will power in his body to keep from running. If he ran, the wolf would follow and would go straight to the field where Gullin and the sheep were, or worse, straight to the house where Beatrice, Ian, Baba and Tanuki were. David had to warn them, but he couldn't think how.

"You have no scent," the wolf continued. "Not even your thoughts. You have been enchanted, or cursed. What are you hiding from me?"

David gulped. He took a deep breath, and his words crept out from his mouth as timid mice. "Y…you are Fenrir, the one who eats the world."

Fenrir's tongue rolled out and he licked it across his lips. David noticed that the wolf was missing one of his fangs, exposing an empty notch in his gums. "I smell the scent of one of the Old Ones, the one I did not consume in the Ageless Ocean. She is of magic, and she must be the one causing me this pain in my teeth. Where is she?"

David's face blanched. He had assumed Baba had eaten the same stew he had to mask her scent as well. Why hadn't she? Didn't she know that Fenrir would have smelled her back at Geras' house? Or had she only had enough magic to provide the scent-masking for one person?

"I don't know who you're talking about," David said.

Fenrir lowered his muzzle so close to David's face that David nearly passed out from the wolf's breath. "You cannot lie to me. You know who I am. She must have told you about me. Is she in the house? Or is this another trick—she has planted her smell here while she is somewhere else? Tell me, or I will shred you into pieces."

David wished he had not left his sword and dagger beneath his mattress in his room. He had nothing to defend himself with, and the wolf would catch him before he could take a step to run. All he could think to do was stall for time. "You don't seem as big as I remember you."

The wolf narrowed his eyes. "We have met?"

"Not face to face, but the Fenrir I saw was much, much bigger. You can't be him."

The wolf leaned back, his head hanging wearily. "My size depends on my strength. I have been imprisoned for more lifetimes than you could count, so it takes much out of me to grow to my true size. Once I have reclaimed what was taken from me, I will have my full strength back and will be my true self again."

"What are you looking for?"

Fenrir glared at David. "You are a kind soul, which makes others feel welcomed to confide in you. You would charm secrets from a corpse. Such men who are easy to talk to are dangerous."

David shrugged. "You can't possibly see me as a danger to you."

Fenrir snarled. "There was an immortal like you, once. He, too, had a silver tongue, and I trusted him. He betrayed me. I no longer assume anyone is safe, no matter how small or weak."

"But you swallowed Geras' house. I saw your teeth through the walls. Someone who can do that, surely, wouldn't be afraid of any mortal man."

Fenrir was quiet, and then he nodded. "You were there with the Old Ones. Yes, there was the scent of a young one, the one whose thoughts I smelled. You were thinking about the sphinx…" Fenrir's paw lashed out and came down on David, pinning him onto his back. "The sphinx! She is more important than the Old One. Where is she?"

David gasped, struggling beneath the giant paw. It was as if an iron slab was pressing down on him. "What do you want with her? If you've been imprisoned all this time, then there's nothing she could have done to you to deserve your anger."

"She has what belongs to me!" One of Fenrir's claws scratched against David's collarbone, not quite breaking the skin but leaving a painful red line in his flesh. "I was immediately drawn to the scent of your thoughts because they reeked of how much you care for her. Does she care for you as much? If I tear off pieces of you and scatter them to every corner of the earth, will that bring her to me?"

"No, that will bring ME to you!" erupted a thundering voice from the other side of the stable. There was an ear-chattering explosion, and David watched as something blasted right into Fenrir's eye. Fenrir reeled back with a howl, removing his paw from David and slamming against the stable wall. The ceiling shook, threatening to fall through from the impact of Fenrir's weight.

"Run!" Gullin came running from the stable entrance, holding what appeared to be a repeating rifle in his hands. David scrambled to his feet, and Gullin grabbed him and pulled him along to escape.

"You had a gun this whole time?" David asked as they ran.

Gullin shook his head. "That's barely going to stun him. If bullets and gunpowder could kill monsters like that, the Master Huntsmen would have been out of business centuries ago." He shoved David towards the house. "Get your blades. I'll lead him off towards the fields."

"But, Beatrice and Ian—"

"They're fine. Ru's gathered everyone and he's taking them to safety. Now go!"

David shook his head. "I'm not leaving you with—"

"I've got three more rounds in here. You better be back by the time I'm done firing them!"

David bolted towards the house while Gullin headed off towards the fields. As David crashed through the back door into the house, he looked over his shoulder to see Fenrir charging out of the stable, ripping through the wooden support beams and tearing up the ground with his claws. His teeth were beared, his ears pulled back, his eyes searching for his quarry.

Gullin fired another shot at Fenrir. It grazed the wolf's shoulder, and the monster barreled down on Gullin, who took off running. David scrambled through the house to his room, reaching beneath the bed's mattress and taking out his sword and dagger. He dashed back outside, to hear two more gunshots ring out in the morning air.

David pumped his legs with all of his strength, flying across the ground towards the mass of black fur that was looming over Gullin. The Scotsman had dropped his rifle and drawn his sword from the scabbard on his belt. Fenrir bristled all over, enraged to be challenged by the tiny mortal.

"You're the big bad wolf?" Gullin scoffed. "You seem more like a runt to me!"

Fenrir gnashed his teeth at Gullin, as the man's sword slashed at the wolf in warning. "You stink of the blood of hundreds of my kindred," Fenrir said. "But you are a lowly man."

"That's exactly what your two pups thought," Gullin replied, "Apparently they were as big-headed as their father."

Fenrir halted. Gullin's face set into a hard, frozen grimace. The two stared at each other, as if speaking a silent language with their eyes alone.

Gullin broke the silence. "You haven't been locked up so long, you don't remember your own pups? What were their names again…Skröll and Hati, I think."

"My sons…" Fenrir hissed.

"Two less monsters in the world," Gullin hissed back. "And I was more than honored to make it that way."

Fenrir's scream of fury was enough to crack the heavens. The Mouth of Hell itself would have closed shut and hightailed it had it seen Fenrir's anger.

David panicked, imagining Gullin's head being bitten off in one clean chomp. He waved his sword in the air over his head, shouting, "Over here! I'm the one you want, you oversized dog!"

The wolf paid him no heed. He lunged forwards, but Gullin ducked and rolled out of the way. Fenrir's paw caught him in mid-roll and held him down, pressing Gullin into the earth. The beast lowered his maw, his teeth wrapping around and clutching Gullin's head.

"Fenrir!" David banged his sword and dagger together as loudly as he could. "Face me!"

Fenrir cringed, his lips pulling back and his jaw locking. Fenrir lifted his head up and looked over at David, his ears perking forwards.

David's breath caught in his throat. He hadn't thought that was going to work. He felt something sticky on his hand. Looking down, he saw that his dagger was *bleeding*. A reddish liquid dripped from the hilt onto his hand.

Fenrir sniffed the air, his eyes widening in anticipation. He flashed his teeth, and David could see the notch where Fenrir was missing a fang was oozing the same reddish liquid as the dagger. "You tricked me, Thief!"

David's mind went blank as the wolf charged straight at him, mouth wide open, revealing the endless tunnel of his throat into which David was going to plunge down in mere moments. He held his weapons up in defense, but they were no more than toothpicks compared to the wolf's mouthful of spears. His heart stopped beating as the bloody teeth prepared to snap down on him.

But they didn't. There was the jarring sound of teeth colliding into teeth, but David was no longer anywhere near them. He was looking down on Fenrir from above, and the wolf had turned to look up at him. There was a shocked expression on the wolf's face, as shocked as David was.

Had David suddenly gained the ability to fly? He heard the flapping of wings, but not from any he had miraculously grown. There was a firm grip around his waist, and a warm breath on his ear from behind. A gentle, soothing voice spoke to him.

"It's all right, David," Acacia said. "I'm here now."

CHAPTER NINE

"Acacia?" David turned to look over his shoulder. The sphinx pressed her nose against his cheek, her long wild mane of dark hair tickling his face. "How did you—"

"Talk is a luxury that will have to wait," she replied. "I'm afraid even up here we are not safe."

As if to illustrate her point, Fenrir jumped up at them, matching their altitude. Acacia veered away before the wolf's teeth could catch them, and the wolf fell back to the ground, causing an earth-shifting tremor.

"I should have known you and the sphinx were working together to keep my fang from me," Fenrir growled. "There is nowhere you can fly that I will not follow you! I will eat you both, even if you fly all the way to Valhalla!"

"Did he say his 'fang'?" David looked at the dripping dagger in his hand. Was his dagger what Fenrir was talking about? How was it possible?

"You will not need to go that far to deal with me," Acacia shouted down to Fenrir. "You need to go back to your prison, Fenrir. It is not your time yet."

"How dare you command me!" The wolf bellowed. "It is my destiny to devour this world, and all worlds! I will not be locked away again in that wretched prison! I will get back what belongs to me. But first...." He turned his searing gaze towards Gullin. "I will have justice for the murder of my sons."

"Your sons got tired of waiting for you. They were going to eat the sun and the moon," Gullin retorted. "We Master Huntsmen do not stand idly by and let beasts like you destroy what is good and right."

"How arrogant humans are, to think they can stand in the way of another's purpose," Fenrir snarled. "You cannot stop the end of your world any more than a blade of grass can stop a storm."

"If you think a blade is so weak, come taste the edge of mine," Gullin taunted.

Fenrir pounced at Gullin, who darted out of the wolf's way a split second before his great paws flattened the ground where the Huntsman had been standing. Gullin smacked Fenrir in the muzzle with his sword, but the wolf caught the blade in his teeth and tried to wrest it from Gullin's grip. Gullin freed one hand to withdraw his dagger, which he planted right into the empty socket in Fenrir's gumline. Rather than open his mouth, Fenrir bit down harder, causing the sword to shatter in two. Gullin tumbled backwards, holding only half a sword.

"Acacia, we have to help him!" David called.

"Help is coming," Acacia said. "It just needed a minute to catch up to us."

That's when David heard a screech from across the fields. An avian with wings that blanketed the heavens tore through the sky at a hurricane-fast pace, shrieking thunder as it came. Fenrir glanced up right as a golden eagle dove talons-first into his nose. The wolf howled, shaking his head madly to free himself from the eagle. At the same time, there was a rumble of hooves across the fields. Four stags—one white as winter, one green as spring, one bronzed from the heat of summer, and one crimson as the changing leaves of autumn—stampeded towards the wolf with their tree-tall antlers lowered for battle.

"Friend of yours?" David asked.

"Let's say they are on loan," Acacia said, as she landed lightly on the ground, releasing David. "They are guardians of the World Tree."

David watched as Fenrir pried the eagle off of his face with his paws and bit down on the eagle's neck, but the bird was buffered from the bite by its thick feathers. A smaller raptor—a silver hawk—fluttered up from between the eagle's eyes, where it had been hiding. The hawk flapped its wings and pecked at Fenrir's eyes, causing the wolf to stagger back. The stags barreled into Fenrir's side, their combined strength sending the wolf tumbling across the ground.

"Should we help them?" David asked.

"They seem to be doing fine," Acacia said. "Not that I don't want to give that hairy brute a good whipping, but it's more important right now to get you and that dagger as far from Fenrir as we can."

Gullin had dropped his broken sword and gotten clear of the skirmish, running over to join David and Acacia. He didn't say anything at first, but then he nodded towards the sphinx. "Mistress…Acacia," he corrected himself.

"It is good to see you, Gullin," Acacia replied, although there was a twinge of sadness in her tone. "We should be away." She made a whistling sound, and from the fields where the other creatures had come, a horse of storm-gray, with sea foam-white mane and eight muscular legs, galloped over to them. David and Gullin gaped in awe at the incredible steed.

"David, Gullin, this is Slepnir," Acacia said. "We might get in a bit of trouble for borrowing him from his owner, but Tyr says he'll take the penance for it."

"Tyr?" David asked.

Acacia nodded. "Our ally. You will meet him soon. Now you two get on. I'm not much for horse riding."

Acacia had to help both men get up onto Slepnir's back, as Slepnir was nearly eight hands taller than a normal horse. As Slepnir took off, David looked back to see Fenrir limping off the opposite direction, as the eagle, hawk, and four stags continued to pursue him.

"I need to find my family," Gullin called to Acacia, who flew on the right side of Slepnir. "I told them to head towards the village, and I'm not going anywhere else until I know they're safe."

"Then we will wait outside the town while you go to them," Acacia replied. "I'll see to it that they have good guardians to protect them, until we see that Fenrir is dealt with."

"Just about anyone would be a more sensible guardian than that scatterbrained Ru," Gullin said. "I swear, he better be keeping a good eye on Beatrice and Ian, or I'll tan his hide."

"I wouldn't underestimate him, Gullin," David said, remembering the time Tanuki had saved Gullin from the belly of the Sleepless Dragon. "I would think you could trust him with your life."

"If it comes to pass that he actually saves my life someday, I'll eat my socks."

While the morning light crept up upon the hills of Moffat, there was no morning light where Fenrir had taken refuge to lick his wounds. The guardians of the World Tree had driven him back through a tear in the Curtain, away from the human world. He managed to lose them in the mist of the Curtain, and made his way to an isolated wasteland within the icy terrain of Jötunheimr. This was a land that even the Viking gods did not wish to visit, for it was home to giants of rock and frost. Such frightful beings, however, did not stir dread in Fenrir's heart.

Fenrir found a cave within the face of a mountain to crawl into, settling into the darkness that had been his closest friend during all those centuries of solitude. He cursed himself for being so close within reach of his fang, and letting it get away. He cursed the human who had slayed his sons, the sphinx and the young one who had deceived him. But he would find them. He would make them pay for their crimes against him.

His stomach grumbled. How quickly his hunger always came to him. He could have devoured those stags and those stupid birds, if he weren't so weak. He would eat them all, soon enough. For now, he could probably find a rock giant for lunch. The taste would be horrid, but it would tide him over.

"That certainly was not a fair fight, now was it?"

Fenrir snapped his head up towards the mouth of the cave. A figure stood there, dressed in a long blue evening coat. He was no taller than a human, but he did not smell of man. It was not a good smell at all—a nasty bitter smell.

"Who dares to approach me?" Fenrir bellowed.

"Calm yourself, my brother. I am no threat. If anything, I would offer you my services." The figure walked into the cave, combing back his faded orange hair with his long fingers. A long, although tattered, tail of matching orange fur swished behind him, the end of it appeared to have been cut off.

Fenrir lowered his head to get a better look at his visitor. "Who are you?"

"Someone who shares your hatred of the sphinx and her little plaything. But they are easy prey. While I will delight in seeing you tear them apart, there is a prize far greater than they. You are destined to devour gods, are you not?"

The wolf curled his lip. "What do you know of me? And why do you stink of Death?"

"Interesting you should mention that, as it has to do with that prize I mentioned." The figure smiled his rows of yellowed teeth. His eyes, once vibrant orange, were now a clouded gray, like ashes from a dowsed fire. His skin, as well, was infected with a pallor that was unnatural for a living creature—although he was far removed from that.

"You see," the figure continued, "I was once employed to a goddess who decided to betray me and strip me of my most precious gift—my intelligence. All for her bratty little incarnation who would succeed her. But I'm not one to be misused so easily. So when she put her Shade inside of me to extract my gift, I decided to take matters into my own hands." He unbuttoned his coat and lifted up his shirt, to reveal a deep, deadly scar across his stomach, a dried ooze staining lifeless flesh. "Ripped that nasty bugger out myself, although unfortunately a few other things ripped out with it.

"Fortunately for me, someone took pity on me in my last few breaths of life," the figure continued, tucking back in his shirt. "By agreeing to pledge myself to him, he gave me a second life…well, perhaps 'life' is not the correct term. But this state has its perks. Detachment of soul and body at will, for example. It's quite fun."

"Is there a point to all of this?" Fenrir barked.

"Patience, brother. You'd think you would have learned that while sitting in your cell." The figure paced in front of Fenrir, tapping the tips of his fingers together. "My point is, we are both betrayed. We are of similar kinship, thus it would be sensible to help each other. I will help you recover your fang and get revenge on your betrayers, if you will return the favor for me."

Fenrir let out a tired snort. "I don't need anyone's help, especially not from some tiny…whatever you are."

"Oh, but I think you will like me as a friend. I can expose weaknesses in your enemies in ways no one else can. I can play upon their fears. I can shatter their minds if I so wish, while they sleep. They will be little more than whimpering rabbits, cowering before you as you gobble them up one… by….one."

"And in return, you would want me to help you destroy the goddess who drove you to this…half-life?"

"The goddess is gone, but her incarnation holds her essence and power. It will be the most divine meal you will ever have." The figure's smile melted into a grimace. "Devour Nyx, the Night, and no other god shall be able to stand in your way."

"Nyx is not the god I wish most to devour. But I hunger, and the Night would be delectable. Tell me what I may call you, friend, and I will consider this our arrangement."

The figure smiled again, bowing to the wolf. "In life, I was called the Teumessian, son of the Great Fox who eternally eludes the hound Laelaps," he replied, "but you may call me Brother Nico."

David and Acacia waited a half mile from Moffat in a pasture away from the main road, while Gullin ran into town to find his family who, he assumed, would take refuge at Beatrice's father's tavern. Slepnir stood by, watching over David and Acacia as a stoic sentinel.

There were many things David wanted to say to Acacia, yet he could not find the voice to do so. Acacia was equally silent, but perhaps she was used to that, after who knows how long she had had Nyx's Shade inside of her. Restraint from speaking had been the only way to slow the Shade's effect, so she may have become comfortable with the silence even after being freed from the soul-draining entity.

The two sat side by side on the ground, the grass swaying lazily around them in the dawn's wind. Finally, David broke the quiet. "Acacia?"

The sphinx gazed at David with her golden eyes. "Yes?"

David suddenly realized he didn't know where to start. "I…I've thought about you, you know."

Acacia nodded. "And I you."

"Thank you for returning my dagger to me. And for the sword."

"They rightfully belong in your hands, David."

"Why?"

Acacia was quiet, as if she wasn't sure how to answer that. "I just…know they do. I feel it. A long time ago, I was taught that sphinxes should rely on their intuition when it comes to human matters. Even we can't always explain how we know what we feel."

Sphinxes have a way of knowing, David remembered Gullin saying. "Was that how you knew where to find me? You just have a way of knowing?"

"It doesn't quite work like that. Even a sphinx has to do a little sleuthing sometimes. We're not oracles, after all."

"Then, how did you know where I was? Or was it Fenrir you were hunting for?"

Acacia scooted a little closer to David. He could tell she was trying to be reserved, but shifted her body in a manner that indicated she was antsy. "I was looking for you. David, there is something that I was shown…"

"By Nyx. The new one," David said.

"How do you know that?"

"A witch showed me your meeting with Nyx, through a spell. He was offering you safety from Fenrir, and then showed you a vision of me killed. But I don't think that was a true vision. Do you?"

Acacia shook her head. "I didn't believe it for one second. The old Nyx may have been honest with her prophesies, but incarnations do not always carry the same traits as their predecessors." She lifted an eyebrow at David. "This witch of yours is Baba Yaga, yes? That's what the cat told me, that she brought you here."

"The cat? Vasilia? Wait, that means you were at my house?"

Acacia sighed. "Perhaps I need to tell you what happened after I met with Nyx. Maybe you know something that can explain to me what madness tried to prevent me from finding you…"

She had had to make sure Nyx wasn't following her after she left her meeting with him—to throw a god off of your trail is no easy task. She surmised that there had to be a reason Nyx revealed the prophesy about David to her. Maybe this new Nyx enjoyed seeing others emotionally ripped asunder, showing them the pains of the future that they could not alter? No, Acacia's intuition whispered to her that there was something more going on. Nyx was egging her on, influencing her to take action. He knew she wasn't going to stand by and risk something happening to David. She would either go to David to protect him, or hunt down Fenrir to stop him.

But what should she do then? Which was the action Nyx wanted her to do, and why? Before she could do anything, she would have to do her best to keep Nyx from knowing what she was up to. There had to be a way to blind his sight of her, to keep him in the dark.

No, the dark was his realm. So she would have to keep him in the light, then.

She thought of Mount Helicon, where the Grecian sun deity Apollo resided with the Muses. It was a land of poetic inspiration, beaming with Apollo's light and bursting with joyful music. A quick pass by shining Mount Helicon would disperse any pursuing Shades of Nyx. Or she could pass through the deserts where her ancestors were exiled and taken in by the lion-men tribes, for Ra of the Egyptian Sun shed his brilliance there and could scatter the shadows. She had not been to either of those places in many a century, but she trusted the folds of the Curtain to help guide her, as they had all her life.

She slipped between the hidden pockets and folds of the Curtain, darting in and out of the mists in a zig-zagging route that had effectively helped her elude predators in the past. But Shades were not limited like those with physical bodies; such evasive maneuvers might slow them down, but they could catch up quickly if they picked up her trail. She hunted for any sign of a land of light, a tear in the Curtain that would call to her with either the symphony of Mount Helicon or the rushing howls of the Egyptian desert winds.

There! She spotted a silvery light flickering in the mist, and traces of melodious voices speckling through the stillness of the Curtain. She could feel the chill of night nipping at her tail, so she flew towards the light and voices, ripping through the wind with a speed that would put fast-winged swifts to shame.

It wasn't until she cut through the tear of the Curtain that she realized that this land of light didn't smell or feel like any place she had ever been before. It smelled not of Greece, or Egypt. It didn't even smell of Earth. This land's aura vibrated with a life-pulse that beat out of rhythm with her own, and she had learned centuries ago how to correlate her life-rhythm with all of the earth. There was no description she could give to this land, and the awareness that she was in a foreign realm stung her with urgent terror.

When she cast her gaze upon this new place, and soaked up the alien music resonating in the atmosphere, her terror subsided into tranquil awe. There were gardens of silver and ivory as far as her eyes could see, flakes of moonbeams dancing through the air, and rivers of liquid starlight rippling in winding ribbons throughout the landscape. She could see this realm's inhabitants below her, staring up at their unusual violet-winged visitor. The people were the most gorgeous creatures that Acacia had ever seen—human-like in many ways, but fairer, willowier, each person seeming to radiate with a light of their own. Acacia had never seen angels before, but she had heard of them and seen statues of them, and her first thought were that these people must be of the heavenly breed. Yet none of them bore wings, and their ear-tips were tightened into delicate points.

Are these the Sidhe? Acacia thought. *The Fair Folk from under the mounds of Ireland? But then, they would smell and pulse with the beat of the earth. Perhaps this is some Heaven after all. But I must reign in my curiosity for the time being. Surely this place will have driven off any Shades that may have been after me.*

She turned her eyes away from the radiant people below, and hunted for an opening that would lead her back to the Curtain. She thought she could make out the shape of a towering structure in the mist-cloaked distance, branching out in a million directions towards every edge of the sky. But it was far too colossal to be a tree, although what else could it be…

A sudden tumble back through a tear in the Curtain thrust her into darkness. Acacia flapped her wings wildly, as she tried to orient herself and adjust her eyesight to the abrupt night. She prayed she would not crash into anything as she slowed down her flight and hovered in space. She blinked, rubbing her eyelids with her paws, and soon could make out dots of muted light beneath her. She realized, as she inhaled the smell of the city below her—the scents of hundreds of perfumes, and delicate cuisines, and horses and people and flowers and everything she knew so well—that she was flying over the human world, or more specifically, Paris.

While it may have been the Curtain that guided her there so quickly, or pure coincidence that she had emerged directly over the city that she had wanted to go, Acacia couldn't help but think, *My heart will always be drawn to the one who owns a piece of it...perhaps even all of it.*

She remained high in the sky, out of the sight range of the Parisians walking the streets. She scanned the city landscape, tracing the roads and alleys, trying to remember which one of the quarters was the one in which to find David's townhouse.

Why must humans make so many of their dwellings look the same? Acacia inwardly griped. *But I remember, he lived not far from that grand building with the golden statues on top, the hall that plays music...the Opera! Yes, he lived a few streets away from the Opera.*

The stately visage of the Paris Opera loomed ahead of her, and the memory of her previous visit—when she had left David his wedding gift on his doorstep—came into full clarity. She circled above the nearby streets with vulture-like attentiveness, until she was sure she was looking down on the one that she had been to before. She softly landed atop the townhouse, lying low on the roof as she inspected the area below. It was, fortunately, a quiet night, with no strangers pacing the street. She unfolded her wings and glided down, alighting on the ground right outside one of the windows that would give a view into David's front parlor.

Placing her paws on the sill, Acacia peeked in through the window. She saw the finely furnished parlor, and a young strawberry-blonde woman pacing the floor. An old woman was with her, gesturing for the younger woman to sit down on the settee. There was a tea tray with a pot of steaming tea and cups, and the old woman offered the young one a cup. The young woman shook her head, keeping her gaze downcast.

Acacia recognized the young woman as David's wife. She was pretty, the sphinx had to admit. She had a kind face, too, and Acacia hoped that her gentle appearance was a reflection of her true demeanor. Yes, David deserved someone like that. He deserved a goodhearted wife who would take care of him, and not lead him into danger, or force him to face monsters, or deprive him of a peaceful, happy life.

Acacia realized then that her claws were bared, and digging into the windowsill. She immediately retracted her claws. *Don't be ridiculous*, she told herself. *Jealousy is a human emotion. And you're not human. No, you're a…*

She shook her head, and turned her attention to the old woman. But… that was not an old woman. There was glamour there, unseen by human eyes, but to sphinx eyes, the glamour was as thin as gauze. Why was David's wife being waited on by a cat?

A cat…this could be fortuitous. Acacia was of feline blood. This cat must be of magical stock to alter its appearance, and might be more willing to answer questions from someone of similar kin than a complete stranger. Acacia bided her time, waiting until David's wife had calmed herself, said a few words to the old woman, and wearily retreated upstairs.

As the old woman went about clearing the teacups and tray, Acacia extended one claw and tapped it lightly on the window. The old woman snapped her face towards the window, pulling her lips back into a hiss. When she saw Acacia's face, however, her snarl faded, and she glided over to the window and lifted up the sash.

"Well well," the cat-woman said, "I've heard about your kind before, but never seen one. I'm Vasilisa. You're the sphinx that Baba Yaga and the boy were talking about, aren't you?"

Acacia stood up taller on her hind legs, trying to peer behind the cat. "The boy? David? Is he here?"

"No, he and Baba went off looking for you. Or someone who might know you. They talked about a wolf that might be after you, and someone in

Scotland who hunts big monsters like that." Vasilisa's violet eyes sparkled, and she patted the windowsill. "Would you like to come in? The mistress of the house has gone to bed for the night, although I don't know if she will stay there. Poor lady can't sleep well, with her husband away."

"Thank you, but I must find David. You said he and this Baba woman went to Scotland?" Acacia knew who they must be looking for; there were few hunters of monsters in the human world, and a single one who lived in Scotland that David would know. "Did they go through the Curtain?"

"Baba Yaga travels by mortar, but it is fast and I would think they would be there by now. They left earlier this evening." Vasilisa tilted her head to one side. "He is a nice boy. You'll see that he is all right, won't you? The mistress would be awfully heartbroken if he gets eaten by a wolf."

Acacia cringed at the memory of what she saw in Nyx's illusion, but she nodded. "I'll do the best I can. You will take care of his wife until I bring him home?"

"Of course. She is a nice lady. Very sad, worried lady, but nice." Vasilisa patted Acacia's paw and smiled.

Acacia departed without another word, beating her wings and ascending into the night sky. She would have to find another tear in the Curtain, for flying all the way to Scotland from France would be too exhausting. She retraced her flight, trying to find the same opening that she has passed through from the land of light. Openings in the Curtain were tricky things; normally they stayed in the same spot and could remain open for millennia, but smaller ones had a way of moving around if the Curtain's folds should deem it necessary.

Or a new tear can abruptly open up and swallow an unsuspecting sphinx whole.

Acacia yelped in surprise as the night sky of the human world blinked out of sight, and she found herself plummeting through a musty, lightless space. She pumped her wings to gain control of her flight, but she landed heavily on hard ground a few seconds later. She groaned, pushing herself up. Her whole body ached down into the marrow of her bones. Her mind was still spinning from the unexpected fall—she hadn't been caught off guard by the Curtain since she had first started learning to navigate it. That was no normal tear that had simply shifted its place within the Curtain; it had felt jagged, frayed, and so raw that Acacia had felt a tingling painful sensation passing through it. It was as if that tear had been torn open, a gaping wound…

Squinting her eyes through the ash-laden wind, she took in her surroundings. It was gray all around, with an overcast sky, solid rock beneath her, and sparse black brambles poking up between stones. It smelled of earth, but also of fear and pain and…a nasty bitter smell…

She realized she was not alone.

Acacia staggered to her feet as slimy, maggoty shapes began to slither up from the rocks. Each wormy creature had a long muzzle full of canine teeth, beady red eyes with white pupils, and pointed triangular ears that lay back against their heads.

"Hyena worms," she muttered under her breath. "I've seen many strange things in my life, but this is a first."

"Actually, they're the Tokoloshe," a voice explained. "Not hyena worms."

Acacia darted her gaze about, but could not locate the sourse of the voice. She looked at the Tokoloshe, wondering if it had been one of them who had spoken. "Whoever said that, I demand you show yourself," she ordered.

Laughter peeled through the stark landscape. "You *demand*? Still as tenacious as ever. Now, where are you off to in such a hurry? Don't you want to play with my new friends?"

Acacia flexed her claws, lowering her head with a snarl in her lips. That voice, it sounded like…but it couldn't be. "Are you too cowardly to come 'play' with me yourself?"

"Oh, I will. I have missed our little games…our witty repartee, our riddles…Haven't you missed me, cousin?"

A tall coated figure formed from the swirling ash in the wind, and it tipped its battered top hat to her.

"Nico…" Acacia willed herself to remain steadfast, although her feet were itching to run. "Nyx changed her mind about taking your intelligence, then. A shame it wasn't the new Nyx that had to deal with you. I think he would have been far less compassionate."

Nico's smile was so venomous, it would make cobras shudder. "Oh no, Madam Nyx was more than eager to take from me what she truly wanted from you. But that's a story that isn't worth recounting, since you won't be living long enough to remember it."

Acacia lifted her head, grinning. "Why, because your little dog-faced worms are going to do me in? Nico, even you can't be that stupid to think I can't handle these mud-crawlers."

Suddenly, the Tokoloshe changed right before her eyes. They grew arms and legs, their bodies fattened into stocky bodies, their hyena faces flattened into visages that resembled a cross between human and bear. They were no taller than children, but these new forms—that and the fact there were several dozen of them—cause Acacia's fur to stand on end.

"Always a trick with you," Acacia spat. "No honesty or dignity. You shame our bloodline, Nico."

"Do you think I care about honesty and dignity? I must be giving you a scare, for you to resort to such words." Nico stepped forwards, and the Tokoloshe advanced on Acacia, their grubby clawed fingers set to snare. The sphinx roared, expanding her wings and flapping a strong gust towards her attackers. Some of the Tokoloshe fell backwards from the gust, and the others halted against the wind.

Nico snickered. "That's how you fight these days, cousin? A gentle breeze, no teeth and claws? That boy has made you soft. Even stupid, I think."

"Watch your tongue, unless you want it ripped out!" Acacia snapped.

"But cousin, you haven't even noticed what's tucked away in your shadow. Any fool can see it plain as day."

Acacia paused. This could be a trick—Nico may want her to look away for a split second so he could make an attack. She kept her eyes locked on him.

Nico smirked, shaking his head. "You've been to see the new Nyx, haven't you? After all, his Shades don't pop into people's shadows all willy nilly. They have to be planted there by either Nyx or someone of his employ. And I can assure you, I did not put that particular Shade in your shadow."

Acacia blanched. There was a Shade in her shadow? How was that possible? She had passed through a light realm, and an exceedingly bright one at that. No Shade should have been able to withstand that. Then again, it might have adopted her shadow's nature—vanishing in direct light, but reappearing now when a shadow could form. How else would Nico have known that she had met with Nyx, unless there really was something hiding in her shadow?

"I've dealt with Nyx's Shades before," she replied. "I will deal with this one, as soon as I am done with you and your friends."

"Aren't you even curious as to why it's there? Why would Nyx have a Shade following you? I don't suppose you were on your merry little way to find someone. Someone maybe Nyx wants you to find, someone maybe he is looking for too." Nico stepped closer to Acacia, and by now the Tokoloshe had her surrounded in a tight circle.

Acacia considered flying away. None of the Tokoloshe had wings or appeared to have flying ability, and Nico was as earthbound as a rock. But his scent was different than it had once been; he smelled like a corpse, but not even as nice as that. She felt there was a pinch of black magic at work here, and that could spell any sort of trouble. "What does it matter to you? Why even point this out to me? I doubt that you're telling me all this for the sake of being helpful."

"Of course not. But any opportunity to point out your stupidity is more than welcomed, even if you won't remember it once I've offered you to my master."

"Your mast—" Acacia didn't finish, because the Tokoloshe rushed her, grabbing on to her fur with such tight grips that she shrieked in pain. She reared up, and slashed at two of them with her claws. To her shock, while the blow had knocked them back—in fact, one of the Tokoloshe was sliced cleanly in half at the middle—there was no blood. Both of the creatures got back up to pursue her again, even the one whose upper half was crawling by its hands, and the lower half was an aimlessly walking pair of legs. Acacia clawed and bit and swiped, but the onslaught kept coming relentlessly. She leapt up to fly away, but the small hands of the dwarves grasped her tail and legs and held her down with surprising strength. She inhaled deeply, and breathed an air of enchantment upon them that would spellbind them to sleep. Yet her breath did not work on the Tokoloshe, not even influencing a yawn.

A realization hit her. The only creatures that her enchantment breath could not work on were those who had no ability to sleep. That would mean either the Tokoloshe were either already spellbound to remain awake—which seemed unlikely—or by nature they could not sleep. If they never slept, and they were stinking of that corpse-like smell…The Tokoloshe were of the undead. And Nico was reeking of the same smell.

Acacia squirmed as the Tokoloshe dog-piled on top of her, pinning her down. She looked up to see Nico standing over her. "You…you're not alive."

Nico rapped his knuckles on Acacia's forehead. "Anyone in there? Did it honestly take you this long to figure that out? You really are getting stupid, cousin." He withdrew a small clay jar from one of his coat pockets, and a short iron knife from another. "Now for the good news and the bad news. The good news, I know exactly how to get rid of that pesky Shade in your shadow. It will simply return to Nyx once it has no living host to be attached to. The bad news, of course, is that you'll have to die for that to happen. But more good news! You'll only be dead until I offer your blood to my master and he will revive you as one of his servants. I've already had a good fill of dragon blood to keep me animated for a time, so I wouldn't want to drink your inferior blood anyway. More bad news: you'll be just like me, so not really alive, not really dead. Actually, not 'just' like me. You'll be a mindless minion who will obey my every order. That was the deal, I'm afraid. I get to control you myself, as long as we both fulfill my master's wishes." Nico scratched his chin in thought. "But I don't think he'll mind if I had you do a task or two for me, as long as it doesn't conflict with his plans. For example, if I asked you to bring me your precious little play thing, so I can make you watch while I cook his carcass for dinner…No, better yet, make *you* cook and eat him for dinner—"

Acacia let forth such a scream of rage that the ground trembled and the ash in the air scattered away. With all her strength, the sphinx pushed herself up and flung open her wings, sending all the Tokoloshe flying through the air in every direction. Nico thrust forwards with the knife towards Acacia's chest.

One clean swipe of her paw made contact with Nico's face, and there was a gooey ripping sound as his head detached from his neck and plopped to the ground, rolling several feet away.

Acacia was seeing a blinding red as she stared at the decapitated head. Nico's body, however, remained standing. It got down on all fours and began feeling around for its missing body part.

"Now that was rude," Nico's head said dryly.

Acacia didn't have time to be sick from the sight, as the Tokoloshe were coming at her again. They had morphed into a hybrid of their dwarf form and their hyena-worm form, sharp teeth gnashing and slimy writhing appendages lashing out at her. She wasn't about to fly away. She wanted payback. She didn't care how many parts she had to chop up these vicious little devils—

A halo of bright silvery light blazed in the sky, coming from the tear in the Curtain that Acacia had fallen through. The tear widened, the light burning brighter, and the Tokoloshe froze in place. They all gaped at the light, shrinking away from it. Acacia squinted to look into the brightness, and saw a figure emerging from it.

Polished leather armor detailed with pendants and gauntlets of bronze, set on a tall, brawny form, materialized from the radiance. It plunged down onto the rocky terrain, sending tremors and cracks throughout the landscape of stone. A mantle of mahogany-brown fur cascaded over his back, and a crimson-and-gold helmet protected its head of moon-white hair. A silver battle-axe that was large enough to split a mile-wide island in half was grasped in the figure's hand.

The figure stood tall, looking down at the Tokoloshe that he could easily stamp out of existence with one foot. "You look a bit small for Dark Elves. Still, twenty against one is not a fair fight. Now, twenty against one plus me..."

The Tokoloshe scrambled like frightened mice back down between the crevices of the rocks and disappeared from sight.

Nico's body had regained its head, and set it back on its shoulders at a crooked angle. "Who might you be?" Nico's head asked.

"I am the Lawgiver," the armored man replied. "I saw this flying lion-beast pass through the realm of the Ljósálfar a short while ago, carrying a thread of darkness with her. It is my duty to keep order between the light and the dark. This darkness is unwelcomed, and must be eradicated."

Before Acacia could question what this all was about, the figure pointed its axe at her shadow. The sphinx leapt backwards as a beam of silver-white shot out of the axe and burned into her shadow, with enough force to make the ground smolder. There was the faintest of wails, and when the light ceased, a puddle of indigo ooze was bleeding on the ground.

"Well, now I know of two ways of getting rid of a Shade," Acacia said, finding the armored man's method much tidier than hunting relentlessly for a Singing Stone, as David once did to entrap a Shade.

Nico contorted his face into a gnarled façade of fury. "I don't know where you came from, but this is between the sphinx and me! Leave now, or my master will possess you with such madness that your existence will be a living nightmare!"

The figure glanced over at Nico. "Those who walk the plain between living and death disrupt the balance as well." He hefted his axe on his shoulder, and started walking towards Nico.

Nico blanched, and he reached down to pick up his top hat that had fallen off when his head had rolled. "No thank you, I've already been dismembered today, and once is quite enough." With that, he tossed his head into the hat, and then the rest of his body was sucked inside of it. The hat sprouted a pair of black wings and flew off, vanishing into the gray sky.

Acacia sat down, winded from everything that had happened. She scanned the armored figure up and down. She noticed that the hand that held his axe was the only hand that he had—his other was missing, with nothing but a stump at the wrist. "Thank you for coming to my aid."

The armored man nodded to her. "I happened to be visiting the Ljósálfar when you were flying through. We have never seen one like you pass through our realm. I have a keen eye for threads of darkness. Forgive me if I was intruding, but it is my sworn duty to maintain balance in matters of light and dark."

"What is that 'Ljósálfar' you keep mentioning?"

"The Ljósálfar," the figure reiterated, as if it was obvious. "Light Elves. Surely you know of them?"

Acacia shook her head. "I'm not familiar with your world, nor Light Elves or Dark Elves. But I am glad you decided to intrude. My cousin is not the savory sort. But I'm afraid I will have to bid you farewell. I have someone I need to find before he is hurt."

The figure slid his axe into a sheath across his back. "Ah, a friend in peril? It would not be gentlemanly of me to allow a lady to wander alone when there is danger about."

Acacia cocked an eyebrow at the man. "I wouldn't use the term 'lady' with me. I know what I am."

"A lady is a lady, whether human in body or…not," the man said. "Admittedly, you are a strange one. I bet you have enough strength in you to rival the mighty Freya herself!"

"I wouldn't know. All I care is if I have enough strength to rival a monstrous wolf and save my friend." She began to pump her wings to take flight, but the man grasped her forepaw.

"Did you say wolf?" he asked.

Acacia noted the sharp tone in his voice. "Yes, a wolf named Fenrir. Do you deal with wolves, Sir…?"

The man's cloudy eyes stared at her, as if he were angry. Acacia's fur bristled, wondering if he was about to attack her for some reason. The man let out a sigh, saying, "So, he's broken free. Odin help us all."

"You know this Fenrir?"

"Sadly, yes." The man rubbed the back of his neck with his one hand. "It would seem it was destiny that we meet. If you are in danger of Fenrir, then I must accompany you."

"If this is part of your 'sacred duty' to protect a 'lady,' you needn't bother. I am capable of defending myself."

"If it weren't Fenrir we were talking about, I'd believe you." He extended his hand towards her. "There's no harm in an alliance between us, is there? Anyone in danger of Fenrir's wrath is my responsibility, and anyone willing to stand against his might is my friend."

Acacia paused, gazing into the man's eyes. He smelled kindly enough, even if soaking with battle sweat, and his eyes were gentle. She extended a paw and shook his hand. "Very well. My name is Acacia."

"I am Tyr," the man replied. "Lawgiver of Asgard."

CHAPTER TEN

David was lost in Acacia's story. It took him a second to snap back to reality when she stopped speaking. "That's the Tyr you were talking about before? The one who lent you all the animals?"

Acacia nodded. "He told me all about the World Tree, how all worlds are connected by it. Even this one. It would seem we are all tied together, and if Fenrir gets his fang back, he will have all of his strength and can consume them all."

David reached into the leather frog on his belt and took out his dagger. It had stopped bleeding, and was clean. "This is it? How can this be his fang?"

Acacia looked at the dagger with disgust. "Believe me, David, had I known all this time that your dagger was Fenrir's fang, I would have buried that thing in the deepest sands of Egypt, or at the bottom of a sea."

"If this is the root of Fenrir's strength, then we need to destroy it," David said. "It can be destroyed, can't it? There must be a blacksmith in this town. We can try melting it in a smithing furnace, or find some tool that can break it."

Urgent apprehension erupted from Acacia's voice. "No, David! Even if it can be destroyed, do you know what happens if you break a talisman of dark energy? Energy doesn't disappear. It is released, becoming one with the universe. The evil in Fenrir's Fang could be unleashed on everyone in this world, in a form we wouldn't be able to contain. I highly doubt it can be destroyed anyway, given that it comes from an animal that's impenetrable to the natural elements and manmade weapons."

David inspected the dagger. How could such a small thing carry so much potential for destruction? It didn't "feel" that evil to him. But maybe that was all part of the fang's deception—if anyone could sense how evil it was, no one in their right mind would keep it. It had even fooled Acacia for years. If anything, the dagger felt like a perfect fit in his hand. It always had.

What did that mean? What did that say about *him*?

Acacia turned away from him. "I've put your life at risk because of my carelessness. I'm so sorry."

David tucked the dagger back into his frog. "Acacia, we're all at risk. Whether or not this dagger fell into my hands or someone else's, Fenrir would still have broken loose and be out to eat everybody. At least we know where his fang is, and we can keep it from him. If this Tyr is as familiar with Fenrir as you say, then we stand a good chance to defeat him, don't we?"

The sphinx was still, but eventually nodded. "I suppose the odds could be worse." She placed her paw on David's knee. "But Nyx's vision will not come to pass. This I promise you."

There was a rustling in the grass. Slepnir pivoted his ears towards the sound, and Acacia turned and growled. She sniffed the air, and relaxed. "Speaking of all things connected, I smell another old friend of ours."

A black-and-white striped head poked up from the grass. Tanuki scurried over to David, chattering rapidly. "You are all right! Mr. Gullin found us at the tavern, and he said you were waiting outside the town, but he wouldn't say why. " Tanuki looked over at Acacia and Slepnir. "Oh, right. Sphinxes and horses with extra legs might scare some people."

"Tanuki, it's good to know you and the Gullins are all right. He must've warned you there was danger in the stable just before he came to save me."

Tanuki shook his head. "Actually, I was only pretending to sleep when you came to wake me up, because I thought maybe if I waited long enough, you'd do all my chores for me." He gave David a sheepish grin. "But then I knew that wasn't right, so I came outside to help you, but I smelled a wolf nearby. I thought it must be coming from the field where the sheep were, so I ran to tell Mr. Gullin. He told me to get everyone in the house and go into town."

David scratched his head. "But, how did you do that, without a horse and cart? Gringolet was..." He sighed with a sad frown. "You didn't have Gringolet to pull the cart."

Tanuki twiddled his forepaws together. "Well, I sort of…well, I mean, I knew I had to get everyone out of there, and I didn't want to scare Mrs. Gullin by turning into a horse to pull the cart, but Baba would never be able to walk such a distance, because she's so old and all, but I didn't have much choice, so..." He had run out of air by this point, so he inhaled loudly to take in as much breath as he could. "So Mrs. Gullin carried Ian and ran alongside of me while I put Baba in the wheel barrow and pulled her myself."

"You pulled Baba in a wheel barrow, all the way here? That was very noble of you," David said.

Tanuki beamed. "Remember, I am the most divine being in Kyoto! Grandson of Raiju! Pulling a wheel barrow with a big fat lady is cub's play. Although I think I pulled something else other than the wheel barrow." Tanuki stretched his back, which made an audible crack. "We got to a neighbor's farm down the road, and Beatrice told them we had to get to Moffat right away, so they let us borrow a couple of horses."

Acacia patted Tanuki on the back, causing the badger's spine to make another cracking noise. "Thank you for protecting Gullin's family and the witch. I'm sure your master Yofune Nushi is quite proud of your courage."

Tanuki's smile crumpled like wadded paper. He began to shiver all over as tears filled his eyes.

"Acacia," David said with soft sadness, "Yofune is dead. Tanuki is certain he was murdered."

The sphinx was so aghast, she was as pale as moonlight. "That's impossible! I know Yofune. He… how could it be so?"

"Yofune was drained of all of his blood. All Tanuki remembers is that he was having a bad dream right beforehand, in which he felt trapped…" David stopped short. Saying the words aloud struck him with a realization. He had been having a dream just like that last night.

Acacia's shock shifted into a wary scowl. "His blood? Dragon blood?"

Tanuki nodded numbly.

The sphinx's teeth clenched together, her lips pulling back into a horrifying snarl. The fur along her backside stood on end. The golden color in her eyes flared with white fire.

David knew what Acacia was thinking. The assassin who took Yofune's blood had to be the same person—no, demon—who had been out for Acacia's blood, the same monster who had taunted David in his nightmare, who wanted both of them to suffer.

Tanuki's anguish was replaced by fear, as he witnessed Acacia's frightening countenance. He scurried behind David, curling up into a ball.

David held up a hand, hesitating to rest it on the sphinx's shoulder, lest she bite it off in her blind fury. "Acacia, calm down. Getting angry right now won't help. Save it for when we find that fiend and make him pay for his evils."

Acacia inhaled deeply, and exhaled. Her expression relaxed, but there remained a hot edge to her look, a tightness around her lips. "I'd say I'm going to kill him, but I've already been cheated of that. Nico will wish he had stayed dead once I'm done with him."

David reached around behind him to pick up Tanuki, and placed the shivering ball of striped fur in his lap. "As much as I hate to say it, Nico may have to wait until we finish dealing with Fenrir. Although it bothers me to think that Nyx hid a Shade in your shadow. Why would he have a Shade following you, when he knew you would most likely go after Fenrir, or me?"

Acacia stood up on her four legs and began to pace. "I have a theory. Obviously that Shade wasn't intended for me, otherwise Nyx would have found a way to put that Shade inside of my body. If that Shade in my shadow was merely to follow me, then Nyx is looking for Fenrir and figured he'd send me to find him, rather than Nyx departing his realm and leaving himself vulnerable. So the real question is, why does Nyx want to find Fenrir?"

Tanuki twitched his nose. "Maybe Nyx wants to stop Fenrir, too? I mean, you all keep saying how scary this wolf is. I heard you tell Mr. Gullin how Fenrir ate those immortal people in the ocean. Maybe Nyx is scared, and he wants Fenrir put back in prison as much as we do."

David scratched his chin. "Fenrir is supposedly destined to devour the gods, according to the *Poetic Edda.* Tanuki could be right. Nyx might be scared of Fenrir. He may have sent a Shade with you to spy on Fenrir, to gage how powerful he is."

"I don't know. This new Nyx doesn't seem to have the same self-awareness of his weaknesses that the old Nyx did. I don't think fear is something he takes into account." Acacia stopped pacing, swishing her tail from side to side. "I feel as if there is more to this than Nyx wanting to spy on Fenrir. I don't suppose your witch friend has a spell that would allow us to look in on Nyx? Maybe he'll reveal something if he's not aware we are watching him."

David shrugged. "Couldn't hurt to ask her. If her magic doesn't reach as far as the edge of the universe, she could at least show us where Fenrir is. Unless your friend Tyr might have a plan as to how to pursue Fenrir?"

"Tyr?" Tanuki looked back and forth between David and Acacia. "Everyone keeps making new friends without me! I don't like it. I'm the spirit guide. What if you both are making friends with all the wrong people, and you don't consult me?"

David rubbed Tanuki's head. "No worries. Tyr saved Acacia from Nico. He sounds like he must be a great warrior." He looked over at Acacia. "But why didn't he come to help us with Fenrir? Why send the stags and the eagle instead?"

Acacia sighed. "He said something about his people are not allowed to come to Midgard—I think he meant Earth. He is sworn to watch over the other eight realms, but there was a quiver in his voice." She leaned in to David and Tanuki, lowering her voice as if someone might listen in. "If you ask me, I think he's the one who's truly frightened of Fenrir."

David lowered his voice as well. "How does he know Fenrir, anyway?"

Acacia grimaced. "I noticed when we started discussing Fenrir, he was rubbing his severed wrist. I bet it has something to do with him losing his hand."

There was a snap of memory that rattled David. The name Tyr hadn't registered with him, but the story about Fenrir from the *Poetic Edda* had mentioned that the god who bound Fenrir with the unbreakable ribbon had had his hand bitten off in the process. How David wished he had the book with him right now, since his recollection of the story was blurry.

Tanuki huffed. "Great good a guy who's too scared to fight Fenrir will do us. It seems to me we need a warrior who's afraid of nothing. Do we have any of those?"

"A warrior who is afraid of nothing is a fool," Acacia said. "Fear is what helps us make wise choices rather than rash ones. I'll see if I can sway Tyr into facing Fenrir and locking him away again. He should know where to find another chain strong enough to bind the wolf."

"Maybe you should do that now. I'll go into town and ask Baba about using her spell to see what either Nyx or Fenrir may be up to." David lifted Tanuki off of his lap and set him down, before he stood up. "Tanuki, why don't you go with Acacia, just in case Nico tries to trap her again? It would be better if she had an extra pair of eyes to keep her safe."

Tanuki shook his head repeatedly. "You want me to go in case the crazy dead fox man is around? If he killed my master, what chance do I possibly have against him?"

Acacia shook her head as well. "Now that I understand what Nico is, I'll be better prepared. The badger doesn't have to escort me, if he doesn't want to."

"I know, but let's say it will make *me* feel better." David kneeled down to be on Tanuki's level. "Tanuki, I consider you Acacia's guardian spirit as much as my own. You will guide her as well as you guide me, won't you?"

Tanuki held his breath for a moment, and then let it out in a heavy puff. "All right. But I want sake when I get back! And a belly rub. And a claw cleaning. And a bowl of boiled potatoes. I've come to like potatoes."

David smirked. "Anything else, oh Divine Being of Kyoto?"

Tanuki thought about it. "I'll make a list."

Acacia scooped up the badger in one of her forepaws. "Come along then, spirit guide. Don't be all fidgety when we see Tyr. The last thing I need is a panicking badger making me look bad." She grinned, to let Tanuki know she was joking.

Tanuki chuckled. "What does the most Divine Being in Kyoto have to be afraid of? Nothing, that's what!"

Acacia lifted Tanuki onto her back, and turned to David. "Tyr said that Slepnir will stay until you command him to return to his realm. You tell him, '*Hvata til Asgard.*' I wouldn't keep him too long, in case his owner gets angry."

David stroked the neck of the mighty horse. "Maybe he can stay a little while longer. Fenrir might come back here looking for me. I'd like a quick escape available."

Acacia nodded, and she took off with a running start before flapping her wings and taking flight.

David could hear Tanuki say, before the wind drowned him out, "Remind me again just how big this Tyr guy is…"

David started walking towards Moffat, but Slepnir followed him, either from an instinct to protect or because the horse did not like being alone. David tried to order the horse to stay put, but not being versed in old Norse—which is what he assumed the language to be, since the *Poetic Edda* was taken from the Norse myths—he couldn't get the horse to obey.

"I don't suppose," David said, despite knowing the horse wouldn't understand him, "that you have some trick to make yourself look like a normal, four-legged horse?"

Slepnir twitched his ears, and stared at David.

"I didn't think so." David reached up and rubbed the bridge of Slepnir's nose. "Maybe it's best if I send you back home. Slepnir…" It occurred to him that he couldn't quite remember the words that Acacia had told him. "Something something *Asgard*…Varti…to…Asgard…you know what I mean, right? Asgard? Go to Asgard?"

The horse didn't budge.

David grunted in frustration. "What am I supposed to do with an eight-legged giant horse that won't go home? I can't have anybody see you. I don't need all of Moffat in a terrified frenzy."

Then he saw a man and woman pass by on the nearby road on a pair of horses. They were looking over at him. David froze, realizing there was no way the couple could miss seeing Slepnir.

"Good day to you," the man called. "Havin' trouble with your nag there?"

Nag? David looked at Slepnir. The horse hadn't changed size or shape.

How was the man confusing him for a nag? David decided it was better not to question. "No, it's fine," he replied. "My horse needed a short rest."

"You're almost to town. Might as well push the rest of the way and get 'im some water," the man suggested. He and the woman rode on, not giving David another glance—although their horses' eyes lingered a while longer before turning away.

David let out the breath he had been holding. So Slepnir must look different to everyone else, like a normal horse. What was it Baba had said? People who see unusual things will decide they were imagining it, because it defies what they know. Either that, or creatures might appear one way in the human world, and another way beyond the Curtain. Whatever the reason, David headed towards Moffat, his "nag" following behind him.

He headed straight to the tavern, leaving Slepnir at the trough outside. David noticed that the three other horses tied at the trough immediately perked forward their ears, staring right at the gray war horse. They bowed their heads and shied away as far as their ropes would allow, giving Slepnir sole access to the water trough.

The horses must see Slepnir for what he really is, thought David. *Maybe bringing him into town wasn't a good idea, if all the horses are going to act strange. Maybe Baba will know the special command to send him back home.*

David entered the tavern, which for this time of day was not busy. There were only a few patrons having quick meals and drinks, and Baba was seated at a table drinking a mug of something steaming. She didn't lift her head when David walked in the door, but as he approached her, she croaked, "You are ridiculously lucky, boy."

"That's arguable." David pulled out the chair across from Baba and sat at her table. "I don't call it lucky to have a…" He looked around at the other patrons, who did not seem to be paying him mind, but he lowered his voice anyway. "…to have a big dog chasing after me and my friends, not to mention a couple others who would like me dead."

Baba glared at him. "Escaping the 'big dog' twice now is not lucky?"

"I don't know if that was luck, or something else. Where is Gullin and his family?"

"Talking to Beatrice's father at his house down the road. They plan to stay with him until Gullin sees that their home is safe. Giving him some excuse about the sheep herd being attacked by a pack of rabid wolves."

David grimaced. "I don't suppose you know that the reason Fenrir found out where we were was because he smelled you. Why didn't you eat the same stew that you forced me to eat? Did you think he didn't smell you back at Geras' house?"

Baba sighed. She ran her finger around the rim of her mug. "Of course I knew he did. I wasn't planning on being around you by the time the wolf caught up. Thought I would be long gone…hoped he would follow me instead."

"What, to lead him away from me?"

Baba leaned back in her chair. "David, I am old woman. My bones ache, my eyes hurt. Dealing with monsters and magic, it is getting too much. Would like a nice, quiet life back home, in my house, in the iron forest. But it will not ever be. Will always be monsters, always be black magic, always be ignorance and fear. You talked about hope once…how we old folk pass it down to the young. Me…what hope have I to give? Bah." She waved her hand dismissively. "So, being eaten by wolf…what care I? I thought once I got you to your friend, sent you on your way, let Wolf come find me. I'm not afraid of sharp teeth." She picked up her mug and took a drink.

David raised his eyebrows. "You're going to let Fenrir eat you? Without a fight?"

Baba slammed her mug with such force on the table, it cause everyone in the tavern to jump. Her scowl could have melted metal. "Fight? Fight for what? Do we not all die someday, boy? We are here, then gone in a blink of an eye. Fight to live a few, lonely years more…" She shook her head. "Bah. You fight, if you want. Fight, if you have something to fight for."

Some people got up and left the tavern, leaving their leftover food and drink behind. David could understand; Baba's wrath was palpable. He stayed seated, however. He couldn't imagine what had happened to her to make her have such disregard for her own life. Yet he couldn't help but feel that it was because she was tired of life, as she was implying. "I think there are people you would fight for, Baba, if you really thought about it."

She shook her head again, staring into her mug.

"What about Vasilisa? She clearly loves you. There's got to be a reason why."

"Because she is stupid cat who loves everyone."

"But wouldn't you fight for her?"

Baba shrugged. "If she wanted to be elsewhere than with me, would not stop her."

David scratched his chin. "Have you ever had a family? Husband, children?"

"No. I am witch. Who would marry witch?"

"The right man."

Baba stood up. "There is no point to these questions. You found your sphinx friend. I did what you asked of me. I am going. Perhaps you should leave business with Wolf to the sphinx and Huntsman, and you go home to your wife."

"Wait, Baba." David was going to ask her about performing her all-seeing spell again, now that the tavern had cleared out, but instead, he said, "You said that I owe you a favor for everything you've done to help me."

The witch stopped short. She gave him a surprised smirk. "Yes, Baba does not forget."

"Then here is my favor to you. I promise I will help you realize that you have something to fight for. I don't know what it is yet, but I will make you see there is something in this world worth saving. And I will make it so you can retire to your home in peace, without any worries."

Baba set her hands on her hips. "I was thinking more along the lines of, I turn you into dog to fetch and do chores for me. But then I have to feed you, walk you, eh, too much work." She rubbed her pointed chin in thought. "I do not think you can do what you say."

David said, "You can at least let me try."

"It is a nice thought. You're a good boy."

"The first thing I can do is make sure Fenrir is imprisoned again, for good. It would help if we could know exactly where he is right now and what he's doing, if you could possibly cast another spying spell—"

Baba's tired smile flopped to a frown. "Ah, so that is it. Act kind to witch and she will perform more tricks for you? I am done with magic. I am too tired to keep doing this."

"Just one more time, please? It's the last thing I will ask of you."

"It will not be last thing." She downed the rest of her drink. She withdrew her pipe and a sachet of herbs from the pouch at her waist. "You do not understand the weight of your curse. You have Huntsman, you have sphinx, you have magic badger with too much loyalty. You think they protect you? Only as long as it is convenient. But they will turn tail and leave you when it becomes too much. Where will your strength be then? With witch? I owe you no such loyalty. If Wolf eats me, it eats me. But I would not throw myself on the sword to save you from Wolf's jaws."

"Then why are you helping me at all, if you truly don't care about saving yourself or anyone else? Why didn't you let Fenrir eat me along with Geras and Elli?"

Baba lowered her gaze. "You remind me of someone," she muttered. "Memories are silly things. They make your chest ache…" She packed the herbs into her pipe, and with a snap of her fingers, she lit it. She took one puff, and choked on it. Baba hacked violently as the pipe burned a foul smell, and the smoke hung heavy like wet cotton in the air.

"Baba?" David came over to her, putting his hands on her trembling shoulders. "Are you all right? Do you need fresh air?"

Baba wasn't paying attention to him. As her coughing subsided, she stared incredulously at her pipe. "Bring me tray and water," she ordered.

After rummaging around behind the bar, David found a wooden tray and a clay pitcher. He ran outside and filled the pitcher from the horse trough, as Slepnir gave him a nervous whiny. David gulped. Even the horse knew something was wrong. He dashed back inside, placing the tray and water pitcher in front of Baba. With shaking hands, she poured a thin layer of water upon the tray, and then tapped the ashes from her pipe into the liquid. She mumbled a few words, and the ashes started to glow a foreboding hurricane green.

The glow fizzled out, as swirls of blackness formed in the water. Then nothing.

"Baba, what is it? Does the spell not work anymore?" David asked.

The old woman slumped back in her chair. She wiped her hand over her face. "Not the spell. My magic…it fails me. Even now I feel it leaving me."

"Why? What happened?"

"I…I don't know. Magic is weaker at certain times. Many things can affect it…the heavens, the earth, the seasons…or perhaps I am dying. The magic would start to leave me, if I am about to leave this world."

A lump lodged itself in David's throat. "Do you…does it feel like you're…?"

Baba laughed weakly. "Death would be quite nervous if that were the case, eh? No, I do not think it is that, yet. Although this uneasiness in my heart, it does not feel like a shift in the heavens or in the earth. I feel like the magic is being called away, that it no longer considers me its master."

David looked down at the water in the tray. He cautiously poked a finger at the murky water, but there was no volatile reaction. "Do you have any idea what might be causing that? Has this ever happened to you before?"

Baba scratched her chin. "One time…a young girl was lost in my forest, and I planned to keep her in my home, to clean and cook. But she ran away, taking one of my enchanted fence torches, to light her way through the forest. I turned into a crow when she did that. I had no powers."

"So, how did you get your powers back?"

"Girl came back to me. When her stepmother and stepsisters saw my fence torch, they turned into ash. Girl had no one to look after her, so she came back to me, and my powers returned."

David frowned. "That's not a very nice story."

"Eh, don't worry. Stepmother and sisters were nasty people. Only evil people turn to ash when they see the light of my torches. Girl much happier with me anyway."

"So, is this time like that time? Has someone stolen something from you that would take your powers?"

Baba shrugged. "Could be. It has been some time since I have been home. I have foolish rivals who would wish to steal from me. But if my magic is failing, I would not risk flying in my mortar to go home and find out, even if it could fly. I suppose you will be on your way now, that this witch is of no more use to you."

David crossed his arms over his chest. "I told you, Baba, that I would make you see there was something worth fighting for. Maybe this is it. Would it be worth fighting for your magic? What if this has something to do with Fenrir, or Nico? Nico's working with very dark magic—maybe he's responsible for you losing your powers."

"Nico? I do not know this Nico." Baba narrowed her eyes. "But whoever is responsible, they will see it is not wise to anger Baba Yaga. What would you suggest we do?"

David sighed, pacing a few feet across the floor. He turned his head towards the door of the tavern. "Well, we may not be able to use your mortar to get you home, but how are you with horseback riding?"

CHAPTER ELEVEN

Slepnir snorted as David and Baba walked up to him.

"That is big horse," Baba noted.

"I figured you would see the true Slepnir. Everyone else apparently sees an old nag," David said.

Baba chuckled. "I know the feeling." She squinted at Slepnir. "You plan to have this animal take me all the way to Russia?"

"He was able to come here from...wherever Asgard is, which I imagine is far away," David said. "He must be familiar with the Curtain. I figured he could take us to your home faster than anyone else, and we could be back to meet up with Acacia and Tanuki in no time. Hopefully by then they'll convince Tyr to help us capture Fenrir."

"Us? What is this 'us' talk? This is my problem, no?"

"Yes, but if you don't have your magic powers right now, you'd be helple—" David paused, thinking of a better way to phrase his words. "—in a precarious position. You said you have rivals. What if there is a thief at your house, or someone who is trying to harm you? Wouldn't you feel better to have someone along to keep you company?"

Baba coughed. "You could rot teeth with your sweetness. I do not need a protector—but maybe, would be faster to search my house with two people than one. Come, we waste time standing here."

David looked up at Slepnir again. "I should mention, it was Acacia who got Slepnir to help us before. I can't seem to get him to do what I want him to do..."

"Never mind. I have way with horses." She clicked her tongue at Slepnir, who lowered his head towards her. She murmured softly, and the horse mumbled back in low noises. It occurred to David that the two were talking to each other. After a few moments, Baba went around to stand at Slepnir's side. She glanced back at David. "Well? You think I can get up on horse this tall on my own?"

After managing to hoist Baba Yaga up onto Slepnir's back in a rather humorous display of effort—anyone watching might have compared it to a ferret hoisting a turkey above its head—David had to climb up a thick braid in Slepnir's mane, as if climbing a rope, in order to get up and sit behind Baba. The horse did not seem to mind his mane behind climbed, as David's meager weight hardly tugged Slepnir's hair. He had barely sat down and secured himself when Baba gave Slepnir quick kicks with both of her feet, and the horse bolted off down the road and across the fields outside of Moffat.

David clung onto Baba and tightened his legs around Slepnir, fearing that the wind would knock him off. He panicked that Slepnir was going to run the entire distance to Russia without use of the Curtain—which at that speed wasn't impossible, but David knew he'd never be able to keep holding on with the force of the wind pummeling him. He had no idea how Baba was staying so calm; the wind speed wasn't affecting her at all.

"It has been long time since I ride horse!" Baba called back to David. "And never one with eight legs. It is exhilarating, no?"

That's one word for it, David thought to himself. How he wished they could've taken the mortar instead.

David was not sure where exactly they were now—Moffat was far behind them, and he thought he may have caught glimpses of a few passing farms, but it was all a blur to him. Slepnir suddenly catapulted over the crest of a hill, and David could see they were atop one of four touching hills, and directly downwards in the middle of the four hills was a steep-sided hollow. It reminded him of a deep bowl in which swirled a foreboding fog.

"Ah, this must be *MacCleran's Loup* that the locals were talking about," Baba said. "They say it is 500 foot drop into dark abyss from up here."

David nearly swallowed his tongue as Slepnir leapt off the top of the hill and down into the abyss, the bottom hidden by the fog.

The lurch in his stomach subsided, and the blistering wind stopped clawing at him. He blinked, his eyes adjusting, but all he could see around him was the shimmering fog. He felt a familiar sensation, one of both anticipation and anxiety, like standing before an enigmatic door that could be housing anything behind it.

The anxiety increased when the fog started to smell like gunpowder. A sharp tingle crept through David's body for a split second, and there was a cry in his mind like a bird having broken a wing. A feeling like a raggedy blanket swept over him—had he just felt the Curtain? But that wasn't possible—the Curtain wasn't something one could feel.

There was a rapid crackling of shots in the air, and Slepnir whinnied and tossed his head, his hooves pounding the earth—for they were indeed back on the ground. David looked about, and turned pale as he saw on either side of him, soldiers engaged in brutal combat. Some men wore uniforms of red and dark blue, and the others smoke-gray. Gunshots intermingled with war cries, and the air stank of bloody bludgeoning. Slepnir was running erratically, barreling into soldiers and screaming in a guttural horse cry.

"Can't you get him back under control?" David called to Baba.

"He is war horse! He is groomed for battle," Baba called back. "It is intoxicating to him."

"Then how do we get out of here?" David squeezed his eyes shut as Slepnir charged towards a line of soldiers, all who raised their rifles in defense.

Another smattering of gunshots rang out, and a cloud of smoke enveloped David, Baba and Slepnir. When the smoke thinned, the sounds of war vanished like candlelight under a snuffer, and the stench replaced by the scents of rain-soaked forest. David cautiously opened his eyes, and saw he was surrounded by the gnarled, scratching fingers of thousands of ashen-barked trees.

Slepnir plodded carefully through the trees, crunching leaves and fallen branches beneath his shield-sized hooves. The quiet of the woods was jarring after the commotion of battle, and after several minutes of regaining composure David spoke.

"What on earth was that??" he said a little too loudly.

Baba winced, shaking her head. “I know those gray uniforms. Russian soldiers. There is war in the south, on the peninsula.”

“I recognized the other soldiers’ colors, the red and blue. Those were of the French army.” David recalled hearing word in Paris about the French armies being sent off alongside the British army to eastern Europe earlier that year, under orders of Napolean III. He never cared much for French politics, however, and had been glad to know Spain wasn’t involved with it. “Why are the French and Russians at war?”

“Eh, why do men go to war? Land, faith, pride…things that matter very little when you are dead. They would probably not waste time fighting if they knew whole world could be eaten soon.” Baba looked over her shoulder at David. “Are you ready to be a soldier, boy? Can you kill your enemy when the time is right?”

David did not answer right away. He would certainly fight, and he had fought some terrible adversaries in the past. If he could kill—especially something relentless like Fenrir, or someone who technically wasn’t even alive, like Nico—he wanted to believe he could if he had to. Yet the thought of killing anyone, even a monster, left an acidic taste in his mouth.

“I’ll do what I have to do,” he answered.

Baba shrugged, and turned back around to face front. “We will see,” she muttered.

They rode on for a time, until Baba leaned forwards towards Slepnir’s ear and mumbled in a low voice. The horse stopped, standing between two thick tree trunks that extended up into a canopy of low-hanging cloud. The roots of the trees, almost as thick as the trunks that grew from them, splayed out around them, grasping the leave-cloaked soil.

David scanned the forest, but noticed nothing of importance through the trees. “Why are we stopping? Did you hear something?”

“We are at home,” Baba replied.

“Oh.” David looked around again, scratching his head. “I thought you would have a house. You live out here in the open?”

Baba rammed her elbow backwards, catching David in the side. “Of course not! You think I live like squirrel? Give me a minute…” She placed her pinky fingers in each corner of her mouth, and let out a long, shrill whistle.

Nothing happened, at first. Then the two trees slowly, creaking, shifted. The roots bent into arcs, scraping the earth, as one of the trees ascended upwards. The roots curled under, and flexed again, as if stretching after a century of standing. The tree placed its roots back down, and the second tree lifted off the ground and performed the same stretching exercise with its roots.

David realized, after marveling at the sight long enough, that the trees were not trees. The roots were not roots. He was staring at a pair of impossibly colossal legs—bird legs, to be exact—with flexing, curling toes. The legs creaked and groaned as they gradually bent, squatting down, and a large shadow descended from the cloudy canopy, the body that the two legs were attached to.

Slepnir plodded casually out of the way as the body lowered down. David fully expected a feathery bird torso to appear, but instead a wooden house came into view, skirted by a veranda laced with a fence, upon which were lighted torches. It was a modest hut, with a red-shingled roof and a brick chimney, and would look welcoming if not for the bird legs, and for the fence, which was built from the bones of every creature imaginable, including man. The lighted torches along the fence were human skulls, with flames emanating from their gaping jaws and eye sockets.

David immediately averted his eyes from the skulls on the fence, remembering Baba Yaga's story about the girl's stepmother and stepsisters.

"Oh, don't be κουτός," Baba said. "You would have been turned to ash already looking at my fence, if your soul was not so good."

David braved to look up, although the grisly sight of the skulls unnerved him. Slepnir carefully kneeled down on his front legs as Baba awkwardly swung her leg over to sit side-saddle, grasped Slepnir's braid and lowered herself down to the ground. She cricked her knees and her back, groaning. "I'm going to make tea first. You count my torches, make sure they are all there. Should be twenty."

As she hobbled up the steps of the veranda towards her front door,

David slid down Slepnir's braid and landed roughly on his feet. He walked in a circle around the house, counting each torch along the fence. One of the skulls clacked its teeth at him, and he jumped back with a shout of surprise. The other skulls clicked their teeth as well, and David got the impression they were laughing at him.

"Would you stop that infuriating chattering?" Baba bellowed from the house.

Instantly, the skulls silenced.

David gulped. He had to remember not to get too comfortable around Baba. If she could order around the dead, who should have nothing to fear, what horrors was she capable of? He finished his skull-counting; all twenty were accounted for. He walked around to the front steps of the house and quietly climbed them. He had reached the door when the bird legs decided they were tired of squatting, and they straightened up. The house elevated into the air, high above the trees and up into the hanging layer of cloud, and then above the cloud cover. David had nothing but the doorknob to cling on to, as he lost his footing and he landed rear-end first onto the stoop.

The house eventually steadied, the wind caressing David's hair. He pulled himself up onto his feet, shaking as he twisted the doorknob and opened the door to Baba's house. He stepped inside, wobbly on his feet.

"What took you so long?" Baba stood at a pot-bellied stove, upon which an iron tea kettle was boiling water.

David was about to reply, but he paused as he took in the room. Everywhere, corner to corner, stuffing the bookshelves, spilling from cabinets, masking the floor, were more random knick-knacks, baubles, toys, papers, jars, books, and bottles than David had ever seen collected in one room.

"They're…all…there…" David said, mesmerized by the clutter in the room. "Baba, did a hurricane pass through here?"

"Ha ha. Boy makes joke. It has been a while since I have been home. No one else to clean up, since my cat is at your house." The kettle screamed with a spout of steam, and Baba lifted it off the stove by the handle. She walked over to a table, swiping the mess off of it so she could set down the kettle. "Now, I know tea cups around here somewhere…"

"How can you possibly tell if anything may have been stolen or not? There is no order in here!"

Baba found a cup amidst the clutter, and set it down on the table. She went over to one of her cabinets and rooted through it. "Then the sooner you start making order, sooner we can see if anything is missing."

David crossed his arms. "You didn't pretend to lose your magic so you could bring me here to clean your house, did you?"

Baba glanced up at him, grinning. "Why, you don't trust Baba Yaga? Can you afford not to trust Baba Yaga?"

David forgot his caution of Baba for the moment, as anger pounded in his temples. "There's a wolf who could eat the world, a fox demon who wants me and Acacia dead, and a night god who may be up to no good, that I need to worry about! And you bring me here, almost getting my head shot off by Russian soldiers—"

"If you want Baba to get her magic back to help you with wolf, fox demon and night god, then start making order."

With a grunt of frustration, David sat down on one of the junk piles and held his head in his hands. He had thought this would be quick; he had thought Baba would instantly notice if something was out of place in her house, and then he could go back to Moffat to meet up with Acacia and Gullin while Baba sorted out her problem. In fact, why didn't he just do that? Baba didn't have any magic right now—supposedly. She couldn't stop him if he decided to leave her here and went back, except she was the only one who could give Slepnir orders. That was if David could even get down to the ground to find Slepnir, now that Baba's house was so high up. He was stuck.

"Fine, how would you suggest I start 'making order'?" he asked. "This mess will take forever to sort through!"

Baba had finally found what she was looking for in her cabinet—a tin of tea herbs—and she waddled back over to the table. She shook some of the tea out of the tin into her tea cup. "Big problem always seems impossible, if you look at whole thing at once. But all big things are made up of many tiny things. Tiny things are not so impossible. If you give attention to tiny things, big things will not overwhelm you so easy."

David groaned. That sounded like something his mother would tell him. "*Niño*, if you pick up one toy off the floor, then another, one at a time, your room will be clean before you know it." He remembered that it still took an eternity, at least to a six year old. That was nothing compared to this. He started picking through the pile that he was sitting on. An inkwell, an earring, a handkerchief, a small birdcage—with a living bird in it, and in sympathy, he let it loose and it fluttered up to settle in the rafters—a spoon, several books, a shoe, a jar of honey, a spool of thread, a straw-haired doll, a necklace, a jewelry box with an unoccupied cobweb inside of it. After a while he managed to sort the first pile into what he thought were sensible categories, and he sighed.

"Now I only have to do that about a hundred more times," he thought to himself.

He paused as he heard a tiny clicking sound at his hip. He looked down to see the little bird he had freed pecking on the hilt of his sword. David watched it in amusement, as the bird would peck for a few taps, then look up at him, and then peck the hilt again. He lightly brushed at the bird with his fingertips to shoo it away, but the bird flittered around in a circle, and landed back on his sword and pecked at it again.

David noticed that the pecking made a different sound this time. Instead of a tiny, metallic click, it had a resonation to it, like the ring of a bell. David gripped the handle of his sword, and the bird hopped down to the floor. It pecked the floor three times, looking up at David, and pecking the floor three times again.

"You're trying to tell me something, aren't you?" He drew the sword out from his belt, holding it horizontally in his hands. He traced his eyes along the blade, on the hilt, but didn't see anything he hadn't noticed before. The bird continued its unusual ritual, pecking the floor thrice, pausing, and pecking thrice again.

David held the sword up, with the tip of the blade pointing downwards. He tapped it on the floor once.

The bird shook its head. It pecked the floor three times.

David tapped the tip of his sword on the floor three times.

He paused. The bird stopped pecking. It fluttered up off the floor and back to the rafters.

David grunted. Apparently, Baba was not the only crazy one in this forest. He placed his sword back into the frog on his belt, and wearily turned around to face the rest of the mess—

Everything was in perfect order.

Baba was sipping her tea at a cleared table, topped with a fine linen and a vase. The floor was swept clean, the kitchen area spick and span, and the bookshelves organized with all their books. Every item was at home on its respective shelf, in its drawer, or in its cabinet. It looked like a completely different house.

"So you had your magic this whole time!" David said, throwing his hands up.

Baba glanced over at him, as if she had forgotten he was there. "Me? I've been sitting here enjoying my tea. I've done nothing."

"Then how do you explain..." David looked up at the bird, who was hopping around on a rafter.

"I told you, pay attention to tiny things to solve big problems," Baba said with a grin. "Of course, it helps if you have power to make order from chaos."

"I...do?" He touched the hilt of his sword. "Did my sword do all this? Did you know it could do that?"

"Ah, you and all your questions." Baba stood up carefully, leaning on the table for support. "You have two blades, yes? Bring them here."

David came over to her, placing his sword on the table and drawing out his dagger to place next to it. "It's this dagger that's causing all the trouble. But I didn't think the sword had anything remarkable about it."

"Dagger causing trouble?" Baba picked up the dagger, tapping the tip of her bony finger on the blade. "Ah, I sense it. Has dark life within it. I perceive the blood of many victims coursing within it."

"It's Fenrir's missing fang."

Baba's eyes widened. "That would explain much." She placed the dagger back down in haste, as if it were a slimy slug. She ran her finger along the edge of the sword. "This was designed to be balance to dagger. If dagger disrupts, sword rectifies. If dagger makes chaos, sword makes order. Halves of same whole."

David touched the hilt of the sword. "But, what is the sword, then? If the dagger was forged from Fenrir's fang, what is the sword made from?"

"What, I should tell you everything? Bah." Baba began to pace around the table. "If sword can make order, perhaps it can fix what is broken. Perhaps can fix my broken magic."

"Fix it? I thought your magic was fading because you might be missing something. Does it look like anything is out of place?" David realized how silly this question may have been. Even though all of Baba's things were organized and on their shelves, there were so many trinkets that it would be hard to know what might be missing without pouring over every nook and cranny.

Baba didn't bother to look around. "Remember, last time someone took something from me, I turned into a crow. Do I look like a crow?"

"So then, you knew you hadn't been robbed?" David was rapidly losing his patience. His fingers coiled inwards into tight fists. "Why on earth did we come all this way, then? If you wanted to see if my sword had the power to 'restore order,' or fix your magic, why couldn't we do that back in Moffat?"

Baba walked over to him. She was staring curiously at his hair. She reached up and plucked something from David's hair, although he couldn't see anything at first. But he felt it—a light pull from his hair, that trailed down to his shoulder, down his shirt sleeve until it stopped at his wrist. Baba squinted at her pinched finger and thumb that was holding whatever it was she had pulled from him.

"This is why we came all this way," she said.

"What is? I don't see…" As David leaned in a little closer, the light in the room reflected off the tiniest sliver of whatever was in Baba's hand, but then it was gone again. He had the impression that it was a spider's thread, but he couldn't see it again no matter how he positioned himself.

"I had suspicion that I hoped was not true. Had to go through Curtain to find out."

David picked up his two weapons from the table and tucked them back into his belt. "The Curtain? What about it?"

Baba hobbled over to a corner of the room, where a battered spinning wheel was sitting. She wrapped the invisible string around the bobbin of the spinning wheel, and fed it around the grove of the wheel. "You have trouble seeing it, as most humans do. But I know thread of Curtain when I see it. Many, many moons ago, I met the Sudice, the three weavers. They showed me how to spin the finest threads of all, those of magic. I never could get it perfectly, but the more I did it, the clearer the threads became to me. I did not need to feel them to know how to weave them. Such threads are the most fragile when loose, but when woven together into an honest purpose, they are unbreakable."

David could see a shimmer feeding through the spinning wheel, like a line of pure diamond. He reached out to touch it, but Baba slapped his hand away. "No touching wheel. Was gift from the Sudice. Only three others like it in all the many worlds. You will taint it if you touch. So no touch!"

David rubbed his slapped hand. "What does the Curtain have to do with *your* magic?"

Baba swatted at him again. "Dumb boy! Curtain hides the world humans do not know about, yes? How does it do this? Magic! All magic, and those who use it, are woven into the threads of the Curtain. If magic starts failing, it is strong possibility that something is wrong with Curtain. And when Curtain starts tearing open in places it should not—say, in middle of a battlefield rather than in Iron Forest where we want to go—it means it is getting weak. Curtain may be starting to unravel." She sat down at her spinning wheel, pressing her foot to the treadle to start the wheel spinning, as she went about her work.

David's initial response was to shake his head. "No, Baba, that's not possible. After all this time, since who knows when, why would it be unraveling now…" Then he remembered the unusual feeling he had when they passed through the Curtain—the feeling of something frayed and scratchy running over him. “Wait, if the Curtain is losing its power, would it…could one physically feel it?”

Baba wagged her finger at him. “It should also not be losing threads that get snagged on a boy’s clothes and hair. This is big, big problem. Soon, not only those who know about Curtain, or who are invited into it, will be able to pass through it. Soon, any clumsy idiot could stumble into it. Those who hide in the Curtain’s fabric will be exposed to the human world. The tide of insanity that would result, is too much to think about…” She stroked her chin. “But your sword and dagger still have their powers. They should be weakening in magic if Curtain is unraveling.”

David shrugged. “Maybe the Curtain’s not unraveling that badly. It might be thinning in a few spots, so not all magic is being affected by it. It could be you alone losing your powers.”

“Oh, what relief,” Baba scoffed. Her face slackened as she stopped spinning. She froze, her eyes fixed on the spinning wheel.

David could see it clearly. A thin line of gray had appeared strung into the spinning wheel, but the string decayed, its strands breaking apart and falling to the floor in broken strips. David knelt down to touch the frayed pieces, but they crumbled into dust under his fingertips.

She sighed, covering her eyes with one hand. “I have lost my talent to weave the magic. I cannot help to fix it. Perhaps it is my punishment. I have not been good woman. Here I hoped to retire in peace, but how can I, when I have caused so much suffering, so much fear? Perhaps I bring this on myself.”

“Baba, I don’t know what you’ve done in the past, but you’re not a bad woman,” David said.

Baba uncovered her eyes, glowering at David. “Someday you’ll know true pain, boy, and then you will see not all people are so good.”

David wanted to bark back at her that he certainly did know pain, and that he didn’t always see everyone as good. He stopped himself from making a rash retort, and instead replied, “Maybe someday you’ll see all people aren’t so bad.”

Baba snickered in her throat, but there was sadness in her eyes. “Would not hold breath about that."

David forced a smile. "I think we're jumping to conclusions. Whether or not the Curtain is unraveling, it doesn't mean your powers are disappearing for good. As you said, the last time it happened, there was an explanation and the problem fixed itself. Your magic will come back. It's not all gone. After all, aren't your house's legs created by magic—"

This was one of those times David wished he hadn't opened his mouth.

The house took a sudden dip to the side, sending everything in the room tumbling in loud clashes and clatters across the floor and against the wall. The house shifted violently back the other way, as the furniture, books and knick-knacks charged across the room, slamming into the far wall. David and Baba bounced back and forth with the grace of wind-tossed laundry, unable to grab hold of anything for stability. David drew out his sword, hoping perhaps the same trick he used before may restore order, but he couldn't secure his footing, let alone tap his sword on the same spot three times. He could feel the house descending, rapidly. His stomach—at least the contents of it—was evacuating into his throat as the house fell towards the earth. Yet the true danger of the predicament didn't truly hit him until he heard Baba scream, a shriek of pure terror.

As he crashed against the wall again, he banged the blade of his sword against the floor three times as quickly as he could.

The door of the house burst off of its hinges as a flash of gray rocketed through it, crashing thunder on the floor. A long braid of wild mane lashed out and wrapped around David and Baba Yaga, with serpentine quickness, and drew them up and onto the horse's back. Slepnir exploded out the window and into the air as the house landed in an implosion of wood, brick and bone on the ground.

Slepnir landed easily on the forest floor, with David and Baba clinging in rigid fright to his back. All around them lay the shattered remnants of Baba's house, including the crumbled pieces of the once majestic bird legs that upheld it, now no more than fragmented pillars of coal. Smoke swirled up from what was left of Baba's chimney for a moment longer, and then it evaporated into nothing.

David finally exhaled. As his senses returned to him, he heard a sound that shook him with the despair of autumn rain.

Burying her face in Slepnir's mane, Baba was weeping.

David placed a hand on Baba's shoulder. "I'm sorry this happened. But maybe I can fix this. Wait here." He slid down off of Slepnir, and walked over to the bulk of the debris. Sword still in hand, he tapped it on the ground three times.

Nothing happened. He tried again, to no results.

"I guess repairing what's destroyed isn't quite the same as putting things in order. It was worth a try." He put his sword away and walked back over to Slepnir. "Don't worry, we'll get your magic back, and then you can rebuild you house. It will be all right."

Baba didn't respond. Her crying quieted, but she kept her face in the warmth of Slepnir's neck. David remained silent for a long while, not sure what to say or do. He could imagine how devastated he would be if his home were destroyed. Unfortunately, he didn't know where someone like Baba could go—where would she live until they could solve this problem?

"Come on," David said. "We should go back to Moffat. Acacia and Tanuki may have returned by now, and I'm sure Gullin's wondering what's become of us."

"Leave me here," Baba wheezed, his voice muffled by the horse's mane. "I don't want to go anywhere. I want to be alone."

"I know. But I'd rather you be alone in someplace warm and dry than out here in the cold. We'll get a room for you at an inn in Moffat. Hopefully if you're in town surrounded by lots of people, Fenrir won't attempt to come after you. Not while he's weak, at least." He patted Slepnir's foreleg. "It would be so much easier to climb on this horse if he kneeled, rather than me having to climb his braid—"

Slepnir tentatively kneeled down on his front legs.

David tightened his lips in irritation. "If you've been able to understand me this whole time, I'm going to be very sore with you."

CHAPTER TWELVE

"Acacia? I don't feel so good," Tanuki murmured as he rode nestled in the curvature of the sphinx's wing.

Acacia walked along the white sands of a vast shoreline, the waves of a teal sea lapping at her feet. The hall where Tyr resided was not much farther now, but an uncomfortable sensation had settled over her. "It's most likely because this place is so unlike where we are from," she said. "I can tell the air here is different. It may take time to become used to it."

Tanuki wrinkled his nose. "Maybe. But I feel an ache all over. Not an 'I've been digging all day' ache, but like thorny vines are growing in my bones. Do you feel that way?"

"Not so much," Acacia said, but she did feel a clawing in her lungs and gut. She thought it was best to not tell Tanuki, however, so as not to worry him. "Do you want me to take you back to the human world?"

The badger curled up tighter in Acacia's wing. "We won't take too long to talk to this Tyr, right? Maybe the aching will go away. Or maybe I'm weak with hunger. Will there be food where we're going?"

The sphinx inhaled and exhaled deeply, hoping it would help dispel the gnawing inside of her. It wasn't so bad, not compared to all the centuries that Madam Nyx's Shade had incinerated her throughout as it drained her cunning away. "I'm sure Tyr may have something to eat. If not, I'll go catch you a fish. There must be fish in this sea."

Tanuki nodded, but his body was shivering. "Tyr doesn't eat badgers, does he?"

"I doubt it. A badger wouldn't be much but a morsel to him. He probably likes bigger game."

"He doesn't eat sphinxes, does he?"

Acacia stifled a laugh. "I'd like to see him try it," she replied.

As she spoke, she noticed that her breath clouded in front of her face as it would in the coldest of winter. But her breath produced a golden haze, smelling of wildflowers. She stopped walking, puzzling over the cloud as it gradually dissipated.

Tanuki lifted his head. "What? Why are we stopping?"

The sphinx knew what she had done. It was her special sleep-inducing breath, but never before had she exhaled it without intent. Now it poured from her mouth and nostrils in tumbling puffs, even when she tried to make it stop. As she exhaled again, she swore she heard the faintest of murmurs, as if her own breath were attempting to speak. The noise was stifled, however, and it resonated louder as she inhaled, the air circulating in her head.

She sat down on the sand, unfolding her wing to set Tanuki on the ground. "I think something is trying to speak to me, through me. I'll need absolute silence for a few minutes."

She said this straight at Tanuki, and another cloud of her special breath poofed in his face. He let out a long, tongue-wagging yawn. "Absolute silence…I can do that…good night..." He flopped backwards onto the sand, legs up in the air as he began to snore.

Acacia closed her eyes, slowing her breathing to the calm pace that echoed the lapping waves on the beach. Her heart's beating receded to the subtle patter of a ticking clock. But she kept one paw dug firmly in consciousness, not releasing herself to nirvana entirely, in the event she should need to awaken immediately. There was risk of her falling asleep if she became too comfortable, and after what Tanuki had told her about Nico's slithering about in others' dreams, she knew better than to leave herself vulnerable either awake or asleep.

She let out a long, drawn-out breath, and this time the smell was different. Her sleep-breath normally smelled of anything soothing, pleasant, and inviting. This smell was of raw, sweaty panic.

Who is calling for me? Acacia braved to ask—not with her true voice, but her mind.

Sphinx! Thank the gods, I have reached you!

Acacia recognized the voice immediately. *Hypnos? Are you talking to me through my breath?*

I apologize for having to take such invasive measures, but I had no choice. I do not have much time. Nyx keeps me trapped, unable to return to my realm. I cannot reach anyone through sleep, and I fear my realm is being usurped. You are the only one who I blessed with the breath of slumber, thus I can slip into your breath as I would a dream.

The urgency of Hypnos' message put Acacia on edge, but she struggled to remain in her meditative state. *Nyx has kidnapped you? Why? How?*

That is not important. Nyx is seeking out all of his kin to force them to reveal the hiding place of my three sisters, the Moirai. They possess something that Nyx wants badly. With it, he believes nothing will prevent him from pursuing Fenrir the Wolf, to steal his ability...

I don't understand! Slow down. Nyx is after Fenrir? What is he after?

Nyx desires something buried within the vast tapestry of the Curtain... Hypnos's voice was fading.

Spit it out! I'm losing your voice! Acacia's thoughts screamed.

He is ripping the Curtain apart...he wants the threads...David...

Acacia's breath chilled, filling her with freezing winter. It caught in her lungs, and she choked on it as the moon-pale face of Nyx flashed in her mind. The solid black eyes bore into her, and the pale lips twisted into a hateful grimace. He didn't speak, but Acacia was smacked with the intensity of Nyx's anger. Then it felt like a hand reached down her throat and wrenched all the air out of her.

She snapped her eyes open, gasping. She saw that her breath no longer clouded in front of her. She inhaled deeply, willing for her gift from Hypnos, and exhaled.

There was nothing. No haze, no smell. Hypnos's breath of slumber was gone.

Acacia sat still, speechless. Numbness prevailed throughout her being. It was not so much that she no longer had her special breath; it was that it had been stolen from her, by that deceitful, hateful Nyx. Her connection to Hypnos was broken, and who knew what Nyx would do to him for having spoken with Acacia, trying to reveal his secret plans. A wail escaped her, as the mournful cry of a lioness who had lost her pride broke the quiet.

Tanuki shuddered awake at the sound. "Acacia? Are you hurt? What happened?"

Acacia swallowed her sorrow, clenching her teeth. With one swoop of her paw, she grabbed Tanuki by the scruff of his neck, throwing him onto her back. She sprang to her feet and beat her wings to increase her speed, running along the shore with a newfound energy that made the badger cling to her fur like a tick.

Let Nyx do his worst. Even a god can be undone, and she would see to it that he would fall. She would have the strongest of Light on her side, and Light would drown the Night, no matter what price she had to pay.

Crossing back through the Curtain the way they had come, David stayed alert in the event that he, Baba and Slepnir strayed into yet another unwanted destination. Given that Slepnir was a war horse, who knew what other battles he might gallop into. The return journey was less arduous, however, as Slepnir traveled at a more cautious pace, even though his speed was faster than what David would have favored. The horse may have been more conscientious of his riders, who were now more somber and shaken than before.

David wished he was more knowledgeable about how, exactly, the Curtain worked. He had always relied on others who understood its folds, its pockets, and its movements, to traverse through it. To him, it appeared as thick mist, occasionally revealing a shimmer here, or a shadow there, but its nature was foreign to him. If Acacia was here, maybe she could sense if it was weakening, or if it appeared different from normal. Once they got back to Moffat, he would ask her if she had noticed anything unusual when she passed through the Curtain.

A horrible thought nibbled at his mind. If the Curtain was fraying, and thus magic was disappearing, what did that mean for her? For Tanuki? How much of what they were was magic, and how much were they flesh and bone as David was? Had Acacia lived for all these centuries because that was sphinx nature, or was it from magical means? Would Tanuki become a normal badger without the Curtain intact? Would either of them even continue to exist? The image of Acacia and Tanuki vanishing into thin air, never to return, struck him so hard that he had to clench his jaw tight to keep from crying out in anguish.

When the mist of the Curtain trailed away—David was relieved to have not felt anything brush against him, so he figured this part of the Curtain was strong—the riders found themselves under a night sky, speckled with stars of a myriad of colors, like an array of gemstones sewn into onyx velvet. The ground beneath them was of an ivory sheen, stretching for miles along the edge of a tranquil sea.

"Where are we?" David was unnerved by how quiet this place was. "Baba, didn't you tell Slepnir to return us to Moffat?"

The witch didn't respond right away. She seemed lost in thought.

"Baba, where did you tell Slepnir to take us?"

Baba looked over her shoulder at him. "You said you wanted us to go back. So I reiterate to horse, 'go back.' Just like you said."

David shook his head. "You knew what I meant. I meant to go back to Moffat! Saying 'go back' could mean anything to Slepnir. In fact, he probably thought you meant...go back home." He rubbed a hand on his forehead. "And home to Slepnir is that Asgard place that Acacia was talking about. This must be Asgard."

"Then you must specify next time," the witch sneered.

"You knew what I meant!" David reigned in his irritation. "Maybe this is where Acacia and Tanuki went to speak to Tyr. They could still be here, or if not, someone might be able to tell us if they've seen a sphinx and badger come through. If there is anyone," he noted, as he couldn't see any homes or towns nearby. Snow-cloaked mountains grew from the horizon on all sides, and forests of the most ancient trees, their tops kissing the sky, filled in the space between the horizon and the shore where they walked. Even in the dim dusk, it was an impressive landscape of primal nature, but everything was too grand, out of proportion with the forests and mountains that David knew in his world. He felt practically puny in this land—even Slepnir was small for this place. Next to one of the trees growing besides the shore, Slepnir was in size the same ratio as a raccoon beside an evergreen tree in the human world.

Baba Yaga tugged her hat down around her ears as a biting wind slinked around them. "If you think to look for them, I suggest we look quickly. I may not have my magic, but I can still sense the deep hostility of this land."

David nodded, and gave Slepnir two quick kicks in the side as he had seen Baba do before. The horse picked up his pace, galloping along the beach into the harsh wind. As David scanned the sea and its churning waves, he thought he spotted the backside of an animal cresting out of the waters and then slipping back beneath the sea froth. He gulped, hoping that any monsters that might be in this sea would stay far out and not come to shore. Who knew, in a land like this, how gigantic such beasts could be.

He turned to look forwards again, and could see a large structure ahead. Slepnir was barreling so fast, he feared they would smack right into what lay ahead. "Woah, slow down! *Cuidado*!"

Baba yanked on Slepnir's mane braid, and the horse stopped so abruptly that both the riders slammed forwards into the horse's neck, almost being thrown off entirely. They had stopped right in front of the structure, which was an irregularly large wooden sign. There was a wooden dock that trailed out into the sea, simple in build but as wide enough for a stampede of ox to cross. There were no boats in the dock, as the dock appeared to have not been used in a long time. Its planks were wood-rotted and cracked, and the sign was wind-worn and the paint faded away. Words had been carved into it, and they were legible, although barely:

"Hymir's Sea Tours: Finest Fishing and Boating Ventures This Side of the Elivigar. Ask for information in the Main Hall up the Hill"

In smaller carving beneath that—a bit more sloppily carved, as if hastily included—stated: "Will not comply to requests to hunt the serpent Jormungandr!"

David read the sign aloud, repeating the name at the beginning. "Hymir…I know him. He's the one who took me out to sea to find Geras." He looked out to sea again. "Was it this same sea?"

"Not same," Baba said. "Wolf drank Geras's sea. Is probably valley or desert now."

There was a twisting in David's gut. As long as he had Fenrir's fang, the wolf wouldn't have his strength all the time, but if Fenrir rested long enough, he could summon another spurt of energy like he had to devour Geras's house. If David and the others didn't track down Fenrir quickly, how soon would it be until Fenrir regained his energy to be big enough to devour another house again? What if he could swallow all of Moffat, and everyone in it? All of Paris? Florence...

"Do you think Hymir was able to escape from Fenrir? Maybe he's in the Main Hall up the hill," David said, pointing to the spot on the sign that mentioned the hall's location. "He was willing to help me before. He might know where Tyr lives."

Baba sighed. "Why not? Is not like I have to go home any time soon..."

She clicked her tongue and gently tugged Slepnir's braid to direct him towards a beaten path that ascended up a gradual slope through the forest. The horse kept a steady trot, as the path wasn't steep, but it was clear after about ten minutes that the "hill" must have been a hill by a giant's standards. The path kept ascending, the trees thinning the higher they traveled. As the trees parted, a warm light could be seen far off at the crest of the hill. Soon the triangular face of a mead hall, built from reddish wood with a bronze-tiled roof and surrounded by cylinder beams on all sides, glowered down at them from atop its hilltop throne. The beams were carved with the images of serpents, boars, horses, and the stoic faces of warriors with cascading beards. Torches as tall as lighthouses stood at each side of the front entryway, their fires blazing bright enough to smother the starlight above.

The closer the riders and their horse came to the hall, the more the mead hall's enormity overwhelmed them. It was by far the largest architectural marvel that David had ever seen, making the Eiffel Tower seem like a lamppost in comparison.

The three paused outside the front door, an intricately carved mural of thousands of men battling with swords, spears and shields. David and Baba Yaga glanced at each other.

"Should we knock?" David asked.

"What's this 'we'? You want to knock on door of giant house, who knows what is inside. You knock."

David nodded. "Very well. But maybe I'll knock while staying on the horse."

Baba veered Slepnir closer to the door, although the horse did so with great hesitation. David lifted his fist, pausing at first, but then tapping lightly on the carved wood.

"Yes, that should do it. Good job," Baba said.

David summoned up more courage, and knocked again with more force. It did not generate much more sound, though, and he started to wonder if there was anything he could do to announce their presence. Then Slepnir pivoted around, his rear end towards the door, and he let go a mighty back kick with his hind legs. His hooves crashed against the door, blasting a burst of thunder that reverberated for several long, heart-stopping seconds.

Everyone froze. Shortly, they heard the sound of heavy footsteps approaching the door.

David held his breath. He hoped that was Hymir they heard approaching, and not another giant. He placed his hands on his sword and dagger, but hoped that if it was something monstrous behind that door, that Slepnir would have enough sense to run away. He wasn't in the mood to fight another giant beast—

The thought that Fenrir might be hiding inside sent stabbing chills up his spine as the door slowly drew open.

It was not a wolf behind the door, nor was it Hymir. A woman, not quite of giant stature but at least eight or nine feet tall, stood in the doorway. She was matronly, not in her winter years but certainly her autumn, with long ropes of golden hair laced with silver. She wore a long white dress, adorned with necklaces and armbands of gold. She smiled kindly at them.

"Ah, you must be more of Tyr's friends," she said. "Please, come in. I have plenty of ale for all. We have a stable in the back for your horse…" She tilted her head, as she looked at Slepnir's legs. "Eight legs…oh, my. I fear my stables are not suitable for the steed of the ruler of Asgard. But I will bring him my finest grains and mead. Come, you need no fear. You may come down and enter."

David slipped down Slepnir's braid, and then helped Baba down to the ground. But he was startled over what their hostess had said—Slepnir was the horse of the ruler of Asgard? He had thought Slepnir's owner had been a friend of Tyr of equal status, not a king. If his memory of the *Poetic Edda* was correct, the ruler of Asgard was an incredibly powerful warrior god named Odin. A god-king! David was filled with dread at the thought that Odin may not have given permission for a human to ride his royal horse, and what repercussions would come of it.

The hostess took Slepnir by the braid, gracefully leading him along the front of the mead hall and around the corner. She called over her shoulder, "Go straight, your friends are in the back of the hall. And do not mind my mother. She has a temper this evening, but she will keep to herself if you do not incite her."

David and Baba walked through the mead hall, their anxiety mixed with awe at the décor of the interior. This must have once been a place of great festivity, judging from the weathered banners and dusty draperies that hung from the ceiling and down the walls. Remnants of past battles—battered shields of every shape and size, the carved figureheads of sea dragons from the prows of ships, swords as long as three men's height, helmets big enough to house a family—littered the hall from front to back. Golden goblets, bronze serving bowls, and jeweled platters were collecting dust on banquet tables that were long enough to seat a hundred humans on each side. From the far back echoed the murmurs of voices, and it took David and Baba four minutes of maneuvering the maze of artifacts to finally see who was at the end of the room.

Seated in a black-lacquered throne with two dragons' heads sculpted on the top, was a white-bearded man who was the most muscular specimen that David had ever seen in his life. Remembering Acacia's story and how she had described Tyr, he knew this man had to be the axe-wielding light-bringer. Yet Tyr didn't sit on the throne as a king or person of nobility would; he leaned forwards, his elbows on his knees, his head hanging down so that his beard swept the floor. The warrior looked troubled, as he rubbed the wrist of his handless arm with a neurotic motion.

In front of him stood Acacia and Tanuki. The badger was nose-first in a bowl of honey-colored liquid, lapping it up and smacking his lips. Acacia, however, gave her focus solely to Tyr, who averted his eyes from her. Even though Acacia's back was to David, he could see her shoulders and spine arched up like a defensive cat, and her tail was swishing side to side in apprehensive jerks.

Whatever discussion was going on, it was not going well.

Acacia's voice suddenly raised from shallow murmuring to sharp barking. "What don't you understand? This is not about you and your dishonor! This is about millions of lives being ended, mankind and the Aesir of Asgard!"

Tyr held up his hands towards Acacia, glancing towards a cavernous door at the end of the hall off to his right. "Please, milady, not so loud—"

"I'm not scared of your grandmother! If she strikes such terror into your heart, maybe I should call her out here to knock some sense into you!"

Tanuki lifted his muzzle out of his drinking bowl. "I think both of you need to relax and have a little refreshment. You won't solve anything having a hot head or cold feet, and a good drink always cures both. Besides, this mead stuff is really good. Maybe even better than sake!"

Acacia rolled her eyes, ignoring Tanuki. "Look, what else are you going to do, Tyr? Just sit here and wait for Fenrir to come for you, after he's eaten everything else in existence? Or maybe wait until Nyx gets a hold of Fenrir? You realize that could spell a fate for all of us worse than being eaten alive?"

David stepped forwards. "What's this about Nyx and Fenrir? Is that what Nyx has been after this whole time?"

Acacia snapped her head around to face David, and her cross expression switched to surprise. "David? How…why are you here? Has something happened? Is Gullin and his family all right?"

"I…It's a long story. The short version is, Baba's losing her magic, the Curtain may or may not be falling apart, and Slepnir brought us here because I'm poor at giving directions."

Acacia stared at David, her head tilted in confusion. "The Curtain is…

no, I can't handle any absurd suspicions right now. We need to stick to the matter at hand. Hypnos was able to sneak me a message that Nyx wants control of Fenrir, and that Nyx is holding his siblings hostage to find three sisters who have something he needs to ensure his victory. So we need to not only stop Fenrir, but keep Nyx from getting his hands on him. The best chance we have is to form as many alliances as we can, with anyone who may have the skills to fight against Fenrir and Nyx. But our brave Tyr here…" She narrowed her eyes on the warrior seated on the throne. "He would rather stay here in Grandmother's house and have Mum pamper him like the big baby that he is!"

Tyr sat up straighter, releasing his wrist and gripping the arm of his throne. There was worry in his eyes, however. "Your intentions are noble and true, milady. But you do not understand Fenrir as I do. Do not underestimate my courage or strength. I have endured more wars than you have lived years. But Fenrir cannot be contained or destroyed. The ribbon that bound him to his prison was supposed to be unbreakable, and yet it failed. *I* failed. To fight him would mean certain doom, and not mere death. One would never truly die within his belly. It would be an eternity of pain and horror, being digested every single moment for as long as Fenrir continues to live and eat. There is no terror that the underworld possesses that would come close to matching the nightmare of being Fenrir's victim."

Tanuki's jaw went slack, and he dropped his drinking bowl. He gulped. "I'm going to need something stronger," he said.

Acacia growled. "That would explain why Nyx wants Fenrir. To have a creature with that sort of power at your command, Nyx would be the most powerful being in the universe, and could threaten any world to bow down to him. No one would dare contest him."

"But why would Fenrir submit to Nyx?" David asked. "I thought Fenrir could eat gods as well as mortals. After all, Fenrir ate Geras and Elli, who were immortal. I don't know if Hymir was a god, but he was a giant—"

Tyr shot up from his seat, staring at David with wide eyes. "What did you say?"

David stepped back, taken off guard by the warrior. "Fenrir destroyed the house of Geras, and swallowed the ocean that Hymir sailed me across. I was hoping that Hymir had escaped and maybe he would be here. Is Hymir your friend too? Has he been home?"

Tyr was frozen in place, and then he slowly sat down again. "Rumors fly fast in the nine realms. I had hoped they were not true. No, Hymir has not returned. He will not return. Now I know why."

"I am sorry," David replied. "He seemed a good man."

Tyr stared down at the floor between his feet. "I cannot honestly say my father was good, but he was blood."

"Your…father…" David closed his eyes and lowered his head. "I truly am sorry. I wouldn't have been so casual about telling you if—"

Tyr raised his one hand to silence David. "You couldn't have known. I'm sure my father would not have mentioned me in the short time you were with him. We were not on the best of terms. I always considered myself more of an Aesir than one of the giants, anyway." He paused, running his fingers through his beard. "Mother told me he had been asked by a god to help a mortal who had been stricken by a curse, by ferrying him to the home of Old Age. I couldn't imagine what mortal would be so important that the gods actually worried about his well-being. But clearly you are an unusual one, judging by the company you keep. No offense, milady," he said, nodding to Acacia. He looked to Baba. "Or to you, dearest elder. Or you…" Tyr pursed his lips at Tanuki, who was now indulging in a stein of potent ale. "Little furry one."

"Hey!" Tanuki slammed his stein down on the floor. "I'm of divine blood too. Grandson of the Lord of Lightning! I am also David-san's spirit guide. I give him words of wisdom." The badger emitted a loud, long belch, followed by a hiccup.

Tyr looked over at David. David shrugged with a smile.

"David was brave enough to face Fenrir himself," Acacia added. "But this is not his responsibility. It is yours, Tyr. You were given the task of seeing that Fenrir remained locked away. It is your duty to put him back in his place. How can you throw your duty upon another's shoulders, someone who deserves to live his life in peace, while you hide like a coward?"

Tyr rubbed his severed wrist again. He looked at David. "You faced Fenrir, and lived? Even weakened, Fenrir would be a deadly opponent. How is it possible you survived?"

"Honestly?" David scratched the back of his neck. "Acacia arrived just in time to save me from Fenrir before he ripped me apart."

"Then, you did not fight him."

"Well, I was able to stop Fenrir momentarily, with these." David removed his sword and dagger from his belt and held them up. "Fenrir is weak because he doesn't have his fang. This dagger was forged from that fang. This sword, too, has special powers, although I don't know where they come from."

Tyr stood up again and walked to David. David was barely half of Tyr's height, and he knew that the warrior could crush him like a grape if he wanted to. Tyr leaned down to get a better look at the two weapons. He tapped the tip of the dagger with his finger, and pulled it back as if he had been zapped by electricity.

"Fenrir's fang. It still carries the same wickedness as the day it did this to me." He cupped his hand over the stump of his wrist again. "And yet it may be the only weapon with the strength to wound the great beast. Not iron, nor steel, nor any metal forged in the furnace of Völundr could pierce Fenrir's hide or shatter his bones, but his own tooth could be his one weakness. You are a rare mortal to wield such a blade."

"By any chance, do you know anything about this sword? It has the ability to put things in order," David said.

Tyr looked at the sword. He ran his finger along the blade with a wistful look on his face. "I suppose this would have been forged around the same time as the dagger. It can instill order, but not repair what is broken, am I right?"

"Yes, that's right," David agreed. "Do you know where it came from?"

Tyr sighed. "What good is Order, if Chaos will destroy and Order cannot undo the damage? Why bother to uphold Order if it all crumbles into disarray in the end?" He stood up straight, walking back to the throne to sit. "What good would it be to return Fenrir to his cell, if he would continue to break free? What good am I, if I cannot keep him there?"

"Will you stop your nonsense?" Acacia hissed. "I thought you were a powerful warrior, balancing the light and the dark. But all I see is a whimpering wimp! You can either sit there, waiting to be devoured along with the rest of your world, or you can stand up and fight back, and give your world half a chance!"

There was a rustling from the other side of the cavernous door nearby. Tyr's face paled. "Please, if you cannot lower your voice, you must leave—"

"I am not going anywhere!" Acacia roared. "You may think you're afraid of Fenrir, or even your grandmother, but you don't know real fear until you've made me angry!"

"What is that noise?" boomed a scratchy chorus of female voices from the foreboding door on Tyr's right. Everyone in the room instantly hushed. Tyr gripped the arm of the throne so tightly, the wood cracked in his fist. His expression was akin to witnessing Death having sauntered into the room and pointed a skeletal finger in Tyr's face.

From the dark archway emerged a gnarled, gangrened hand that was so enormous that it had trouble fitting through the doorway. It was too large and too fast to avoid, and in one swipe it snatched David, Acacia, and Tanuki in its withered clutches. It drew them into the adjoining room, as Tyr leapt forward to grasp onto the hand. He tried to pry it open in vain, all the while shouting, "*Mor mor*, please! They are my guests! They mean you no trouble!"

Baba Yaga shuffled after them, muttering to herself, "I swear, these young buffoons have no respect…"

David did not dare to move, praying this disgusting hand would not crush him and his friends. For what felt like hours, he, Acacia and Tanuki huddled inside the rank, pus-oozing fist. When it opened, holding them up on its palm, the sight that they beheld made David gag, Acacia cower, and Tanuki pass out on the spot. Their captor was a bloated, bulbous, tree-bark-skinned mass, covered in tumorous burls and dripping all over with what may have been sap, but it was more viscous and greenish. It was what was atop that body, however, that made David's eyes pop out of his skull. He remembered what Hymir had told him back in the boat: "Bet your *modir* doesn't have 900 heads to scream at you with."

CHAPTER THIRTEEN

Spanning out from where the neck of the giantess should have been were hundreds of limbs and branches, and instead of leaves, there grew clumps of what appeared to be grayish-green hair. Dangling from the branches, like overripe fruit ready to drop, were female faces of every description: crones, children, mothers, maidens, but what they all had in common was the penetrating hatred blazing red in all of their eyes. David wasn't about to start counting, but he wouldn't doubt for a second that there were 900 heads, all glaring right at him.

"How dare you raise your voice in my house!" the giantess thundered with all of her voices at the tiny intruders in her palm. "I did not give you permission to intrude in my home!"

David could understand now why Tyr was so terrified of this…woman?… but also why he braved to live in the same house with her. Even Fenrir would think twice about intruding here in his weakened state, if he knew about Tyr's grandmother.

Tyr was clinging onto her thumb, and he hoisted himself up onto her palm next to David, Acacia and the comatose Tanuki. He stood tall and steady, but there was a quiver in his speech. "*M-m-mor mor*, these are friends of mine. They are unused to our ways. They intend no harm. Please, release them and I will take them somewhere else to finish our talk."

"What is in my house belongs to me," Tyr's grandmother bellowed. "They will not leave unless I permit them to. We could always use more servants, ever since your father and his friends squashed the last ones."

"Accident," Tyr whispered to David and Acacia. "Giants are notoriously clumsy."

Acacia, despite being shaken by the giantess, cleared her throat and stood her ground. "I apologize for disturbing you, oh Great Mistress of this Hall. But we cannot stay. Millions of lives are in danger from the one called Fenrir, who would destroy this world and all worlds. We need your grandson's help to capture him, so we must be on our way, if you will be so kind as to give us leave. Surely you understand the urgency of this matter."

"Do not impugn my 'understanding' of your meaningless problem," retorted Tyr's grandmother, speaking through the mouths of a hundred middle-aged heads. "What care I about millions of lives I know not? I have always been here, and I will continue to always be here. I do not fear the children of Loki, not the wolf or the serpent or any of them. I am as timeless as the World Tree. I will do as I please, and I will do as I please with you and your company."

"That's telling them!" Baba Yaga cackled as she finally arrived, hobbling over to stand at the feet of Tyr's grandmother. Baba kicked at one of the long, twisting toes that mimicked a knotted tree root. "These children, think they can go doing whatever they please, right? No respect for us old folk and all we've had to endure."

Tyr's grandmother leaned her heads forwards to look down, the branches swaying. "Who is down there? I did not hear anyone else in the other room."

"Because I know better than to blabber my head off without proper introduction," Baba shouted up. "Would you be so courteous as to give me lift, so I don't have to shout? My voice gives out faster than it used to."

Tyr's grandmother reached down with her free hand, scooping up Baba and raising her up to be on level with her other hand.

Baba steadied herself on the giantess's open palm. "Much better. I am known as Baba Yaga, Keeper of the Iron Forest. Always people getting lost in my forest. Unwanted guests, such a bother. Not that I get many visitors. Not even my bratty grandson comes to see me!" She gestured towards David. "Look at him, such fine clothes, the elite of society, but does he care for his old grandmother? Ha!"

David opened his mouth to say something, but then he shut it. What on earth was she up to?

"This is your grandson?" Tyr's grandmother raised her hand higher until dozens of her faces were within a yard of David, scrutinizing him.

"You wouldn't know it, from the way he treats me," Baba groused. "What is it with grandchildren, eh? No manners these days."

Tyr's grandmother let out simultaneous sighs from all of her heads. "I know! Back in my days, we knew how to treat our elders. Now this one…" Her eyes turned to Tyr. "Always complaining, 'but I have to go fight the Frost giants,' or 'the Dark elves are causing trouble,' or 'my honor' this, 'my duty' that. Too busy to listen to *Mor mor*!"

David and Tyr side-glanced at each other. Acacia wiped a paw down her face. Tanuki twitched in his unconsciousness.

"All I know is I raised my children properly," Baba said. "Something got lost between our children's generation and their children's. It's not our fault!"

"Valhalla, no!" Tyr's grandmother agreed. "I blame that no account son of mine, for my little Tyr's aloofness. Always with his scatterbrained ideas, his parties, his drinking! So obsessed with those brewing pots! He cared more about those bottomless cauldrons and all the ale they could brew than his own flesh and blood! Is it any wonder his son is such a soft brain too? Mighty warrior, peh!"

Tyr looked away, scratching his nose absent-mindedly. But David, meanwhile, was starting to brew an idea. He remembered Hymir and his odd cooking pot, the one that magically produced ale. Hadn't he said something about having a much grander one, that was a mile deep? That one, he had said, was now owned by his son. David looked over at Tyr.

A cauldron that was a mile deep…could it hold something other than ale? Could something be put into it, rather than come out of it? David was about to ask Tyr about this, when the hand they were standing on shifted abruptly and they all toppled over.

"Oh, poor Hymir! Where did I go wrong?" wailed the 900 heads of Tyr's grandmother.

"Now now, no need to get upset," Baba said, patting the giantess's thumb. "When was the last time you had a nice, warm cup of tea? I make the best tea in Russia, and I think I have my freshest herbs with me, if you would like to split a pot."

The 900 heads sniffled, but then all of them smiled. "I can't think of the last time we had tea. It's always ale and mead around here. Yes, tea would be wonderful."

Baba nodded. "Then how about you and I enjoy a cup—or two, or a hundred—while the children go tidy up your main room? Let the young ones do the chores around here, I say."

Tyr's grandmother slowly lowered both of her hands to the floor, allowing everyone to disembark (although David had to carry Tanuki, who remained incapacitated). In the doorway stood the tall golden-haired woman, her face creased with concern. David understood now that the woman must be Tyr's mother; there was enough resemblance between the two to see it.

"My dear, would you show me where your tea kettle is?" Baba said to Tyr's mother. "We would like to make some tea."

Tyr's mother nodded with a smile, and led Baba back into the other room to gather what she needed. Everyone else followed, not daring to glance behind them.

"That was clever thinking from your friend," Acacia said to David. "Makes me think I'm losing my touch."

"Baba has that effect on people," David said. "She even won Gullin over in no time, and he's wary of witches. Besides, that doesn't make you less clever. If it were a riddle contest..."

The sphinx stood up on her hind legs, as she often did, as she was a comfortable on two legs as on four. "Oh, is that all I'm good for? Riddles?" She shot him a sharp look.

David blanched. "No, of course not! I was trying to say—"

Acacia laughed, pushing David's shoulder with her paw. "You're still so innocent, David! Here I thought married life might have hardened you up."

David grinned. "Trust me, Florence does a good enough job keeping me in line."

The sphinx's smile dropped. She didn't look sad or angry, but she tightened her lips and was quiet for a moment. "I'm sure she does," she eventually replied.

The badger began to squirm in David's arms. He fluttered his eyes open. "Oh, David, Acacia. I had another bad dream! This one, there was this giant scary lady with lots and lots of heads…"

"It's all right, Tanuki," Acacia assured him. "But, let's all remember to keep our voices down, all right?"

Tanuki nodded, but then the meaning of Acacia's warning sunk in, and he snapped his head around, looking everywhere. He scrambled up onto David's shoulder, watching the door where the monstrous hand had appeared.

"Settle down," David said. "She really not as bad as all that."

"Ha!" Tyr slapped his hand over his mouth, surprised that his laugh has slipped out. He lowered his voice. "Pardon me. But you have no idea what *Mor mor* is capable of. The fact that we all got out of there unscathed is… maybe the first time that's ever happened."

David began rummaging through the artifacts scattered on the floor. "Tyr, your father told me that you might have a magical cauldron that you won from him in a bet, a pot that is a mile deep. Do you still have that?"

Tyr blinked in surprise. "My father's prized brewing cauldron? Yes, of course. Why do you ask?"

"Tell me about it. Does it only brew, or can it do other things?"

The warrior stroked his beard. "To tell the truth, I never tested its power much. I won it from my father because the other Aesir had run out of ale, and I knew that cauldron would provide everyone with enough drink for the rest of time. But once we brewed what we needed and bottled it all up in the Asgardian cellars, I haven't used the cauldron since."

"Is it here?" David picked up one ornate silver bowl, looking it over, and then putting it off to the side.

Tyr glanced around the caliginous cluttered hall. "It very well could be. I think I re-gifted it to Mother for her birthday, but I can't remember."

"Not as if you could possibly find anything in this mess," Acacia noted. "This is worse that Pharaoh Tutankhamen's tomb in Egypt. Not that I know what his tomb looks like." She darted her eyes away, and then looked back. "You would have to pick around this place for days to find anything."

David drew out his sword. "Not necessarily. Hopefully this still works." He held the sword by the hilt, blade pointed downwards, and tapped it on the floor three times.

The items in the hall all scooted a few inches one way or the other, and then paused.

"How did you do that?" Tanuki asked.

Acacia sniffed at David's sword. "I always thought this sword smelled odd. I thought any magic it had was dormant. No one else I've seen wield it could make it do anything of the magic sort."

David tapped the sword on the floor again. The artifacts shifted, but not much.

'I don't understand. When I did this at Baba's house, all of her things went to their shelves and cupboards immediately," he said.

Tyr put a hand on David's shoulder. "Little household trinkets are always willing to listen and comply. But these are the remnants of great Viking fighters. They take orders from those who command leadership and courage. You have to give them a reason to follow your order."

David held his sword in both hands, the flat of the blade resting on his palms. "Then maybe you should use this."

Tyr held up his hand, shaking his head. "If you were not meant to wield this sword, the remnants would not have moved at all for you. They want to listen to you. Give them a reason. Show them who you truly are."

Who I truly am? How can I do that when I'm not sure who I am? David thought. He gripped the hilt of the sword in both hands, blade pointing out towards the objects. He took a deep breath. "I am David Sandoval of Cervera. I have outwitted the Teumessian…passed the test of the White Buffalo…survived the World-Devouring Wolf…I am Guardian of the Last Sphinx, Ally of the Most Divine Being in Kyoto, and I have stood against the will of the Night Goddess. I strive to bring Order to Chaos, and…" He paused, thinking. "…and Hope to those who despair. May the cauldron I seek present itself, so I may fulfill my quest. May all that surrounds me be brought to its proper place, this I command you!"

Silence.

David shrugged his shoulders. "Please?"

The room sprang into a whirlwind of motion as all the artifacts started to roll, bounce, and float around the hall. Shields found their hanging hooks on the walls, helmets made their way to sit aligned on shelves, and stray weapons and battle gear slid into place along upright racks. Cobwebs and dust were shaken away, and rugs unrolled themselves to blanket the floor. In one minute, the hall was a clean and shining paradigm of orderliness.

"There is a reason they call 'please' a magic word," Tyr said.

"That is all well and good," Acacia said, "but where's the pot we were looking for?"

A rumbling sound was heard, and an iron pot, no bigger than a tea kettle, came rolling out of the adjoining room where Tyr's grandmother was. It sloshed hot tea on the floor as it rolled, and it teetered to a stop at David's feet.

Baba shuffled in, holding a tea cup in her hand. "What is the idea, calling our tea kettle away? You will have to make us a new pot, you know."

Tyr slapped his hand to his forehead. "I knew I had re-gifted it to Mother! She must have thought it was a tea kettle, but she doesn't make tea very often."

Baba shook her head, sipping her tea. "Bah, that made the tea taste too metallic, anyway. But good news. I have been talking to your grandmother, Tyr—lovely lady—and I told her it would be a good idea for you to go with David and the sphinx to capture big Wolf. It will teach you to keep your responsibilities and toughen you up. Plus, it will help you build character."

Tyr's jaw dropped open to his chest. "You…told my *Mor mor*…what?"

"And she would like you to bring back nice wolf fur coat. She always wanted a nice warm coat, but no animal is big enough to make a coat her size. But I said, Wolf is plenty big. Could make coat and nice pair of slippers."

Tyr's face reddened to the hue of a tomato. "She wants me to WHAT??"

Nine hundred voices boomed from the other room. "Do not raise your voice in this house! I have decided you will go, so you will go! NOW!"

In two swift motions, Tyr wrapped one arm around David and Tanuki, and the other arm around Baba. Acacia grabbed the iron pot and flew behind Tyr as they made a frantic dash out the front door of the Main Hall. Tyr's mother was already waiting outside with Slepnir beside her. Without breaking stride, Tyr bounded up and straight onto Slepnir's back, and the horse took off running down the hill, the flying sphinx close behind them.

"Do remember to visit more often, son!" Tyr's mother called, waving goodbye. "I'm so glad you finally have friends to bring over to the house!"

"So, why did you want this thing?" Acacia asked, turning the iron pot over in her paws.

The camp they had built was a simple one, but they were well guarded by the titanic trees of the forest. Tyr had started a good bonfire, even with missing a hand, and Tanuki scuttled here and there to gather twigs and grasses for kindling. Baba had found a stump twenty feet away from the camp, and she sat on it, trying to smoke her pipe. She hacked every now and then, but managed to lightly puff on it. David wished she wouldn't be so far from the camp, but she had said she needed some time to think.

"I had a thought," David replied to Acacia. "If that pot can go a mile deep, it could hold something really big, right? If it can brew as much ale as anyone could possibly want, then it must defy physical space and dimension, I would think anything put into it wouldn't be able to break out of it. It would be like tumbling through a void, right?"

Acacia looked puzzled at David's analysis, but then it dawned on her. "Wait, you're not thinking of…capturing Fenrir in this pot, are you? Even if something can be put inside of it, he would never fit through this small brim!"

Tyr scratched his chin. "Now, hold on. There's one thing I know that pot can do." He came over, taking the pot from Acacia. He placed it down on the ground, and started to pull at its mouth. David worried that Tyr was going to crack the pot, but gradually the pot began to expand, as Tyr pulled it wide like taffy. Eventually, he could not pull it any wider or taller, but the cauldron was six times bigger than it had been.

"But it is still too small of an opening for Fenrir," Acacia pointed out.

David thought for a minute. "Wait, Fenrir changes size too! He was big enough one day to swallow a whole house, but the next he was small enough to fit inside a stable. His size depends on how strong he is. If we can wear him down enough, could he become small enough to catch him in that pot?"

"It's possible," Tyr admitted. "But that would take a lot of wearing him down."

"First, we need to test if it will actually take in something and keep it there," Acacia said.

"Oh, that's easy," Tanuki said. He picked up a rock from the fire pit, and brought it over. He tossed it into the pot.

Everyone looked inside. There was blackness, as far as anyone could tell. They never heard the sound of the rock hitting a bottom. Tyr picked up the pot and flipped it over, shaking it, but the rock did not come back.

"But would that work on a living thing?" David asked. "What would keep Fenrir from jumping back out again?"

"Simple. Once he's inside, just pull the pot back to small size again. Maybe you could even pull the rims together to seal it," Tanuki said.

Tyr smiled at the badger. "So you are as wise as you said," he said, using one finger to ruffle the fur on Tanuki's head.

"But could Fenrir break the pot open, once he is inside?" Acacia asked.

David, Acacia and Tyr looked at Tanuki,

"What? I'm supposed to answer everything now? That's the burden of being a Divine Being, I suppose." The badger scratched his head. "How about this. I'll go inside, and I'll transform into the biggest thing I can, and see if I can break out."

David shook his head. "No, you could get stuck inside and not come back out!"

The badger thought on this. "Tie a rope around me, and pull me back out once I tug on it. It'll be like eel fishing."

"Plus, if he can break the pot from the inside, then it's no good to us anyway," Acacia said.

David paused. He felt like they were making assumptions about this pot that may or may not be true. What if Tanuki went in, even with a rope, but all they pulled back out was a severed rope? What if whatever went into the pot didn't get trapped, but disappeared entirely? Tyr didn't seem to know much more about how this worked than the rest of them. Maybe if they were able to keep Tanuki in view, lower him in a few feet or so, it would be enough to test their theory.

"No one will force you to do this, Tanuki," David said. "But we'll let you down inside a few feet so you stay in view. You should be able to test the pot's durability without having to go in too far."

Tanuki gave him a big beaming smile. "You worry too much, David-san. I am your spirit guide, remember? You are stuck with me, whether you like it or not!"

Tyr had a rope around his waist that he was using for a belt, so he removed it and tied one end around Tanuki's middle. Tyr dangled Tanuki off the ground, and slowly lowered him into the iron pot. Letting the rope slide through his calloused hands, Tyr let down the badger one meter, then two, until Tanuki was a foot away from being out of visible range.

"Stop there," David said, and Tyr grasped the rope tightly to halt Tanuki's descent. David called down into the pot, "Tanuki, are you all right?"

"Of course," the badger called back, his voice already sounding distant. "It's strange in here. I think I can hear the ocean! And it smells like cucumbers."

"Be careful. Try changing size and see what happens."

There was a pause. David thought he could see Tanuki wriggling at the end of the rope, and then the rope started swinging. Tyr tried to control it as the rope smacked the sides of the rim of the pot. As Tanuki swung, he flashed in and out of the visible light, diving in and out of shadow.

"Tanuki, stop swinging the rope!" Acacia called down.

There was a frightened, urgent chittering coming from inside the pot. Amidst the squeaking and squealing, they heard the words, "Wrong! Up! Something—wrong!"

Immediately, Tyr yanked the rope, and in a flying catapult out of the pot, Tanuki soared upwards. David's heart rapped wildly as he saw Tanuki tumbling back down, not turning into a feather or a bird as he normally would to slow down a fall. Acacia pounced up, catching Tanuki in mid-air, and then gently floated them back down to the ground.

The badger was shaking all over, his eyes so wide that they could see the rims of white around the black irises.

"What happened in there?" David asked. "Could you not transform while inside the pot?"

Tanuki looked down at his forepaws, as if the answer might be there. He squeezed his eyes tight for ten seconds, and then opened them again.

"No, I…I can't change at all!" he squealed.

All was quiet for a long time after that. Tanuki lay curled up in David's lap, his face covered by his paws. Acacia went out to the nearby sea to catch fish for dinner, while Tyr was sharpening branches with a whittling knife so they could cook them when she returned. David didn't know what to say or do. He was glad that Tanuki hadn't been hurt while testing the pot, and at least they knew for sure a living animal could be put in the pot. But was it the pot that had caused Tanuki to lose his shape-shifting ability…or was the Curtain continuing to fall apart, and now it had affected Tanuki as it had Baba?

"David?" Tanuki's voice was small, nearly a whisper.

"Yes?"

"I lied before."

David furrowed his brow. "About what?"

"I said I thought I liked mead even more than sake. But I don't. I like sake best. I love sake."

David didn't quite understand what Tanuki was talking about, or why his drink preference was so important. But then Tanuki looked up at him, tears streaming down his furry nose, and David understood.

"You miss Yofune," David said.

Tanuki sat up, leaning back against David's stomach. "While I was in the pot, hearing the ocean, and smelling cucumbers, it made me think about how Yofune and Kappa and I would sometimes go to the beach in Suma in the summertime. We would disguise ourselves as humans, of course, and I'd carry Kappa in a basket along with fresh cucumbers, carrots and bamboo. I think Master Yofune would have rather stayed at home, but he knew Kappa and I liked the beach. Maybe when this is all over—this wolf business—maybe I can dig a burrow there. Would you come visit me if I do that, David-san?"

David patted Tanuki on the head. "You could come live in Paris, if you'd like. There's a nice public garden not too far from where we live where you could dig a burrow, or maybe I could convince Florence to let us have a badger in the house. Or once you get your shape-shifting back, you could pretend to be a cat. I think Florence likes cats."

"What if I can't shape-shift ever again? Will you still be my friend?"

David scratched Tanuki behind the ear. "Of course. You're my spirit guide. You're stuck with me as much as I am stuck with you."

Through the trees, the back end of Acacia emerged as she tugged and dragged something large through the grass, a pungent fish smell filling the air. She struggled to bring a shimmering blue-green fish, as long and wide as a shark, that she had caught into the circle of the camp. Tyr came over to help, hoisting the fish by its tail with no effort, and he set about skinning and gutting it near the fire.

Acacia sat down next to David, panting. She was soaked in sea water. "That was not an easy one to catch. Takes me back to catching crocodiles in the Nile."

"But you're a Grecian sphinx, aren't you?" David asked, feeling a little silly that he should know this about Acacia. "You keep talking about things in Egypt."

Acacia shook the water out of her mane. "When my mother was exiled from the city of Thebes by King Oedipus, she escaped to Egypt where she had heard about a tribe of lion-men living in the desert. She found them and they accepted her into their lot, so most of my earliest sphinx-hood I spent in the tribe. It wasn't until I was older that I returned to Greece to learn about our original home."

"There's so much I don't know about you," David said.

Acacia smirked. "We sphinxes are enigmatic. But there's much about me you wouldn't want to know." She let out a yawn. "Although, I meant what

I said the first time we dream-talked together. I would like to know more about you, what you're willing to tell me."

David chuckled. "There isn't much to tell. Eighteen years is like a single breath in your lifespan."

"Then it will be easy for me to remember it all."

They both could feel eyes watching them, and both David and Acacia looked over at Tyr. He was sitting with his chin in his hand, grinning at them as one might at a pair of cuddling lovebirds.

"You two remind me of Thor and Sif," he said. "I always wished everyone would find their soul-mate the way those two found each other."

Acacia bleated a laugh that was neither happy nor humorous. If anything, it sounded angry. "We are not soul-mates. We are friends. That's it."

"Oh. Forgive me." Tyr tore a piece of meat from the gutted fish, and jammed it onto one of his sharpened sticks. He started roasting it over the fire. "Should be a few minutes to cook."

Acacia went over to the fish, sliced off a piece with her claws, and brought it back over to her spot next to David. She ate the fish raw, her feline fangs tearing into the meat ravenously. She held out a piece to David.

"I'll wait for Tyr to finish cooking that piece," David said, waving the fish away.

"I'll have it!" Tanuki bounced up and snatched the meat from Acacia's claws, and nibbled away on it.

"Baba, do you want dinner?" David called out to her, but the old woman remained fixed on her stump, not replying.

"She'll come over when she's hungry," Acacia said after swallowing another mouthful. "You take care of yourself, David."

David yawned, his eyelids dipping down. The weight of the long day was seeping into his bones. "I'm not very hungry. But I'm really, really…" He snapped to attention, sitting up urgently, causing Tanuki to roll forwards off of his lap.

"What is it?" Acacia asked.

David rubbed his eyes. "It's…I don't know if it would be a good idea to go to sleep. Nico…"

Acacia swallowed the last bite of her fish. "Nico is good at frightening others, but he's a coward. Besides, he can't really hurt you in your dreams. If he comes into your dreams tonight, we'll show him a thing or two."

"We?" Acacia unfolded her wing and put it around David's shoulder. "We're together now. Even without Hypnos, we know where we are, so I can be with you in your dream. There's nothing Nico can do in a dream that I can't best him. I'll protect you. I promise."

"I don't want him to do something that will damage your mind, Acacia! Why don't we sleep in shifts, so if it looks like one of us is distressed while sleeping, the other can wake them up?"

"Then we'll just keep waking each other up all night long, and no one gets any sleep. No, we need to stop this now. It's not only us Nico might be affecting, David. What about Gullin and his family?" David had forgotten about that. Nico could have access to anyone in the Sleep realm. What if he was manipulating Gullin's dreams right now? Or Beatrice, or even little Ian?

"I'll stay awake and watch you both," Tanuki said. "If you start acting funny, I'll wake you up."

"And I'll keep watch on the camp," Tyr said. "Eyes on all fronts. I never need much sleep." Acacia folded up her wing, settling down on all four legs, resting her head on her forepaws. "You can lay your head on my wings, David. Better than lying down on the hard ground."

David leaned his body over and tentatively placed his head on Acacia's violet-black wings. Her feathers were so soft and warm, and she smelled of lilacs.

"Are you ready?" the sphinx said with a heavy tone, as she was already slipping off into slumber.

David didn't answer, as weariness took hold of him in seconds. His final thought, before drifting off, was, *We're together now. I'll protect you.*

The snarling, seething voice was burning in David's ears.

I was wondering how long it would take you two to fall asleep. It's rude to keep one waiting, you know. But it will have been worth the wait. How much more fun this will be, to make you and my cousin suffer together...

CHAPTER FOURTEEN

"Nico!" David somehow found his voice in the dream, but he was surrounded by the empty void. He could not see Acacia anywhere, and he worried that Nico was somehow keeping them apart. "Show yourself, coward!"

No response. David willed himself to move, but there was nowhere to move to. "This is unimaginative, even for you!" he called. "I've had dreams about bunnies scarier than this!"

Still, no answer. There wasn't any presence of malice, or any hint that anyone was paying attention to him. David wondered how it was, for all of Nico's pompous pride in his "cleverness," that the fox-man was so mediocre at creating a dream atmosphere. Hypnos had built a realm of millions of dream-paths, a swirling garden where all dreamers and dreams could connect. The lifeless void surrounding David was not unnerving; it was dull.

Then it made sense. Nico was not Hypnos by any means. Nico was unskilled at manipulating a dream atmosphere, and trying to balance millions of dreams would be far too great a task for him. Nico was not interested in that, anyway; he was focused on tainting David and Acacia's dreams.

Dios mío, Acacia! What if that was why Nico wasn't tormenting David? The fox-man most likely didn't have the talent to invade two different dreams at once. He would have to pour all his attention into one dreamer at a time. Where was Acacia?

At the thought of Acacia, a pinprick of light appeared in the black void. David couldn't walk to it, since there was no ground to walk on, but he was drawn to that tiny shard of light. He willed his mentally-projected self to broaden the light, to tear through the void. He reached out, hooking a finger into the spot of light and pulled. The blackness gave way easily, ripping open at his touch. David did not need to pull the rip open too wide, as he found he could slip through it like liquid through a funnel.

Hot sand pushed up between the toes of his bare feet. The whispering wind whipped his hair and clothes, but its abrasiveness was muted. It was the impression of sand, the impression of wind that David felt, for a small part of him remembered that this place was not real. Vast stretches of desert extended to meet the cobalt blue sky, high in which a white-fire sun beat its rays down on all below.

Panic took hold of him. Was he trapped here? Was he doomed to wander a desert of solitude forever? Could he starve or die of thirst here, or blister into a sundried piece of *charqui*? No, no, this was a dream. Remember it's a dream. There's got to be something here. This desert appeared because he had thought of—

Acacia. Find Acacia.

There was a temple before him. It hadn't sprouted from the sands, or appeared in a puff of smoke. It was there as if it always had been. Two square outer walls faced him, with an entryway in between that was flanked by two statues of seated royals with tall pointed crowns. Beside the statues stood an obelisk tattooed with symbols and images that David recognized as hieroglyphics. A smooth avenue extended out from the temple for well over a mile, and along both sides of the avenue were rows of sandstone altars. Atop every altar, creatures were chained down to them, forced into lying positions as they struggled to stand up.

Sphinxes. Hundreds of living, breathing sphinxes. Men's faces, young and old, were set on lion bodies that each had their own distinct fur color, musculature, and sheen. They roared and screeched, their claws scratching uselessly on the altar-tops. Human guards, brandishing spears, shouted and jabbed their weapons at the sphinxes to keep them under control. A dozen humans stood at the end of the avenue in front of the temple: the head of the group was a tall sun-bronzed man, wearing white linen robes, jewelry of gold and precious stones, and a golden-and-black headdress with matching armbands. The others wore long brown robes with hoods covering their heads. One of the brown-roped men held a thick book made from papyrus paper.

David had books on ancient Egypt in his home library, and he could tell by the head man's attire that he must be of high status, possibly a pharaoh or king. The other men, he couldn't tell what they might be. The man with the book raised a hand and began to chant a string of archaic words, the tips of his fingers emanating a bluish glow. The other robed men did the same, their fingertips glowing as cerulean fireflies. David realized the men must be sorcerers.

The sphinxes howled in pain at the sorcerers' chanting, and they thrashed against their binds to no avail. Some sphinxes even cried out in human voices, pleading, shrieking.

Their cries were instantly silenced as all of them turned into stone.

A wave of nausea swept over David. Hundreds of lives, snuffed out in a second. Even worse, none of the sphinxes possessed their own faces any longer. Every single one of the statues bore a facade that resembled the pharaoh, headdress and all. And the pharaoh, who saw the handiwork of his sorcerers, couldn't have beamed prouder.

The pharaoh and the sorcerers turned and walked into the temple, followed by the procession of guards. From within the temple came song and music, the sounds of a great festival, but above the joyous melodies, one lingering cry echoed through the desert. The cry was that of a child's, and David could make out a form standing in front of one of the stone sphinxes.

He approached cautiously, not sure if the crying person would be aware of him or not. As he got closer, he recognized the violet-black wings and the golden fur, the mane of dark hair that shrouded the feral but beautiful human face. This version of Acacia, however, was smaller, the wings not fully formed as bits of grayish down poked out from the feathers. She cried uncontrollably, her paws pressed against the altar of the petrified sphinx before her. David looked up at the statue, seeing that this one statue did not perfectly mimic the pharaoh's face. This one had the sorrowful face of a woman, set on a sleek feline form. It was also the only stone sphinxes that had two nubs on her shoulder blades—right where a pair of wings would have been, but hers appeared to have been sliced off. To his horror, David could see how much this doomed sphinx resembled Acacia.

David knew that the human heart did not truly possess strings, but as Acacia's despair became his own, he could hear his heartstrings snap. "Acacia… *Dios mío,* I…I am so sorry. I can't believe they would do this to your people, to your... Please, please don't cry. This is a dream. It's not really happening." He knew his words would do no good. Dream or not, it didn't make the memory less painful. Acacia did not acknowledge his presence, as she wailed and clawed at the statue.

"Acacia, you need to wake up." David tried to grab a hold of her, but his hands were stopped half an inch from her. There was a force keeping him from making contact with her.

David felt a shadow creep over him, and a wicked chuckle burned in his ears.

"Poor little kitty," Nico said dryly. "Couldn't do anything to save them. How many times, do you think, can someone relive such a soul-breaking moment before she loses her mind? Let's find out. How about we keep her asleep long enough to experience this again and again, a thousand times over, or at least until I'm bored with it."

David spun around to face Nico, venom in his eyes and voice. "You're not going to hurt her again, Nico. Your mind games are over."

Nico grinned in amusement. "Good, you're as foolishly optimistic as ever. It's more fun to break a boy who has a shred of hope. I knew you would find your way here. That makes less work for me, not having to jump back and forth between your dreams and hers. But don't worry, I have something delightful for you, too."

David swung at Nico to land a punch to his face, but again he was stopped half an inch away.

"Do you think you can hurt me here? Or in the real world, for that matter? I'm beyond physical pain now." Nico tapped his foot on the ground, and David sunk downwards. He was sucked into the earth up to his waist, and then the ground solidified around him. David pushed as hard as he could to get out, but he was stuck.

"But do you know who's not beyond pain, David?" Nico knelt down, bringing his lips within an inch of David's ear. "Your pretty wife."

David lashed out with his fists again. Nico darted back about ten feet, not to avoid the punches but so he could remove a glass orb from within an inner pocket of his coat. Inside the glass orb was a miniature Florence, who pressed her hands against the glass, trying to see out. She was shouting something, but her words were inaudible from within the orb.

"How...how did you..." David stammered.

"She does nothing but dream about you while you're away. It made it easy to find her. Pathetic." Nico tossed the orb back and forth between his hands. "I would have thought you'd prefer a lady with a stronger will. She succumbed to me with no resistance."

David clenched his teeth. "This is a dream. You can't hurt her."

Nico twirled the orb on his fingertip. "Physically, you mean? No, I can't kill her, per se. But it's amazing what one can do to the mind in dreams. For example, I could destroy her memories, her thoughts, her ability to think, until she's no more than a bedridden vegetable. Or I could induce such insanity that the only place for her will be the asylum. Oh, the options are endless..."

"She's done nothing to you. If you want to turn someone into a vegetable or a lunatic, do it to me!"

"I might. Although, the notion of brainwashing you into adoring me, pledging yourself to be my unquestioning servant...that tickles me. But I'll give you the option: should I destroy your wife's consciousness first, or make you watch as I break my cousin beyond repair?" Nico slapped a hand to his forehead. "Of course, easy answer! I'll just do both at the same time!"

Nico did not get the chance to do either, however, as a black-and-white whale dropped from the sky above and smashed directly on top of the fox-man. The glass orb popped out of Nico's grasp, rolling along the avenue until David could reach it and snatched it up.

"That's for my Master Yofune, you monster!" the whale bellowed in the familiar voice of Tanuki.

David gawked at the whale. "Tanuki? What are you doing here?"

The whale turned his eye to David. "Sorry, David-san. I must have fallen asleep. But I could sense you were in trouble. So I thought of you, and here I am!"

"You're incredible! But how are you shape-shifting again?"

"David-san, this is a dream. You can do anything you want in a dream!"

David couldn't believe his own foolishness. Of course he could do whatever he wanted! Nico could manipulate him as much as David allowed him to, but David's will had to be stronger. With one final push, he broke free of the ground, leaping up onto his feet. He brought the glass orb up to his face, smiling warmly at Florence inside. He pressed his hands against the sides of the glass, imagining his wife standing before him, free and unafraid. The next thing he knew, he was holding Florence's hands in his, her sweet face gazing at him.

"David, is that you? Have you come home?" she asked.

"Florence," he said, holding her close. "You'll be all right. I'll come back to you. But for now, you need to wake up. The next time you sleep, you won't have any nightmares. Dream of me, and I'll come to you." He kissed her forehead, and then released her hands.

Florence gradually floated up into the air, and she reached down for David's hand again. "Wait! Don't leave! Please, David, please…"

"I'll come home, Florence. I love you," he said.

Florence ascended higher, until her dream-self faded away. David could no longer feel her presence in the dreamscape, and he knew she had awoken. Seeing Florence, for that short time, filled him with a pining sorrow, and he knew he had meant what he said. He would come home to her.

Tanuki let out a deep low as he was hoisted upwards, Nico lifting the whale above his head. To say he looked furious was a gross understatement. "You think you can make a fool out of me?" He threw Tanuki with the ease of tossing a cushion, and the whale soared across the sky, landing straight into a whirlpool of quicksand that Nico materialized. Tanuki changed into an eagle to fly out, but the quicksand sucked him down, not allowing him to escape.

"If you don't want to play my games," Nico growled, "then I'll just shred your mind apart right now!"

David could feel himself being pulled in different directions, and a tearing agony in his being that set his soul on fire. Nico was literally ripping him down the middle, but David summoned all his will, resisting. Nico was unrelenting, as the two opponents struggled against one another. David pulled himself inwards, imagining that his body was steel armor, sealing himself inside. But Nico changed his attack, as he summoned a dozen warhammers and swords around David. The weapons pummeled at him mercilessly, bending and cracking the armor.

David visualized the ground beneath Nico crumbling, and the fox-man found himself tumbling down as the stone avenue beneath him broke apart. Nico leapt up to avoid falling through, but as he jumped, David directed one of the warhammers to spin around and fly smack into Nico mid-air. The fox-man was flung so far, he became a speck on the horizon where the desert met the sky.

David knew Nico would be back any second. He allowed his armor to vanish, and he rushed to Acacia, who remained trapped in her memory. He hoped Nico's hold on her had faded, given David's distractions. He reached out for her, and his hands fell on her shoulders. "Acacia! Can you hear me? Do you know who I am?"

The young Acacia faced him, her eyes red with tears. She peered at him curiously. "You...you don't belong here..."

"Yes, I do! This is a dream. You're reliving a memory that happened a long time ago. Do you know who I am, Acacia? Can you tell me my name?"

The sphinx locked eyes with him. Recognition dawned on her face. "D...David. Your name is David."

David helped her to her feet. "Yes, Acacia. Right now, I need your help. We need to stop—"

The whole temple collapsed around them, the rubble cascading over them in a tidal wave that buried them in an immovable tomb. The young man and the sphinx pushed upwards to find freedom, but the weight of the rubble grew heavier and heavier. David could hear Nico laughing above them.

"You two can remain buried together, for all I care! You'll never wake up! Your bodies will be useless. Nothing will be able to revive you. But you'll feel it when the crows and vultures pick your bones clean!"

It was dark beneath the rubble, but David could feel Acacia's paw in his hand. "Acacia, I know he's your family, but I'm sick and tired of your cousin."

Acacia squeezed his hand. "I've been sick of him since before the fall of Rome. So let's teach this weasel in fox's clothes a thing or two."

"Suggestions?"

"Oh, I have one…"

Nico's laughter stuck in his throat as a hot geyser blast blew up from beneath the rubble, blowing the pile of stones as well as Nico sky high. The geyser wrapped around him, forming a lion's paw, swooping back around and slamming the fox-man on the ground. A female voice came from within the water. "It was about time you had a bath, Nico!"

Meanwhile, David was hanging on to the tail of the geyser stream, which was in fact Acacia, as he followed her out of the rubble. He could see Tanuki was fighting with the quicksand, staying afloat in the form of a dolphin but unable to free himself. David let go of Acacia's tail, willing himself into the form of a three-masted ship that sailed on top of the desert sands. As he circled the quicksand, he threw out a fishing net at Tanuki, catching him and pulling him out of the whirlpool. Once they were clear of the quicksand, the two shifted back into their normal forms, man and badger.

"You were a boat! Why didn't I think of that?" Tanuki said. "It looked like fun!"

"'Fun' is not the term I would use right now," David said.

The desert around them was no longer the tranquil stretch of sand that it had been. It was now an arena of duststorms churning around them, the sky clouding over with tombstone-gray thunderheads. Nico had quite enough of Acacia drowning him in her geyser grip, so he transformed himself into lightning, setting the clouds afire and spitting electric shocks down at his liquefied adversary. Acacia altered her form, becoming a metal obelisk that absorbed Nico's lightning, trapping and sending his energy into the earth beneath her. But Nico became an earthquake, cracking the ground to swallow Acacia and crush her. In response, Acacia became a river, filling the fizzure to flush Nico out. Nico chose the form of an icy wind, breathing over Acacia's river to freeze her over, but she retaliated as a twirling tornado, pulling Nico's wind into her spiraling vacuum.

David scooped up Tanuki into his arms, bracing himself against the winds and ice and flying debris. "This is crazy! They'll go on until they destroy each other's minds!"

"This is a bit out of my league, David-san," Tanuki squealed against the howling wind. "What are we going to do?"

By now, Nico had become a firestorm, a cylinder of raw raging flame, and Acacia was a tsunami, preparing to extinguish him. David sent his voice up into the clouds, amplifying it and filling the entire space of the dreamscape. "STOP!"

The firestorm and the tsunami froze in place. Both twisted around in David's direction.

It was the first time David was being stared down by two natural disasters, and he took an extra moment to find his composure. "This is going nowhere! You both could do this until the end of time, and no one will win. We need to end this, in the way most fitting. No shape-changing, no tricks. One final test, one indisputable winner."

The firestorm and tsunami paused. They didn't change back, as if waiting for the other to resume normal form first.

"For Pete's sake." David imagined the firestorm and tsunami disguises stripped away, and moments later, the fox-man and the sphinx were standing before him.

Nico looked down at himself in surprise. "Now that's hardly fair."

"The back-stabbing dream-corrupting madman knows what's fair," Acacia snarled.

"You both like riddles, right?" David said. "Then let's see who truly is the most clever. No cheating, no mind-killing. There will be one indisputable winner."

Nico rolled his eyes. "We're going to play this idiotic game? I know every riddle there is. There's no riddle my cousin can propose that I cannot answer."

"That's why I'm going to give the riddle," David said. "One riddle, for each of you. If Acacia answers hers correctly and you don't, you will swear on your master that you will stay out of our dreams. If you break your vow, I'm sure your master will be cross that you blasphemed his name."

"And if I win?"

David bit his lip. "Then do what you want with me. Make me a vegetable, or a lunatic, or your servant. Whatever you prefer."

Nico scratched his chin. "No protecting my cousin, human. I'll do what I want to both of you. And the badger, if I feel like it."

Tanuki gulped, but Acacia replied firmly, "Deal."

"Such confidence in your plaything," Nico sneered at her. "You trust that he can give a riddle that will actually stump me?"

"It seemed to work well enough last time," David replied.

Nico glowered at David, remembering the last time he had incorrectly answered a riddle that the young man had invented. "It won't happen again, I assure you. What if we both answer our riddles correctly?"

David paused. "Then you still win."

Nico lifted his eyebrows. "Really? So, whether or not my cousin answers her riddle correctly, as long as I answer mine with the right answer, I win?"

Acacia gave David a stern look. Tanuki tugged David's pant leg, shaking his head.

"The odds would be in your favor," David replied.

Nico snickered. "Then, by all means, let's play riddles. I'll even be sporting and let my cousin answer her riddle first. Not that it will matter, but you know how much I love crushing one's hopes."

"First, swear to your master," David ordered.

Nico groaned. "Fine. I swear to my malevolent master of madness, Lord of all Insanity, may he stricken me with smallpox and have maggots feast on my innards, so on and so on." He drew a cross over where his heart should have been with his finger.

Acacia took one step towards David. She held her head high, her voice unwavering. "Very well. Tell me your riddle."

David held his hands out, and a small wooden box appeared in his hands. It was the size of a cigar box, smooth on the outside with no carvings or markings. "What's in the box?" he said.

Acacia's eyes went wide. "Excuse me?"

Nico looked equally baffled. "Not that I agree with my cousin, but that's not a riddle."

"It's no different than a riddle. One hint: it's small enough to fit in this box," David said.

Acacia stared at the box. Her jaw went slack. "David, that's not fair!"

"It's fair enough that you and Nico know as much about this box as the other."

The sphinx continued to stare at the box, as if she could see through the wood. After a minute, she shook her head. "A…a key?"

David frowned. "I'm sorry, it's not a key."

Nico grinned ear to ear. "Wow, not even giving your friend a chance. That's as cold as…well, what I would do."

David turned to Nico. "Your turn. What's in the box, Nico?"

The fox-man's smile withered. "Wait, I get the same riddle?"

"She couldn't answer it. Now you try."

"That's preposterous!"

"So, you're not smart enough to figure this out."

Nico bared his teeth, and a trail of saliva dripped from his lips as he growled. "I know exactly what I'll do with you after I win this. I'll render you brain-dead, find out where your body is, and I'll hunt it down to eat your heart!"

David stared at Nico coolly. "What's in the box?"

"No matter what answer I give, you'll just change whatever is in there before you open it!"

David knelt down, turning his back to Nico and facing Tanuki. He opened the box towards the badger, showing him what was inside. He snapped the box shut again and stood up. "There, Tanuki can be witness to what's in here. He won't lie. So, are you done wasting time, or do you give up?"

Nico tightened his lips. He glanced over at Tanuki, and was about to pry into the badger's mind to find out the answer. But he found he couldn't—as he had blocked David from Acacia before, David was now mentally blocking him from the badger. Nico grimaced. Honestly, what was the point? No matter what the outcome, this boy didn't have the willpower to keep Nico out of his dreams forever. And who cared if he stayed out of their dreams, even if they could make him? He would find them in the waking world soon enough and slit their throats. This whole game would be for naught.

"Fine," Nico said. "There's nothing in the box. Right? It's such an old trick. People have been pulling that one for centuries."

David didn't reply.

Acacia's face blanched.

David turned to the badger. "Tanuki?"

Tanuki shook his head. "Nope, not the right answer. There is definitely something in the box. Badger's honor."

Nico frowned. "So what? She didn't get it right either. That's a moronic riddle. There was no way anyone could answer that!"

A smile drew across David's face. "Exactly."

"What do you mean, 'exactly'?"

David tapped his fingers on the box. "You know, Nico, you really should have asked me what happens when both you and Acacia lose."

The fox-man was knocked silent. He stared at David, and the boy's smile filled him with dread. "What happens?"

"*I* win."

Nico shot his gaze back a forth between Acacia, Tanuki, and David. "W-what? But, you didn't…you said…" He threw his hands up. "Not that it matters! You want me to stay out of your and the sphinx's dreams? Make me, if you can. But you can't protect the dreams of your Huntsman friend, or your wife, or anyone else! I can turn the whole world against you, if I wish! I can influence your wife to despise you! I can make the Huntsman want to kill you!" He laughed wildly. "On second thought, the Huntsman won't be killing anyone, after what I've done to him! After all, dead men don't dream!"

"What did you do to Gullin??" Acacia bared her claws and teeth, her fur bristling.

"Oh, you'll find out," Nico said. "That's just the start. I know there's a lily-livered warrior with you. I could strike him with a madness that will convince him to turn his axe on you!"

David opened the box. Inside was his dagger, Fenrir's Fang. He took it out of the box, gripping it tightly.

Nico almost doubled over with laughter. "Are you stupid?? You can't kill me, you idiot! Not in this world, and not in the real world!"

"No, I can't. But what I want isn't for you to stay out of Acacia and my dreams."

David raised the dagger and plunged it into Nico's skull. Nico hadn't bothered dodging, knowing the dagger wouldn't hurt him. But a jarring sensation rippled through out his being, as an oozing heat seeped inside him. He quavered like a reflection in a pebble-tossed pond.

"You are going to stay out of *everyone's* dreams. Fenrir's Fang is a weapon that destroys anything, Nico. If Fenrir can eat the heavens, can devour souls, then this fang can destroy the intangible as well as the physical. Your mind is already broken, so there's nothing more I can do to damage it. But I can destroy the part of you that allows you to dream, Nico. You will have no more connection to this realm. You've had your last mind game, and you better pray your new master doesn't find out what a worthless simpleton you are like your last master did."

With a bellow of rage, Nico disintegrated, his consciousness obliterated under the power of Fenrir's Fang.

David opened his eyes. Violet-black feathers brushed against his face. He could feel Acacia's body beneath his head, her breath calmly inflating and deflating her sides.

"Acacia?" he whispered.

"That was the best dream I have ever had," she replied.

From the other side of Acacia, Tanuki peeked his head over her wings. "David-san, you are scary. Amazingly, wonderfully scary."

CHAPTER FIFTEEN

Rain was gushing in torrents over Moffat as Slepnir galloped back into the human world through the Curtain's opening in *MacCleran's Loup*, carrying Tyr, David and Baba on his back. Acacia flew close behind, with Tanuki perched on her shoulders. David knew he had to get into town and find Gullin. Nico could have been bluffing about having done something to him, for all David knew, but he had to be sure that his friend was all right.

David and Baba Yaga had to be the ones to go into town, since Tanuki could no longer disguise himself, and Acacia and Tyr would be more than conspicuous. There was a farm nor far from Moffat, where the badger, sphinx and Viking snuck into a barn to hide, hoping that the landowner wouldn't stumble on them. David and Baba rode Slepnir into town, the witch huddling beneath her hat while the rain pelted David's head. David had a moment's hesitation, as he wondered if the Curtain's decay would mean that Slepnir's true form would be evident. As he and Baba rode up the main road, meeting townsfolk along the way, no one gave them frightened stares or screamed, so he figured that Slepnir must still look like a normal horse to them.

A crowd was assembled inside of the tavern owned by Beatrice's father. It was not the usual crowd of patrons, but the local watchmen were there as well. David and Baba dismounted Slepnir, climbing down his braid, and entered the tavern.

Beatrice was standing among the throng, speaking frantically. Ian was in the cradle of her arm, crying. When she saw David and Baba come in through the door, Beatrice ran over to them, throwing her free arm around Baba's neck.

"*Seanmhair*!" Beatrice said, hugging Baba tightly. "And David! Dear Saint

Andrew, please, please tell me you have seen my husband!"

"We were actually coming to find him," David said. "What happened?"

"I don't know! I wish to God I did! He…he wasn't himself! And now he's gone!"

Baba patted Beatrice's back as she wept. "There there, dear. Tell us what happened."

Beatrice sniffled, pulling back. Baba held her arms out to hold Ian, who quieted as he rested his head on Baba's shoulder.

"We've been staying at my Da's house," Beatrice said. "In the middle of the night, Alasdair awoke in a sweat. He started screaming, tearing out his hair, saying, 'the wolf! The wolf! It's eaten my wife and child!' I tried tellin' him it was a dream, that Ian and I were right there, but he didn't recognize us! He didn't know who we were, or where he was. He ran out of the house in his nightshirt, took my Da's horse and took off like the hounds of 'ell were after him! I'm afraid he's going to hurt himself. He's never acted like this before. I don't know what to do…"

David wished he had done worse to Nico than severing his connection to dreams, and he vowed he would make the demon paid tenfold when he saw him in person. "Did Gull—Alasdair say anything else? Where he was going? What he was going to do?"

Beatrice sat down in a chair, as one of the watchmen passed her a handkerchief to wipe her nose. "I don't remember all he said, it was incoherent rambling…although, I think he said something about…two giants, and a road over the water… 'burn the wolf with the Chimney Stacks, and crush him with the Giant's Boot,' I think he said."

"That sounds like the Giant's Causeway," a man in the tavern said. "There're stone pillars there that make strange shapes. The Chimney Stacks and the Giant's Boot are the names of some of those pillars."

"But that place is clear across the channel into Ireland! It's nearly two hundred miles from here!" said one of the watchmen. "There's no way a man could go that distance on a horse alone."

Beatrice brought her hand to her lips. "But, why would he want to go there? There's nothing out there but rocks and hills. And to cross the channel, he'd have to take the ferry, but he didn't take money with him."

David put his hand on Beatrice's shoulder. "He wasn't thinking clearly. He may have headed in the direction of the channel, but either his horse will tire long before he gets there, or he'll stop in the next town for rest. We should send someone that way to see if they can catch up to him."

"He may come to his senses and come back on his own," Baba added.

"I pray so," Beatrice said. "*Seanmhair*, David, please, help me find him. Anything you can think of, anything we can do to reach him…"

Baba looked down at Ian, hugging her arm. The boy looked up at her, mumbling "shen-he-vuhr."

"What's this word you keep using on me?" Baba asked Beatrice.

"It's our way of saying 'grandmother.' I hope you don't mind," Beatrice said.

Baba's face went blank, and then a sad smile crept into her lips. She looked up at David, determination set in her eyes. "David, we go to find him. Now."

David and Baba reconvened with the others in the barn, shaking off the rainwater and inhaling the smell of cows.

"Did you find Gullin? Is he all right?" Acacia asked.

David shook his head. "What Nico said was true. He drove him mad, and Beatrice said he took off in the middle of the night. He was rambling words that imply he was heading towards the North Channel, towards a place called 'the Giants' Causeway.' "

Acacia shifted uncomfortable on her feet. "I remember Gullin telling me about that place once, back when he traveled with me in the caravan. Terrible dealings went on there, very terrible things."

"What did he say about it? Why would he be driven to go there?"

The sphinx shrugged. "He told me about how there was a legend of two giants, one from Ireland and one from Scotland, who wanted to best one another in a fight, so they built the causeway in order to join their two countries to meet. Ever since, brutal duels have been fought there, often between the Master Huntsmen and the monsters they pursue. It's the place where…" She looked away.

"Where what?" David insisted.

"Gullin said he was sent by the Master Huntsman Guild to slay two wolves that would have eaten the sun and moon. He chased them for months, finally cornering them at the Giants' Causeway and…well, did what he had to do."

David remembered Gullin had taunted Fenrir back on his farm…*Skröll and Hati, two less monsters in the world…*

"Oh no…" David clutched his hair as a thought occurred to him. "We need to get there before Gullin does!"

"Where is this Giants' Causeway?" Tyr asked.

"One of the watchmen said it's in Ireland, almost two hundred miles away. I don't know how Gullin is going to get there before wearing his horse or himself out."

"If that place is home to a legend about giants," Acacia said, "giants who were there one day and gone the next, I'm betting there is an opening in the Curtain there. Gullin wouldn't need to ride all that way, if he entered the Curtain at the four hills, and then could exit it over there."

"But can Gullin navigate the Curtain by himself? How would he know where to go?"

Baba's voice darkened into a grave, solemn timbre. "If it is Madness that possesses him, Madness will show him the way."

Gullin's scent had become a permanent pigment in the pallet of aromas that Acacia had memorized over the years, so she led the way back through the Curtain as Slepnir carried the rest of the cavalcade, and he sped at a full gallop after her. Her flight was straight and true, as she picked up on Gullin's distinct odor and pursued it with a falcon's fervor of the hunt.

David sat foremost on Slepnir's back, with Baba directly behind him, and Tyr on the end with Tanuki huddled under his mantle. The weight of three people and a badger—although Baba and David were piccolos compared to the grand piano that was Tyr—was straining Slepnir's muscles, but he kept up his speed, refusing to lose track of the sphinx in the mist.

Both Acacia and Slepnir were so driven down their path, they didn't acknowledge that there was something going on within the Curtain around them. The others noticed it right away, as the mist, normally the shimmering gauze that rises from a hot spring, was sullied into the char-black of furnace secretions, pressing in around them with the impending wrath of a williwaw.

David tried to see what was causing the darkness, but at the speed they were going, it was too difficult to focus on any one spot. There was movement within the Curtain, that much he could tell. Flashes of colors, bioluminescent neons, zipped in and out of the fog, and David could swear the colors took the forms of coiling tails, and lashing tentacles, and spindly spider legs.

"There's something here with us!" he called to the others, as a chorale of indistinguishable rasping grinded into their ears. "I can't tell what it is!"

"Not what 'it's is, lad," Tyr replied, "but what 'they' are. They're tawdrier than the last one I saw, but no doubting these apparitions are the same as the one I blasted out of Lady Acacia's shadow."

Acacia had heard what Tyr said. She darted her gaze about, catching the flickers of gaudy colors among the fog. She buckled mid-flight, falling back and landing smack against Slepnir's nose, The horse continued its full gallop, neighing in panic at the mincing menace around him. Acacia hunched up, wrapping her limbs around Slepnir's face.

David leaned forwards, trying to take hold of Acacia's paw as she clung to Slepnir. "Acacia, what is it?"

She had her eyes squeezed shut, her teeth clenched tight enough to crack metal. "Sh…shades, David! There are Shades everywhere!"

David could understand her terror at seeing so many Shades of Nyx. After the inextinguishable pain that one of Madam Nyx's Shades had put her through for so long, seeing a whole legion of them must have been horrific. "Don't look at them! We need to get out of the Curtain, but you need to guide us. The sooner we find where Gullin went, the sooner we get out of here!"

Acacia opened one eye to look at him. "I can't have another one of those things inside me, David! I…I'll die if I do!"

"They won't get you. You fought a Shade, and survived. You're stronger than they are." He stretched forwards farther, placing his hand on top of her paw. "You're stronger than Nyx! You're the strongest person I know!"

The sphinx opened her other eye. Her grip on Slepnir loosened. "What if I'm not strong enough?"

"You've got us to help you! You've got me!"

I wish that were true, she thought.

She unfolded her wings, took a deep breath, and pushed herself off of Slepnir's nose, thrusting herself back into flight. She spiraled through the air, keeping her eyes straight ahead and forbidding the Shades to enter her line of vision. She picked up Gullin's scent again, letting it fill her nose and throat. It was thicker now; she knew they were getting closer.

We'll be there soon, Gullin, she thought. *Don't do anything crazy before we get there. Please, be safe. I can't lose any more family…I can't…*

The pathway narrowed into a tunnel, fog and Shades spiraling around them and pressing in closer, creating the experience of racing down the middle of a vortex. Acacia shut her eyes, allowing her nose to guide the way, but the crescendo of the Shades' gnashing was getting to her again.

Tyr reached to the sheath on his back, extracting his axe and holding it over his head. "Fear not, milady. Allow me to light the way!"

His axe erupted in a blaze of silver light, pushing back the black fog and its infestation of Shades. A barrage of the swarming Nyx-spawn scattered out of their way as Acacia and Slepnir came powering through the Curtain. Billions of threads netted them, but they slammed into it with such force that they broke through, hearing a rattling rip as everyone tumbled through.

Almost everyone. David, Baba, Tyr and Tanuki were all thrown from Slepnir's back as they fell, and David flipped head over heels through the air. He caught a glimpse of Slepnir behind him, neighing at the top of his voice as the horde of Shades swamped the war horse and pulled him backwards into the folds of the Curtain. Half a second later, David plummeted into the froth of flesh-chilling, lung-stopping waves.

David coughed out the salt water clogging his windpipe, and peeled his eyelids open. Cold rock was beneath him, and even colder water lapped at his legs. With a groan, he forced himself up onto his arms, craning his neck to look up.

He was no longer in the Curtain, but where he was now was no less foreboding.

Column upon column of hexagonal stone surrounded him, invading the shoreline as far as the eye could see. The pillars fitted together in tight clumps, and formed the façade of tiered pyramids and winding staircases. The shore stretched up into green hills, and towers of stacked gray disks fortified the hillsides like hundreds of human spines. Basalt chimneys—a perfect image for the formations that Beatrice had alluded to—balanced atop outcroppings from the hills, somehow standing steady against the wind even though they looked as if a simple nudge would tip them over. Nearby, David spotted an unusually shaped boulder, curved into a smooth-edged L—although the longer he looked at it, the more it gave him the impression of a boot. A Giant's boot.

David rose to his feet, careful not to slip on the channel-soaked rocks. A drizzle drooled down from the overcast sky, the clouds as slate gray as the pillars around him. He looked about, spotting a ball of wet fur wedged between two mussel-encrusted stones about twenty feet away. Running over, David scooped up the soaking, shaking wad of badger, who immediately shook off the water, causing his fur to fluff up.

"Badgers are made for digging, not swimming!" Tanuki bleated. He cast his gaze across the shoreline. "No…no sand or dirt? No place to dig? What kind of cruel joke is this?"

"This isn't a joke. This is the Giants' Causeway." David set Tanuki down. "Can you smell if Acacia or the others are nearby?"

Tanuki sniffed the air, and snorted. "Too much water. It's washing over any scents. But it would be awfully hard to miss the horse or the big guy with the axe."

He had a point. Slepnir and Tyr should be easy to see if they were anywhere in the area. Acacia in flight would be bigger than any bird, and David scanned the skies, hoping to catch a glimpse of her. "We better look for them. Maybe we'll run into Gullin while we look."

They hiked along the stairs of stones, searching by not daring to call out for their friends. If David's suspicions were correct, there might be a giant of a different sort somewhere among these lava-molded monoliths, and he didn't want to draw attention. He hoped that Fenrir wouldn't be able to pick up on their scents due to the North Channel temporarily washing them away, as it had been with Tanuki.

A short ways down the shore, they spotted a squat, round form sitting on one of the shorter pillars, ringing water out of her hat. David and Tanuki rushed over to her, but she gave them an impatient glare.

"Took long enough," Baba huffed, slapping her wet hat back on her head. "Have a good swim, while rest of us were drowning?"

Tanuki licked the palm of his paw and tried to flatten down the puffed-up fur on his scalp. "It wasn't exactly a picnic for us either," he said.

"Have you seen Acacia or Tyr?" David asked.

Baba rolled back her shoulders and stretched her neck, which made a loud crick. "Not yet. But maybe you go try and wake up friend, yes?"

She pointed inland towards the top of a high pyramid of the igneous pillars, where a brawny copper-haired man stood on top of the very tallest column, right in the middle of the pile. He was dressed in a full-body mud-splattered nightshirt and a pair of boots, and he held a cleaver in one hand that dangled limply at his side. His back was to them, and his head was craned upwards, locked in a paralyzed trance.

David raced over to the pile and bounded up the stacks of stones towards Gullin. He stopped short a few feet away from the Scotsman. "Gullin?" he spoke in a low voice.

Gullin didn't acknowledge David. He continued to stare out, and a faint mumbling dripped from his lips.

David ventured closer to Gullin, wary of the cleaver. "Gullin, can you hear me? Say something if you know I'm here."

When Gullin didn't turn to look at him, he took another step closer. David kept one hand on the hilt of his dagger, in case Gullin should suddenly turn his cleaver on him. "We need to leave. Beatrice and Ian are waiting for you back in—"

The Scotsman let loose a roar that cracked the air itself. He raised his fists above his head, jabbing his cleaver at the adolescent dawn. "I'll gut the beast that killed my wife and son! I'll skin him alive and smash his bones!"

"No, Gullin! Beatrice and Ian are fine! You've been possessed!"

"Show yourself, monster!" Gullin continued to bellow, as his voice wavered to hold back his sobs. "You'll pay! You'll pay for the lives you took from me…" He shook all over, his knees going weak as misery took hold of his being.

David took a chance, stepping forwards to swipe the cleaver out of Gullin's hand. Gullin didn't struggle, but instead let the cleaver go so he could cover his face with his hands. "My Bea…my beautiful Bea…"

"Gullin, listen to me!" David dropped the cleaver on the rock next to him, and grabbed Gullin by the back of his shoulders. "Nico has affected your mind. He gave you a nightmare that made you think Beatrice and Ian were eaten. They're alive! And if you want to see them again, we need to get out of—"

The hill in front of them suddenly grew to twice its height. That was how it appeared, as the hill was masked in shadow from the rainclouds drowning out the first hint of morning light. It became quickly clear, however, that the hill wasn't growing—something was rising up from behind it. A pointed head full of death-dealing teeth rose to look down at them from over the hilltop, and its yellow eyes ensnared them with barbed vehemence. Waterfalls of acidic saliva poured out from the curled-back lips, burning up the grass on the hill below his chin into withered black ash.

If David had thought Fenrir was terrifying before, seeing the wolf ten times larger was beyond his belief. The fear he felt turned his entire body numb, striking him with both heat and ice throughout his skin and skeleton, and a part of him wanted to resign itself to death right then and there. Instead, he forced his hand to draw his dagger, pointing the fang-forged weapon at its original owner.

Fenrir's gaze burned into David. The wolf appeared neither furious nor pleased to see him. "Thief, you have come to join your friend in death."

Gullin snapped his head up at the sound of Fenrir's voice, and twisted his face in primal fury. "You foul beast! I'll break your neck with my bare hands!" He darted forwards to make good on his word, but David grabbed him in a bear hug to hold him back. It took all of the young man's strength to restrain Gullin, who thrashed about trying to break free.

Fenrir raised his head higher, and he placed one paw on top of the hill in front of him. "I traced the smell of my slaughtered sons here. This is the place where you robbed me of my legacy, Huntsman. Now, I will rob you of your life, and then I will fulfill my purpose, starting my final feast with your world."

The wolf's head snaked up and over the hill, its opening jaws striking towards Gullin and David with surprising swiftness for his size. David reacted without thinking, making a desperate grab for his dagger and thrusting it upwards at Fenrir while still holding back Gullin with his other arm. The dagger spurted a spout of blood as it had done before, and Fenrir reeled back with a snarl, the empty socket in his gum-line weeping red.

"You will stay away from my friend, and this world," David ordered.

Fenrir's ears folded back, as he stood with his front paws on top of the hill. His weight deflated the hill by about ten feet. "You have brought my fang to me. I have ached for my missing tooth. Give it to me!"

"NO!" David hollered.

Fenrir pulled up the section of his lips right under his nose, to flash his front teeth in an odd smile. "Is that all? That single word will save your planet? Even Odin does not command such power. Perhaps I will leave you for last, so you may watch as I eat everything and everyone in your world. Or I will leave you for the dead fox. He seems to have a fervent desire to do you in himself."

David froze. The dead fox? Nico? Don't say that Fenrir and Nico were working together! Anger swelled up inside David merely at the thought of Nico, and a brazen tongue wriggled forth with newfound, possibly foolish, courage. "Are you stalling, Fenrir? If you want your fang back so badly, then come down here and take it from me, if you can!"

Fenrir was no longer amused. He was infuriated by the taunt. He propelled himself clean over the hill, his backside arcing up to brush the heavens, his front paws aimed straight at David and Gullin with the intent to squash them into paste against the rocks.

A blinding streak of silver light flew like a comet through the air and smacked into the right side of Fenrir's muzzle with a deafening clang. The wolf was knocked out of his trajectory and tumbled off to the side, landing on a cluster of pillars and shattering them into a fragmented heap. Fenrir instinctively convulsed to get up and face his attacker, but out of his right eye, where a silver axe had struck right beneath it, he recognized the crimson-and-gold helmet, the trails of white hair that flowed from underneath it, the mantle of brown fur, and the pale, intense eyes. The wolf's eyes broadened, and his long tail tucked itself between his back legs.

"It's been a long time," Tyr said, yanking his axe out of Fenrir's cheek. The axe had done no more than a slight nick in Fenrir's skin.

"Lawgiver…" Fenrir growled with the deepness of a canyon. "You dare show your face to me, after your betrayal?"

Tyr hefted his axe on his shoulder. "I did what had to be done, Fenrir. As far as betrayal, I think you got your revenge for that." He held up his severed wrist.

"You will not lock me away again!" Fenrir swung his head around and snapped his jaws at the warrior, who jumped back and readied his axe for another strike.

As David looked on at the fight, Gullin's eyes fell on the dagger in David's hand. "That dagger…it can kill him…"

David had heard Gullin, but he couldn't put his dagger away fast enough. Gullin wrestled it out of his hand and shoved David aside, sending him rolling down the pyramid. Gullin took off towards the wolf, the dagger clenched in his raised fist.

David landed heavily at the bottom of the stone pile, his body battered and bruised from the rocks. He heard a fluttering of wings above him, and then gentle paws trying to help him up.

"David!" Acacia saw that there was a gash above David's left eyebrow, and her feline instincts instructed her to lick it clean.

David groaned at the sting of Acacia's tongue on his wound, and he jerked his head back. "No, Acacia! You have to stop Gullin. He's got Fenrir's Fang!"

The sphinx turned to see Gullin dashing towards the battle between Tyr and Fenrir, and she took off, pumping her wings against the strong wind. She flew past Gullin and circled around to land on all fours, blocking his way. "Gullin, stop!"

Gullin halted, but there was no recognition in his eyes, only a wild determination. "Get out of my way!" He raised the dagger over his head, preparing to bring it down on her.

Acacia side-stepped Gullin, darting around his side as her tail swiped at his legs. Gullin tripped over her tail, but he retained his footing and didn't fall over. He spun around to face her again, slicing the dagger out at her. Acacia could feel the dark energy radiating from the dagger, and even though it had not made contact with her yet, a searing pain shot through her chest as Gullin swiped at her.

Of all times not to have her slumber-breath! Yet there was a chance she could put Gullin to sleep nonetheless. She looked deeply into his eyes, trying to reach him as she might in her dream-talks. She hoped that she could still tap into people's minds through her hypno-stare, without her special breath, it required all of her concentration, and she did not like to use it in a fight because she could not return from her hypnotic gaze quickly enough to fend off a blow. But she had to try it, otherwise she would have to risk hurting Gullin.

She could see it. Buried in Gullin's eyes, in the recesses of his mind, was a swirling blur of incoherent shadows and paranoias. It was an abstract barrage of emotion and sickness, craving chaos and murder. Pure, raw madness.

It was too overwhelming for her to calm Gullin while the madness was still inside of him. If she could dispel it…if she could drive it out of him…

David forced himself to stand up, although his legs screamed. Tanuki scampered over to him. "David, please tell me you have a plan! What do we do?"

David drew out his sword. "It looks to me like a little order is needed here." He had no idea how rocks would respond to his orders—would they be like Baba's trinkets, easily willing to comply, or would they take a firm command like Viking artifacts? Would rocks respond at all? He didn't have time to experiment, so he decided the safest thing to do was put his foot down.

He held the sword out in front of him, shouting, "Stones of the Giants' Causeway! I know there is an ancient life within you. This world, the earth from which you were born, will be destroyed by Fenrir the Wolf if you do not help stop him! I beseech you, help me stop the wolf! As this causeway was once built by giants, I now rebuild you to bind a giant!"

He thrust his sword down into a crack between two stones. As soon as the sword touched the ground, pillars uprooted themselves, popping out of the earth as if they were spring-loaded. Disks of rock shot up from under his feet and all around him, spiraling through the air. The stones hurtled themselves towards Fenrir with a magnetic force, and Tyr blanched as the hurricane of stones came raining down on them. He managed to jump aside in time, as the pillars crashed on Fenrir, pummeling him unrelentingly. The wolf yelped, more so out of confusion than pain, as the rocks shattered against his hide. The pillars stacked up around Fenrir, enclosing him in a pen, and the rocks continued to pile over him until they had created a sealed dome around him. It lasted for five seconds until Fenrir burst through it, sending stone chunks flying in all directions.

David ground his teeth together. There was nothing around that was strong enough to attack Fenrir with! He held his sword in both hands. If the dagger was strong enough to pierce Fenrir, he prayed that the sword could as well.

Fenrir barked at Tyr. "Using your old tricks, Lawgiver? Ordering the elements of the earth to do your bidding? I would have thought I had taken that power from you, when I bit off your commanding hand."

Tyr huffed. "Your mistake was spitting my hand back out. Just because it's no longer attached to me, doesn't mean it lost its power."

David was cautiously approaching, his sword at the ready. If he could land a strike on Fenrir, while Tyr was distracting him…

Gullin lashed out at Acacia again, who bounded out of the way. She had to drive the madness out of him, but how? She had dealt with madness before—eons ago, she had encountered Lyssa, the goddess of insanity that held sway over the Greeks. Lyssa, for someone who inflicted madness on others, had had an ironically logical demeanor. What had she said… "I do not use my powers in anger against friends, nor do I take joy in visiting the homes of men." It was a hypocritical statement, however, as she had turned around and infected Heracles with insanity at the goddess Hera's order, causing him to murder his family. But Lyssa didn't use madness to turn friends against one another—did that rule apply to the madness that affected Gullin?

She locked eyes with Gullin again. "Gullin, I know you. You are strong. This madness that grips you, you can overcome it. I will help you. I am your friend. Trust me, and we can free you from this."

Gullin swayed on his feet, the tightness in his angered expression slackening. Then he shook his head. "You are a monster! You must be slayed as well!"

Acacia concentrated, reaching deeper into the vortex of insanity that drove Gullin. There was one more thing she could try. It would take all of her will, all of her mental prowess, and if it didn't work, it would spell her demise. But if she could find that one tiny spot in Gullin's brain—

Gullin launched himself forwards, bringing the dagger down and impaling Acacia right between her collar bone and neck. The sphinx didn't scream, but her face froze in a shocked visage. She collapsed, as bright red blood seeped out of her flesh in torrents, staining the rock beneath her.

All the rage fled Gullin as he looked down on the bleeding sphinx before him. The blindness that had cloaked his sight was gone. He knew this creature…oh God, Acacia! He fell to his knees beside her, a scream of pain pouring out. "Acacia! What have I done??" He pulled the limp body into his arms, weeping into the soft, warm fur and tousled hair, shaking all over as the horror of his deed shred him apart.

The sphinx's body stirred, as she nestled her nose in the crook of his neck. “It’s all right, Gullin. I’m all right.”

The Scotsman, tears streaming down his face, pulled back to look at Acacia in his arms. There was no wound, no blood! She looked up at him, smiling. “I’m sorry, but I had to trick you. When Heracles was stricken with madness, his sanity was restored to him when he saw that he had killed his wife and children.”

“But…but I stabbed you!” Gullin said.

Acacia shook her head. “I made you think you stabbed me. I was able to use my hypno-sight to alter the place in your mind that interprets what you see with your eyes. You saw the dagger strike me, but really you were a foot off the mark.”

Gullin wiped the tears off of his face. “Thank you for freeing me of my madness. But don’t ever, ever make me think I hurt you again!”

David’s knuckles were going numb from how tightly he gripped his sword. Fenrir’s left flank was towards him, as the wolf faced away from David. Fenrir stared down Tyr, but he shifted uneasily on his feet, his tail switching from being tucked under to raised half-way up. It was as if his tail didn’t know whether to be submissive, or challenge Tyr for dominance.

Tyr could see David trying to sneak up from behind, but he kept his gaze on the wolf so as not to give David away. “Fenrir, understand that what I had to do was for the good of Asgard, for all the nine realms! But destinies can be changed. If you could prove to the Aesir, to Odin, that you would not devour the worlds, and pledge your alliance and loyalty to us—”

“Loyalty? The betrayer speaks of loyalty?” Fenrir lowered his head, advancing on Tyr. “You would treat me like some common dog. You would have me for your pet! Never!” He jutted forwards, jaws open, and clamped his teeth around Tyr. But Tyr pushed with all of his strength against the roof of Fenrir’s mouth, forcing the wolf’s jaws to stay open. Fenrir lifted his head high, and shook it back and forth with such ferocity that Tyr’s helmet and armor were flung away.

“Stop!” David wasn’t being careful anymore. He ran up behind Fenrir, sword raised, and brought it down with all of his strength on the wolf’s back paw. There was a resonant ringing as sword clashed with one of Fenrir's claws, and the high-pitched ring made the wolf cringe. He swiveled his head around to look at David, with Tyr still propping his jaws open.

"Spit him out!" David cried. "This sword is a match to the dagger made from your fang. It upholds everything that you would tear down! It wields the power of Order. I am David Sandoval, Protector, Fighter, and Scholar, and I order you to release Tyr and go back to your prison, Fenrir!"

The wolf cocked his head at David.

Tyr shook his head. "If only it were that simple. But that's not the kind of 'order' that my hand could influence."

"What? Your hand?" David looked at the sword. "Are...are you saying this sword was made from your hand?"

"The bones of it. This sheep in wolf's clothes bit off my commanding hand when I put the binding ribbon on his neck, and then he spat it back out. Odin ordered for the bones in my hand to be forged into a weapon to balance out the evil of Fenrir's tooth. I figured, what else would I do with a bitten-off hand? Pickle it?"

"Ood ou heez hut ut?" Fenrir said, trying to speak past Tyr in his mouth.

"Don't you tell me to shut it—" Tyr started, but then Fenrir curled up his tongue that Tyr was standing on, causing the warrior to lose his footing and fall over. A thunderous snap of Fenrir's jaws, and Tyr was gone.

"Tyr!" David swung the sword again, banging the blade against Fenrir's ankle. The wolf picked up his foot, but there was no wound from the strike. He positioned his back paw over David, bringing it down to smash him. David staggered back, falling on his backside as the paw missed him by inches. Fenrir turned around and lowered his head down to David's level, and the boy knew he was looking Death in the eye.

"I can finally smell something about you," Fenrir said, inhaling deeply, the vacuum of his nose drawing David closer. "Even an enchantment cannot mask your thoughts forever. You smell of kindness, and loyalty, and love. Such traits are for the weak. You will be devoured, knowing you are too weak to save your friends or your people. You will burn forever inside of me, along with all the other fools who thought they could defeat me. Relish your world for one last moment, mortal."

As Fenrir's massive red tongue emerged from between his teeth, coming to lap up David as a miniscule appetizer, there was a gouging sound of flesh being ripped. Fenrir pulled back so fast, David flinched in shock. Fenrir rubbed at his head with his paw, and David could see Gullin was standing right behind the wolf's ear. There was another ripping as Gullin dug the dagger into Fenrir's scalp and pulled, tearing a gash into the skin. Acacia was up there with him, and she stuck her head right inside Fenrir's ear, letting loose a bombastic lion bellow. It rattled inside Fenrir's head, disorienting him and making him unsteady on his feet.

"Look at the big bad wolf now!" Gullin called, as he slid down the front of Fenrir's face and gripped the beast's brow. He brought the dagger right in front of the wolf's eye, pulling his hand back to deal a blow straight into the retina.

Fenrir threw his entire body towards the side of a hill, against a wall of the stone pillars. He smacked his face into the rock, intending to flatten Gullin, but the Scotsman let go of Fenrir's brow and dropped down, catching hold of a whisker to keep from falling to the ground. He swung on the whisker, avoiding hitting the wall, but the dagger dropped out of his hand, clattering on the rocks below.

Acacia took to the air, swooping around under Fenrir's chin to catch Gullin. The Huntsman started to shout to her, but the horrid tongue flicked out from between the wolf's lips, snagging Gullin and pulling him into his mouth.

The sphinx screeched, and she clawed at the side of Fenrir's face, latching onto his muzzle with her teeth and biting with everything she had. Fenrir swatted her off with his paw, slamming her into the wall. She tumbled down the wall, hitting the rocks below. She laid still, her tail twitching.

David couldn't believe it. Gullin...no, he couldn't be gone. Gullin had once been in the belly of a dragon and survived. This wolf wasn't going to have him!

He scrambled over the stones, spotting where the dagger had fallen. But Fenrir had spotted it too, and was lowering his head to snatch up his long-lost fang. Either that, or he was aiming for Acacia, who was about fifteen feet from the dagger.

"Acacia! Get the dagger!" David called, but she was barely stirring. He ran faster, sword in hand, clashing the blade against Fenrir's front paw as he dashed past it. It generated the same high ringing as before, but Fenrir was too focused on his fang to let it bother him. David lunged for the dagger, his hand coiling around it as Fenrir's mouth came down on him.

David flipped over, thrusting the dagger upwards, intending to slice the wolf's tongue down the middle as it was cascading down over him.

But the dagger did not connect with the tongue. Instead, it jammed into Fenrir's gumline, right where the empty socket was. In a single moment, David was no longer holding his dagger. He was holding the tip of a stalagmite of a tooth, which had grown out of the notch.

Fenrir had his fang back.

The last thing that David felt, as the jaws closed in around him, was the feeling of soft feathers enveloping him, and two paws holding him close to a furry body, and a voice whispering into his ear, "We're together now…I'll protect you…"

CHAPTER SIXTEEN

Baba and Tanuki watched, petrified, as Fenrir snapped his teeth around David and Acacia. He lifted his head, and swallowed. He bared his teeth, licking his tongue over his regrown fang. As Baba and Tanuki huddled behind a rock formation, they could see Fenrir grow even larger, his coat took on a lustrous sheen, his muscles strained as they inflated, his claws grew longer, and his eyes burned with the fires of the underworld.

He turned his shaggy head up towards the sky. He sat back on his haunches, lifting his front paws off the ground, so that he looked as if he were begging. He opened his mouth and inhaled, and the clouds above swirled down into his maw, a twirling tornado that was sucked down into his gullet, until the sky all over Ireland's north channel was free of clouds. The sun was no longer hidden by the layer of cumulus, and Fenrir smiled widely at the shining beacon in the heavens.

I shall enjoy eating this world, he thought, *but first I will fulfill my sons' destinies in their stead. I will start with consuming this world's sun.*

He opened his mouth again, and streams of golden rays trailed into his throat, pulled in by his ravenous craving. The sun's fire poured into him, and the sun itself was slowly changing color, glowing a little redder, fading a little dimmer.

"Baba, what can we do??" Tanuki whispered.

Baba picked him up, holding him in her arms. "World will be in total darkness soon. There is no place we can go, that is safe. We can be brave, little one. That we can do…"

*

David and Acacia slowly opened their eyes.

They hadn't quite known what to expect, inside of Fenrir's stomach. But this was different from what they would have guessed.

A miniature galaxy spread out before them. Hundreds of thousands of bubbles, as small as eyeballs to as large as planets, floated about, their surfaces swirling with iridescent soapy polish of every color in the spectrum. Palm-sized white flames leapt about the space, shooting up from an abyss below like a battalion of comets. Chunks of land, like meteors traversing through a solar system, bobbed among the bubbles and flames: patches of green forests, blocks of icy tundra, trays of dusty deserts, and bowls of blue ocean. Amidst it all were random objects of every sort, including buildings and bridges, ships and sleds, monuments and museums, tornadoes, hurricanes, thunderheads, and jagged-edged blocks that appeared to be broken-off sections of skies from whatever worlds they were from. David and Acacia hovered in the space, holding one another in fear that they would fall if they let go.

Acacia sniffed the air, and hacked. "At least the stench is as I expected."

David observed a bright green bubble as it floated past him. He was tempted to poke at it with his finger, but then a ghastly shadow of a face rolled over the surface of the bubble. The face's mouth was stretched open in an agonizing scream, and the eyes were wide empty holes staring out into nothingness. It silently floated on, but David was as shaken as if the face had shrieked bloody murder in his ear. But then he did hear something, as one of the white flames flickered by him. It wailed as it rocketed past, in a distinct male voice, the howl of a man in never-ending torment.

"Acacia, do you—" David started.

"Yes, I see and hear them," she replied. "Those are the faces and voices of the victims Fenrir has consumed. Eventually we'll be digested and broken down as well, our bodies fused with the acid of Fenrir's stomach while our souls and minds are released, to wander aimlessly until they, too, are melded to the burning inferno of this eternal gut. But that could take weeks, months, years possibly."

Even now, David could feel they were slowly sinking downwards, and far, far below, he could make out a boiling, steaming swamp from which the bubbles and the white flames were rising.

"Can't you fly us out??" David demanded.

Acacia looked all around. "Fly us where? I can't tell where 'out' is!" She flapped her wings, and they hovered upwards an inch before an abrupt pull of gravity forced them downwards even faster. "It's no good. Everything is drawn in towards the pit of his stomach. The more we fight it, the faster we get pulled in."

"So this is it? This is how it ends, digested by a giant wolf?"

"Not exactly how I was planning to meet the reaper, either," came a voice directly below them. Gullin was sitting on a floating oasis under a palm tree, resting his head in his hand. "I'm sorry, boyo. We did our best. But how do you stop the end of the world?"

Even farther down, Tyr was trying to make his way upwards, jumping from island to building to any object he could reach. "I knew this wolf would be the death of me. I just wished I could've undone some of the wrong I allowed to go free." He ran out of breath, and sat to rest on a wandering piece of volcanic rock. "I vow, upon Odin's spear, that I will make Fenrir pay for his crimes, even if the worst I can do is give him bad indigestion."

Indigestion…David had a shard of hope. "Wait, is there anything that would make Fenrir sick? Anything that might make him regurgitate what he's eaten?"

"If there is, I wouldn't know it," Tyr sighed. "This brute's stomach is as steel-clad as his hide."

Acacia watched as an ancient moss-covered temple hung in the space a ways off. It was different from the Grecian or Egyptian temples she was used to, but it brought tears to her eyes nonetheless. "I guess there's no point in keeping my thoughts to myself anymore. Oh David, there's so many things I would have loved to show you. Atlantis, Mount Helicon, Olympus—from a distance, of course, but it is so beautiful, when the sun is setting behind it, washing it in scarlet and orange light."

"For all we know, they could be in here," David said, in a poor attempt to elevate the mood. "Or they will be soon. Then we can visit them."

"That's a horrible thing to say, even if it is true," the sphinx replied, although she didn't sound angry. "Just because all the world will be here, doesn't mean it will be the same. It's like saying the dinner on your plate will be the same after you eat it. Everything and everyone is born with its own special life journey, not just to be prey for a predator. Everything and everyone has its place, and the right to be in the world. That's all I wanted for you, David, to have the place in the world that you wanted to be. Even though I missed you, even though I knew that you belonged to someone else...you being in the world, is enough."

David had no words. He wiped a tear from Acacia's eye, holding her close, wary not to cut her with his sword—

His sword! He still had his sword!

"Acacia, you're right!" he said. "Everything does have a place. Every world has its own order. And none of that is in here. Everything needs to be put back where it belongs."

Tyr stood up, realizing what David was going to try. "Son, I'll be honest. I've never tried commanding whole worlds with my hand. I have no power over souls or free will, nor have I ever tried to command freedom for prisoners trapped in an inescapable void!"

David didn't allow Tyr's words to dampen his hope. He held his sword in both hands. "Acacia, this may not work, but...if I have your strength, your spirit, with me, I think I can do this."

Acacia positioned herself behind him, wrapping her arms around his chest and laying her head on his shoulder. "You gave me my name, so the least I can do is give you my strength."

Even as she spoke, David could feel a wave of energy course into him. He held out his sword before him, willing all of his might to command it.

"I am David Sandoval. I may be mortal, but my spirit is unbreakable. I may not be a great warrior, but my strength comes from my friends, and that is a greater strength than all the storms, and typhoons, and giants of the world combined. I may be young, but I have learned much, and I use what I learn for the greater good."

The sword began to glow with a brilliant white light. The light grew brighter and hotter as David's voice grew louder.

"I stand for Order. I stand for Light. I stand for Knowledge and Wisdom.

I stand for everything that deserves its place, deserves its freedom. I am Protector, I am Fighter, I am Scholar. I am a beacon of Hope, and I would pass hope along to all those who despair. With all my strength, with all my spirit and hope and heart, I command all within this space to break free, to return to your rightful place! I order all of you to reclaim what you lost, and to return Order to your worlds!"

The light from David's sword spread out among everything in the belly-galaxy, alighting every bubble, island, building, comet, and element with a glowing radiation. Far, far below, the glow spread out like a vast ocean, setting ablaze a churning, frothing and whirling swamp that must have been the acid at the pit of Fenrir's stomach. The acid frothed higher, and bubbles and comets erupted up from it in ever growing numbers. Everything began to tremble, shaking with anticipation, as the light became blinding. The tension of the energy was on the verge of explosion, and yet there was still a pause, still a lingering moment where all things were held in rapt attention, waiting for David to complete his order.

David paused, until with an exasperated huff, he screamed, "PLEASE??"

Everything all at once blasted upwards in an eruption to challenge the force of Mt. Vesuvuis, and David, Acacia, Gullin, Tyr, and everyone within Fenrir hurtled up with it, one with the maelstrom of star-hot light.

Fenrir stopped his consumption of sunlight. Something was not right. He clamped his mouth shut, feeling an incinerating sickness rising up.

The sudden upsurge from his throat tore his jaws apart with such force that several of his teeth shattered, and his reclaimed fang broke loose from his mouth. The cyclone of light ripped loose from him, shooting up into the sky, as everything he had ever eaten escaped to return to their rightful homes. Millions of souls cried out in joyful ecstasy as they were summoned to the many sanctuaries that spirits call home, ready to meet the ancestors and descendants that they had been torn away from. As all things departed from Fenrir's belly, so did his energy and power, and to his horror the wolf was shrinking, shrinking…

Baba and Tanuki had to avert their eyes from the towering tornado of white fire, and they remained huddled together for a long time even after the light finally faded away. Baba ventured to peek open an eye. The cyclone was gone, and the wolf was gone. The only sound to be heard was the calm lapping of the water against the rocks.

"I…I think it is over," she whispered to Tanuki.

Shivering, Tanuki cautiously opened his eyes. He looked up at Baba. "Is the world exploded?"

"No."

"Are we dead?"

"Me, getting there. You, no."

Tanuki patted himself over, checking for any missing pieces. "Well, then, I say it's turned out to be a much better day than I expected."

Baba stood up from behind their hiding rock, and for the first time that Tanuki had ever seen—perhaps the first time anyone had seen in a long time—a smile of joy brightened Baba Yaga's face. "I do not believe it!"

Down the far hill, walking their way, looking no worse for wear, was David and Acacia. Behind them were Tyr, and behind him was Gullin, still in his nightshirt and looking visibly shaken. He was riding a burly white horse that Tanuki immediately recognized.

Tanuki jumped from Baba's arms and ran across the rocky ground to the group. "You're all alive! And you blew up the wolf! And you found Gringolet too! What else was in there? Did you bring me back anything?"

David and Acacia gave Tanuki a hard look, but then Acacia chuckled. "Next time we're in the belly of a giant world-eating monster, we'll remember to grab you a souvenir."

"I wouldn't start friendly banter yet," Tyr said, as he walked away from the group towards a shape lying among the basalt pillars nearby. He stopped as he stood over the broken, withered, feeble form that was all that remained of Fenrir. The wolf was no bigger than a sheepdog, his fur faded to ashen-gray, the sinister light in his eyes extinguished. He weakly turned his head up to look at Tyr, but he didn't have enough strength to even snarl.

"Fenrir," Tyr said, his voice tender and calm. "It is over. It is time."

The warrior removed the iron pot that he had hung on his belt, and stretched it wide until it was large enough for its intended prisoner. Tyr stooped down and picked up Fenrir in his arms. He did so with unexpected gentleness, and hesitated as he looked down into the cauldron, and looked back at Fenrir.

Fenrir shivered, understanding what was about to happen. He closed his eyes, his voice barely audible but sounding like he had aged a thousand years. "Tyr…don't do this to me again. I trusted you once. You made me believe that someone understood me. I think I could be better if you give me another chance. I…could be good."

Tyr paused. He sighed. "I know you could."

"Could you forgive me, for what I've done?"

The warrior held the frail wolf closer to his chest. "I'd like to think someday, we will forgive one another. But that day cannot be today. I have my duty to balance the light and the dark. I pray that one day, light will find its place in your heart. I am sorry, Fen."

Tyr knelt down, and carefully allowed Fenrir to slip from his arms and fall into the cauldron. The wolf fell with a mournful howl, his pleading eyes staring up as he was swallowed into the mile-deep blackness. Tyr grabbed hold of the rim of the cauldron, pushing it back down to its small dimensions. He remained kneeling for a while, his eyes closed. Such sadness was on Tyr's face, and he whispered as he rested his hand on top of the sealed pot: "Forgive me, my friend."

David came over to the warrior, placing a hand on his shoulder. "It was the right thing to do, Tyr."

Tyr removed his helmet, raking his fingers through his moon-pale hair. "Right isn't always easy. But I think you best retrieve what's yours over there."

David looked over to where Fenrir had been laying, and he saw that his dagger was there among the rocks. He went over and picked it up, and returned to Tyr. He took his sword from his belt as well. "If you're going to be guarding the cauldron from now on, you probably want these back."

Tyr looked at the two weapons. "David, those weapons won't work for me anymore. I may keep balance between the light and the dark in my world, but to me, it looks like someone should be keeping the balance here, in your world."

Acacia went up to David. "But no one will force you to accept that role. You've worked hard for a life of peace and security. If that is what you want, I can take those weapons back and find a safe place to hide them, until they may be needed again."

David weighed the weapons in his hands. "I don't know what to say. I know I have to go home, and keeping these means that something could come after me again. But, Fenrir's Fang, and the Sword of Order, also brought you, and Gullin, and Tanuki back into my life. Giving these up could mean I'll never see any of you again after this."

Acacia stood up on her hind legs, placing her paw against David's cheek. "As long as we are both in this world, we'll never be apart."

"Maybe I'll hang on to them a little longer," David decided, sheathing them on his belt. "Then, if they are needed elsewhere, it will give you a reason to come see me."

Tyr had the goofy smile on his face again, watching David and Acacia. He stood up, picking up the cauldron in his one hand. "Well, best be bringing this to Asgard, see what the council wants to do with it. Hate to lose track of this—"

There was a loud rip as a tear in the fabric of space opened up directly behind Tyr. He didn't have time to turn around before two monstrous wings of inky indigo extended out and encompassed him, David and Acacia, drawing the three into the rip of the Curtain. Gringolet whinnied and reared up, throwing Gullin from his back and sending him straight down onto the rocks, smacking the back of his head. Dozens of clawed Shade hands stitched up the tear behind them with the threads of Night, trapping the kidnapped victims inside.

Tanuki stared dumbfounded, jaw hanging limply open, at the spot where his friends had disappeared. He scurried over, his forepaws searching frantically for the tear, but it was nowhere to be found. He sniffed about, desperate to pick up his friends' trail, but their scents were gone. The harder he sought for them, the more anger burbled up within him.

"Give them back, you...you...whatever you are!!" he squealed, throwing himself about as if he too had been stricken with madness. "You evil, nasty, friend-stealing—"

He was grabbed from behind and hoisted off the ground, and Tanuki wriggled in the arms holding him. "Let me go! That thing took my friends! I can't let anything happen to them!'

"Tanuki," Baba said, and the badger was stunned into silence that, for the first time, she had addressed him by name. "Hush. Hush."

Tanuki looked up at Baba, who was wide-eyed and tight-lipped with fear. He could feel her shaking, even though she was doing her best to contain it.

"What...what can we do?" Tanuki cried. "Baba, I can't change shape anymore. You don't have your magic. What are we going to do..."

Baba then did something Tanuki hadn't expected. She hugged him, resting her cheek on his head.

"If there is anything that boy has shown me," she said, "it is that people are capable of great things without magic. We will find them, Tanuki. You are spirit guide after all, no?"

Tanuki gave her a small nod.

Baba turned to Gullin, who was sitting upright on the ground at Gringolet's hooves, rubbing the back of his head. "Well, hunter? What would you say we do?"

Gullin slowly stood up, grunting at his bruises from having been thrown, and placed his hands on his hips as he stared pensively at the sky. He was quiet for a minute, but then he tightened his jaw and nodded to himself. "There is someone we can go to for help. It might cost me my skin to show my face to those blokes again, but I don't think we have much choice." He placed a hand on Gringolet's neck, who continued to shiver and shift unsteadily on his feet. "I think Gringolet can carry us all, since the groundhog's so small. Both of you, get on. It's time we go have a talk with my old Guild."

"That was impressive, even though I had foreseen that you would trap the wolf. It is admirable, for a mortal."

The voice was unfamiliar to David, but he didn't have to guess who it was.

He, the sphinx and the warrior were standing upon a cold, black-marbled floor within a circular room. Twelve pedestals with glowing bluish-purple orbs stood around the edges of the room, and above them was the endless ceiling of deepest night, sparkling with its diamond-dazzled constellations. Before them was an obsidian throne that resembled a chariot in shape, two carved horses set under the arms. One of the horses was extremely large, with a long braid in its mane and its mouth frozen open in a panicked whinny.

"Slepnir..." Tyr whispered.

Hanging in the air near the throne were five silver birdcages, all with birds inside them, fluttering about. One was a vicious white hawk with a steel beak, pecking wildly at the cage bars. Another was a black raven with a bone-colored face, staring out with cold glassy eyes. The third bird was green and purple, clutching a golden apple in its talons. The fourth was a scrawny brown gull that had lobster claws instead of wings—and David had a sinking feeling he knew that bird.

The last one was dark blue, and rather than having normal wings, its wings grew out of the side of its head.

Dios mío! Hypnos!

David started to run over to the bird cages, but he froze as a shadow appeared on the throne. The shadow solidified into a youthful man, skin as pale as waning starlight, long hair that swirled around his head like tentacles of deep ocean. The same wings that had kidnapped them grew from his back, feathers as shiny and slick as oil. His eyes were two spheres of solid black opal, and all the universe was contained within them—all creation, all destruction, all wonder, all horror. The one thing that they did not contain was compassion, nor did anything in the man's sharp-chiseled face express this.

Those eyes. David had not forgotten those eyes. They were the same as when he had first met this being, back when this shadowy man had appeared as a ten-year-old boy clinging to Madam Nyx's dress. The new Nyx had grown into a direct parallel of his mother in many ways, being her incarnation, but where Madam Nyx had instilled the dread of a looming nightmare, this Nyx *was* the nightmare, ready and ravenous.

"Do you remember me?" Nyx asked, his voice ice.

David hid his hands behind his back, so Nyx couldn't see how badly they were shaking. "I do, Lord Nyx," he replied.

Lord Nyx pressed the tips of his fingers together in a steeple. "You were admiring my collection. I'm sure you recognize some of them. They were being uncooperative, so I made them more aesthetically pleasing. But now I have what I want, so I will have to consider keeping them as pets or getting rid of them."

"What do you want, Lord Nyx? Why have you kidnapped Hypnos, and why have you brought us here?"

Nyx frowned. "My predecessor may have allowed you to speak so impetuously to her, but you will speak when I ask you to. I will pardon your rudeness this time, however, since you have captured the wolf for me."

David looked back at Tyr, who was still holding the cauldron. Tyr stood up straight, tightening his grip on the pot. "I so happen to be a god in my realm, so I will speak to you as an equal. The wolf is not to be touched. I am taking it back to Asgard with me."

In the sheen of the marble floor, the bioluminescent Shades swam beneath them like fish beneath a layer of ice. They seeped up from the floor and in seconds had swarmed Tyr, coiling around him and binding him in place while one of the Shades yanked the cauldron from his grasp. Acacia was about to go after the Shade when it turned and stared at her. She was paralyzed, her face blanching as the Shade inched towards her. She locked her jaw, covering her mouth with her paw, and stepped back. The Shade slithered across the floor over to its master, handing Lord Nyx the pot.

David went to Acacia's side, putting his arm around her. "It's okay. I won't let the Shades get you."

"I'm sorry," she croaked, trying to hold back her trembling. "I'm so sorry..."

Lord Nyx sneered at them. "My predecessor was right about one thing. Love makes even the most intelligent creatures blind. But it matters not to me. I will discourage this foolish love nonsense once I have everyone in all the worlds worshipping me. It will be a new age of clarity and prosperity, with Night lording over all."

"No one will worship you, cold-blooded rogue!" Tyr shouted.

"What choice will they have, now that I possess the gift I have always needed—the power to destroy any and all worlds?" He smiled at the cauldron in his hands. "But I will be merciful. I sense you have some attachment to this dog, so I will let you have him, once my Shades finish draining his power from him. Even within the void of this cauldron, my Shades will find him and retrieve for me what I need. And unlike Madam Nyx's Shades, which took so pathetically long to drain someone of their talents, I am more powerful than she was. My Shades should finish the job in days."

Acacia bared her teeth. "Do you understand what you're doing? You can't force people to bow down to you! You'll have everyone, every god and divine warrior, in all the worlds after you! If everyone banded together—"

"That would be amusing. But Fenrir was able to devour gods as well, and so shall I. I appreciate you finding a way to trap the wolf, so I did not have to risk being devoured myself."

David grimaced. "Fine, you have what you want. So release Hypnos and your other siblings, and let us leave!"

With a flick of his hand, Lord Nyx propelled David across the floor straight towards him. He clutched David around the mouth with his freezing hand. "It is only because you will cease to be a threat to me in mere moments that I do not punish you for your audacity. I have the gift of prophesy, mortal, and I know that no matter what torment I inflict on you, it would not keep you from getting in my way." He released David, dropping him to the floor at Nyx's feet. David crumpled onto his hands and knees, and found that he was paralyzed in place. He could move from the neck up, but no more than that.

Acacia ran forwards towards David, but a line of Shades emerged from the floor to block her way. She roared, "You will pay if you hurt him, Nyx! He has done nothing to you!"

"You are right, Sphinx. Nor will he do anything to me." Nyx leaned forwards, bringing his face close to David. "Do you know why I brought my siblings to my home? Do you know what else I was seeking?"

David clenched his teeth, swallowing back his fear. "You…you were looking for something else…you had your Shades unraveling the Curtain…"

Lord Nyx arose, pressing his hand down on the crown of David's head. "Not all of the Curtain. They were to seek out any threads of the Curtain connected to you. You see, the Curtain isn't comprised solely of woven magic, as the witch told you. It also contains the Threads of Fate. Everyone's fates. The three weavers who spin these threads, my sisters—or sister, it depends what mood she is in—have hidden themselves well from me so I would not force them to do my bidding. Fortunately, once my Shades started to tear down the Curtain and remove magic from the worlds, my brother Sleep caved in and told me where I could find your threads, David. He's familiar with your threads, and your fate."

David looked up at the cage that held Hypnos. The god of Sleep turned away, ashamed.

Nyx opened up his hand, and from his palm sprang a small tapestry, shimmering with reds and golds and greens. "It is a beautiful fate you have, David Sandoval. One of the most stunning for a mortal that I have seen. I knew of it long before, seeing with my prophetic eye. But it has one small, ugly blemish on it. The thread that foretells that you will undo my work. You are destined to keep me from achieving my true glory. I could scarcely believe it at first—a mere mortal, interfering with my plans? But I will not be the fool that Madam Nyx was. In her lame attempts to defy Fate, she brought about her own undoing. I believe she allowed you to live because she, too, saw that you could bring about my downfall."

Acacia had had enough. She barreled through the Shades, and they clawed and scratched at her, pulling her back. She struggled forth, disregarding the pain the Shades were trying to inflict. "You…will…not… have…him…" she growled.

Lord Nyx watched her inch closer, as more and more Shades tackled her. "I meant what I offered you before, Sphinx. I will give you refuge in my realm, for it is inevitable that I will have to destroy the lesser worlds in order to encourage the faith I will require to garner my followers. You are a rare specimen, and you will be valuable to me in converting others to my worship."

"NEVER!" she roared again with vehemence. "I'd rather die than be your servant!"

Nyx shook his head. "I was not asking you."

A sixth silver cage appeared among the other five. Acacia was no longer on the floor, but in the new cage. She clawed and bit at the bars, to no effect.

David could scarcely breathe, he was so mortified. "I implore you, I beg you, Lord Nyx! Set Acacia free. I will pledge myself to you, be your devoted follower, do anything you wish as long as I live. Just let Acacia go!"

Lord Nyx was quiet, as if considering this proposal. "Such an offer would be tempting to your enemy Nico, but he is a fool. To allow you to persist, even as my follower, would allow your fate to come to pass."

"I threaten you so much, yet you won't kill me—"

Lord Nyx's laugh tolled like a death bell. "You have seen that even Death can be defied. There is one who would delight in having me kill you, so he could claim you for himself, bring you back as an undead device to oppose me. I will deal with him, as I will all those who deny me."

Nyx opened his other hand, and a ball of purple fire sparked from it. "Do you know what happens to a man who had no fate, David Sandoval?"

David's body ran cold.

"He ceases to exist," Nyx said.

He set David's Threads of Fate aflame.

Acacia's scream pierced the heavens. David could feel the fire deep inside of him, and he thought he would disintegrate into ash from the inside out. As he watched his tapestry burn up, wither away into nothing more than smoke, he felt all recognition of the place, the people around him, himself, being stolen away from him…

Then he was stolen away, spirited through time and space, across the universe and beyond everything he could comprehend. His life was in reverse; he has fleeting images of Fenrir at the Giants' Causeway, Gullin and his family in Moffat, Geras' house and the ocean…

As his memory of his home in Paris zoomed past him, with Florence waiting by the door of their townhouse, watching for him, he yelled for her, reached out in a desperate attempt to keep hold of her, his life—but it slipped from his grasp like grains of fine sand.

Fine sand, everywhere.

He spat and coughed, as he awoke to a mouthful of sand. It was in his hair, in his clothes and sticking to his skin. He rubbed it from his eyes, and looked up at a blue sky. There was sunlight, and birds riding the gentle winds past white puffs of cloud. Upland of the beach, white cliffs faced him, topped by green grass and wildflowers.

Where was he? This beach felt oddly familiar, but he couldn't place it. He couldn't place much of anything at the moment, but a word pressed up in his mind. He forced it to rise—where am I? What is this place?

France. He had been here before! It was a beach in northern France. Yes, he had vacationed here this past summer. He had been here with…

With…

The name refused to surface.

David sat up. He stared out at the ocean, as the sun set its orange shell down on the horizon. He held his head in his hands, desperate for his mind to give him something, anything, to remember why he was here, where he needed to go, how he was supposed to get home, wherever home was.

There was an echo. He couldn't tell if it was in his mind, or if a voice was resonating off the cliffs from some far-off spot. But the words were clear, even though they meant nothing to him.

We'll be together… we'll be together…

TO BE CONCLUDED

GLOSSARY OF MYTHOLOGICAL CHARACTERS

Baba Yaga (Russian Mythology)—a witch that reoccurring appears in several Russian folk legends. She lives in a bird-legged house in the forest, and typically plays a villainous role, although sometimes she provides help if given the right incentive.

Elli (Norse mythology)—the female personification of Old Age. In the Norse myths, Loki tricked the god Thor into wrestling Elli, as the thunder god believe Elli was a frail old woman. Elli beat Thor in the wrestling match, since no one can overcome Old Age.

Fenrir (Norse Mythology)—a giant wolf, one of the sons of the trickster god Loki. It is said that during Ragnarok (the final battle of the gods), Fenrir will devour the gods and the world. He had two sons, Skroll and Hait, who would eat the sun and the moon.

Geras (Greek mythology)—the personification of Old Age. One of the goddess Nyx's sons. The Greeks revered and feared Geras, as many do with growing old.

Hymir (Norse Mythology)—a giant, father of the god Tyr. He had a boat he would take on the Elivigar Sea to fish, until Thor had him take him out to sea to catch the Midgard Serpent. Hymir grew so frightened of the serpent that he cut the fishing line as Thor was reeling it in. Hymir owned a mile-deep cauldron for brewing ale, which his son Tyr won from him in a contest.

Hypnos (Greek mythology)—the god (personification) of Sleep, one of Nyx's sons. Described as a male with wings above his ears.

Ilomba (African Mythology)—In Zambia, it is a destructive snake usually created by a witch doctor. It is said to take the face of the one who created it, and can grow two heads. If the Ilomba is wounded, the creator feels the pain as well.

Jormungandr (Norse mythology)—Also known as the Midgard Serpent, and was a son of Loki. Jormungandr was a sea serpent who was long enough to wrap its body around the entire world. He was also the arch-enemy of the thunder god Thor.

Nyx (Greek mythology)—a primordial Night goddess, daughter of Chaos and mother to Hypnos (Sleep), Thanatos (Death), Geras (Old Age), the Fates, Strife, Blame, Woe, and Deceipt, as well as others. She was also said to have an incarnation, which was male.

Odin (Norse mythology)—The Allfather of the Gods, and ruler of Asgard, the home of the gods (who were also called the Aesir).

Slepnir (Norse Mythology)—The god Odin's steed, which has eight legs. Because of its speed, it helped Odin immensely in battle.

Sphinx (Greek mythology)—One of the original monsters of Greece, with the body of a lion, the wings of an eagle, and the head of a woman. The Sphinx stood at the gate of Thebes, challenging anyone who wished to enter with a riddle; if the visitor could not solve the riddle, the sphinx killed them. King Oedipus solved the sphinx's riddle, and according to legend, the Sphinx threw itself off a cliff (or so everyone was led to believe).

The Sudice (Russian) / **the Moirai** (Greek)—Many cultures had their own versions of the Fates, normally symbolized as three people (commonly women) who had weaving abilities, and thus "wove" peoples' fates.

Tanuki (Japanese mythology)—Tanuki are real animals in Japan; they are a subspecies of raccoon dog. However, in folklore, they are said to have shape-shifting powers and are mischievous and generally good-natured. In English translations, they have often been misinterpreted as badgers, although they are an entirely different species. Tanuki in this book, who is in fact a badger, is a Tanuki in clan name only, although he is related to the Lightning God Raiju, who has a connection to badgers.

Teumessian Fox (Greek mythology)—a monster that terrorized ancient Greece, it was an enormous fox whose fate dictated that it could not be caught. However, the dog Laelaps was sent after it, as its fate was that it would catch anything it hunted. Because of this paradox, Zeus, King of the Gods, turned the fox and the dog into stone. Nico is a descendant of the original Teumessian fox.

Thor and Sif (Norse mythology)—Thor is the God of Thunder, wielder of the hammer Mjölnir, and he was married to Sif, the corn goddess.

Tokoloshe (African Mythology)—In Zulu folklore, an undead dwarf, or a dog-faced worm, but it can take on other forms as well. They are called on by malevolent people to cause trouble for others.

Tyr (Norse mythology)—the Lawgiver of Asgard. Normally associated as being one of Odin's sons, some versions of the myth say he is son of the giant Hymir. He is the god who convinced Fenrir to allow a ribbon to be placed around his neck, since Fenrir was certain no chain could bind him. But the ribbon was enchanted and unbreakable, so Fenrir could not break free. In the process, Fenrir bit off Tyr's hand.

MOMENTS OF HISTORY

David and Baba on the Battlefield (**Chapter Eleven**): From 1853 to 1856, the Crimean Wars took place between Russia and an alliance between France, England, and the Ottoman Empire. As Russia continued to expand and gained possession of the Ukraine, this caused direct conflict with the Ottoman Empire. French emperor Napoleon III declared war on Russia in 1854 because he would gain Catholic support if he attacked Eastern Orthodoxy, as sponsored by Russia.

Acacia's Nightmare (Chapter Fourteen): The temple in this sequence alludes to the Luxor Temple in Luxor, Egypt (once the ancient city of Thebes) founded in 1400 B.C. The Avenue of Sphinxes, which extends for two kilometers outside the temple, was originally built in the 18th dynasty. However, it was reconstructed later by the 30th dynasty king Nectanebo I (380-362 B.C.). Most writing of King Oedipus in Greece began around 5th century B.C., thus the "recreation" of the Avenue of Sphinxes would have fallen after the time of Oedipus and thus would be concurrent with Acacia's timeline.

The Giants' Causeway (Chapter Fifteen)—This is a historical sight in northern Ireland, about three miles from the town of Bushmills. The 40,000 interlocking stone columns are from an ancient volcanic eruption, but the legend of Finn MacCool (Ireland's mythological giant) and the Scottish giant say that the two built the Causeway as a means to meet so they could fight. Being an Irish legend, Finn wins, although how he wins has several variations.

Made in the USA
Middletown, DE
24 March 2015